Shadows Over Bishop Hill

Mary R. Davidsaver

Mary R. Davidsaver

PSC Press – Davenport, IA

PSC Press

An imprint of Park Square Crafts

1451 W 40th St.
Davenport, IA 52806
www.parksquarecrafts.com

This book is a work of fiction. Names, characters, places and incidents are either products of the author's imagination or are used fictitiously. Any resemblance to actual events or locales or persons, living or dead, are coincidental and not intended by the author.

First Edition: July 2021

Cover design: Kaitlea Toohey

Cover photograph: Mary R. Davidsaver

ISBN-13: 978-0-578-90825-0

For my guys

The original MAD man.

The son who is MAD II.

The son who is free of acronyms, KJD.

CHAPTER 1

Monday, June 9, 2008

A solitary robin awoke and began singing its cheery morning song encouraging others to join in. They forced me to abandon the disaster of my bed. I had tossed and turned throughout the night fretting over events I had no control over. I used the faint predawn light to get dressed in worn-out gym clothes and tiptoed out of the red brick house. I hoped going for a walk on Henry County backroads would help me manage the tangled mess of my problems. Ordered chaos would be an improvement over fruitless rumination.

I stopped at the edge of the Smoketree Road to study the Ox-Boy Campground on the other side. All was quiet with the newest visitors. My plan was to take the loop around to Bishop Hill, but which one. Starting out to the south would go downhill and once past the bridge over the Edwards River everything leveled out to form a shorter circuit. Going north presented an uphill climb along wooded meadows, all that remained of the Bishop Hill Colony's woodlots, important assets for the mid-1800s Swedish communal society. I heard an owl calling to its mate and chose to stay close to the trees.

I held a brisk pace until I got to a high spot on the main road and saw the northernmost Welcome to Bishop Hill sign in the distance. I slowed. The asphalt road climbed into the village after crossing the bridge over the Edwards River. My goal, The

Lutfisk Café, was almost in sight. The cozy one-story wood-framed building stood tucked away on the right, well before the stately colony-era structures that clustered around the village park.

Talli Walters, the owner and a trusted early riser, usually unlocked the café and put the coffee on by six. I had counted on getting into the village in time for a leisurely cup of milky coffee, an order of toast, and watching the gradual awakening of a sleepy village as seen from the café's broad front porch.

The aroma of fresh coffee wafted out to meet me as I opened the screen door. Talli called out a friendly "Mornin'. How ya doin'?" from behind the counter. When she got a better look at me her cheery tone changed to the incredulous. "Girl, someone chasin' you?"

"You know," I answered, "you're not all that far off base." I stepped away and busied myself with selecting a coffee cup. Some cups were off limits, as regular customers could be quite territorial about their favorites. I chose carefully, raided the tall cooler for some real milk, and made my way outside with my caffeine fix. I located an isolated seat away from the other early birds hoping Talli would be too busy to look for clarification on my cryptic comment.

I was wrong about Talli. She followed me out to the picnic table at the end of the porch with her own cup of black coffee and sat down opposite me. After a thorough inspection of what I'm sure was my tangled perm, flushed face, and bloodshot brown eyes, she issued a terse order. "Spill it, Ms. Michelle Anderson."

"What?" I answered, as I finger combed stray curls away from my eyes and tugged at my sweaty T-shirt. I couldn't hope to pull any kind of innocent act with Talli; she knew me too well.

Instead, I followed up her question with my own. "Why so formal? I'm not Shelley anymore?"

"Oh, well, of course you are." She relaxed and took a sip of her coffee without taking her eyes off me. "I can just tell somethin's really botherin' you."

"You're right." I heaved a heavy sigh. "I've got a lot of things on my mind." I took a long draw on my cup before launching into an abbreviated rundown on my list of complaints. "Last weekend started out terrific. I cleared the air with Teeny Mom." I paused long enough to note her satisfaction on hearing me use my adoptive mother's pet name. "I had a great meeting with my boss, Mr. Hemcourt. He wants me to stay on at Nikkerbo. I have a job for as long as I like. Even made me his interim director. It's a good thing, since grad school is on hold." I didn't try to check my frown before adding, "Then things seriously slid downhill." I took in another dose of caffeine and rested my eyes on the sun's glow peeking above the tree line of the cemetery. "I'm sure you know all about the standoff in the archives room and how I had to be rescued by a deputy. I was the only one there without a gun."

Talli reached out for my hand. "Thank goodness for Deputy Johnson and Michael getting there in time." She gave my hand a gentle pat but continued to look puzzled. "I thought you had plans for more college, somewhere far off and fancy?"

"You've been talking to Uncle Roy. He'd consider anything further than Galesburg far away and frivolous."

Talli nodded. "That's puttin' it mildly."

"Well, like I said, my grad school plans are on hold for a while. Probably a year, at least. I have to build up my savings." I stared into my cup and sighed again. "That's why being on Mr. Hemcourt's good side is so important. I've got to prove myself up to the challenge of being his interim director while David Ekollon is out of the picture."

"Come on," Talli said, "you've been around the history of the Bishop Hill Colony your whole life. You could run that museum with your eyes closed. David has good reason to be envious of you."

Such unwavering confidence perked up my spirits. "You know what would really be helpful right now?" Talli gave me a quizzical look. "An order of whole wheat toast with peanut butter and jelly. I am starving."

"Comin' right up, Sweetie," Talli said. I saw more gray shading the temples of her dark hair as she pushed her stout body up from the picnic table's wooden seat. Could it have been a trick of the morning light?

Talli let the screen door slam shut behind her as she entered the café. It squeaked open right away. I looked up to see one of my least favorite people in the whole world headed in my direction.

Rune Gunnarson, an ex-boyfriend, walked up with his coffee cup in hand and asked if he could join me. I made him wait while I considered some fanciful, and admittedly painful, options.

"Shelley," he said, his tone serious, "it's important. I wouldn't bother you if it weren't."

I thought about making him stand and suffer a bit more, but people were starting to notice us. My voice had a frosty edge to it by the time I said "Well, if you must." I waved for him to sit. He gave me a curt nod and took Talli's vacated seat opposite me.

I started with a drawn out, "Sooo." I wanted him to squirm. "I imagine you're busy cohabitating with Marsha Ellen, my cousin, my best friend since forever, and you need my help with what exactly?"

He studied his coffee cup for a moment before he leaned forward to whisper, "I think you wanted to say cohabiting."

"I don't believe it. You came all this way to play grammar Nazi?"

"No," he said, looking uncomfortable. "Look, they make us journalism majors learn how to spell and such. I know, for obvious reasons," he cleared his throat, "that cohabit is a verb, cohabitation is a noun, and I think 'co-habi-tating' is something you made up." He paused. "And personally, I prefer to think I'm more of a wordinator than a war criminal."

Not a bad comeback. The guy's sense of humor was always one of his better qualities, but I was not about to return the semi-smile that was creeping across his lips. *Don't focus on the lips.* I stayed silent and waited for him to get on with his excuse for "bothering" me.

"I have appointments for a couple of interviews today. Sort of near here." He cleared his throat again. "I could be headed for my first big break." He studied his hands as they massaged his coffee cup.

I picked up on his nervousness. "Then you do need something from me."

He seemed to take forever to finally spit out, "Marsha Ellen is mad at me."

I have been accused, on occasion, of being a drama queen, so I gave him my best I-am-so-shocked face. "What did you do? Tell me you haven't turned frat rat on her? Or did you take a few liberties with her writing like you did with mine?"

"No, of course not," he said. "Look, I've played it straight with Marsha Ellen. And come on, we worked on that project together."

"Exactly. And when it got published my name was strangely missing from the by-line. You got full credit and I got what? Nothing. Nada. Zip." I would have added more sarcasm, but he held up a hand to stop my rant.

"I can explain. Really." Small beads of perspiration appeared on his upper lip and just above his eyebrows.

"Too late. That one got away." I crossed my arms in front of me as if daring him to continue. "What have you done to Marsha Ellen?"

"Well, it started when I told her I was coming here to see you, alone." He used a paper napkin from the table-top dispenser to dab at his face.

"Let me guess … it made her jealous? Smooth move there, Romeo." I had to admit the little kid inside me began bouncing around until I got it under control. I did *not* want this guy back.

"Yeah, it started a big fight … and I never got a chance to explain, that is, properly."

"For an up-and-coming journalist, a 'wordinator' and all, you sure have trouble with personal communication."

"I know, I know," he said. "That's why I tried to write it all down. I slipped it under the bedroom door last night."

"Oh, this is going to be good."

He looked sheepish and nodded. "I got this back." He produced a folded piece of printer paper from a wallet-like creation made out of duct tape that looked familiar in a way I couldn't immediately place. I focused on the note he handed me.

The paper didn't feel sticky or anything, but I unfolded it carefully anyway. "You typed it out in block form?"

"That's how I write," he said with a shrug. "Remember."

Of course, I knew that. I shook my head as I read Rune's clumsy attempt at an apology. The plea for forgiveness. Then noted the poison prose of Marsha Ellen's refusal scrawled across the bottom. That's when I uttered my opinion of the whole moronic mess. "You are gonna die." I scanned it all a second time. "Yup, dead, and none too soon."

"Come on, Shelley, give me a break."

"Why should I?"

"Because I really want her back." His cheeks took on a rosy glow that threatened to spread down his neck.

"You idiot. With your vocabulary, your style, you should have tried a poem. It might have spared you this dose of venom." I shook the paper at him before letting it drop to the table. At that exact moment, I didn't have a lot of sympathy for Marsha Ellen, and none at all for Rune. "I want no part of this." I made a show of using my cell phone to check the time. "I have to get ready for work. Some of us have real jobs."

"But Shelley, she's the *one*. I want to propose. I went and got my Gran's ring and everything. Come on, *please* help me."

His pleading was too much to take. Ignoring his protests, I rose and took my coffee cup inside like the well-trained local I was. Talli reached for it with soapy hands and gave me a disappointed look while letting out an exasperated sigh. I knew what she was getting at. If I wanted to keep a boyfriend, I'd have to be nicer. Blame it on the stress of the past week, the unknown challenges coming up, or the lack of sleep, whatever, I was not inclined to be accommodating.

I muttered, "I can't help it."

CHAPTER 2

I was not about to have anyone think I was running away. I set a casual pace toward the Edwards river and got across the two-lane bridge before any cars showed up. The shortest route home was to cut across the meadow and go up the gentle rise to the red brick house. On the way, I paused long enough to send a text message to Lars Trollenberg asking him to cover for me in case I was a few minutes late. I thought extra caution might be a good thing. The coming week's work schedule was made up yesterday and should be an easy task for him to set it in motion, deploy the troops if you wanted to think of it that way, should I be sidetracked by any other unforeseen distractions.

Back at the red brick house, I found Teeny Mom sitting in the room we used as a formal dining room when we needed more space than the smaller, cramped kitchen could provide. The sun-filled room held two sets of the old-fashioned six-over-six double-hung windows. One set offered a view of the Bishop Hill road as it approached the two-lane bridge from the north. The other set overlooked the Edwards River, a modest-sized stream with banks lined in a combination of stately old trees, younger saplings, and the brushy undergrowth common for summer. There was enough greenery inside and out to make this spot perfect for morning coffee.

She started to say, "You look—"

"Terrible, I know," I finished for her. "Talli and I have already covered the basics."

"You must have walked to The Lutfisk."

"Well, I had such a bad night sleep-wise that I thought getting out of the house early for some exercise might be a good idea. I walked most of the way around the north loop. I'm not in good enough shape to do much running." I helped myself to another cup of coffee before sitting down. This one had the pleasant aroma of hazelnuts. "I hope I didn't wake you."

"Strange, I didn't hear a thing." She stirred more cream into her cup and handed the carton to me. "What was keeping you awake?"

I sighed. "Too much to think about." I quickly sorted through the list I'd given Talli and decided to skip all those issues and chose to focus on the one I hadn't mentioned. "What am I going to do about Great Auntie Pearl's cloud-inspired dream? How do I tell her about finding the portrait? What might be Olof Krans's last painting." I fidgeted with the cup weighing whether or not to do anything at all. "I guess I have to decide which Anderson I should talk to. I'll probably see Michael first, but maybe I should start with his mom, Amy."

"Amy is Great Auntie Pearl's primary caregiver. She'll want to have a say about Pearl's wellbeing. Talk to her first. And don't be so nervous about Pearl. After all, she started her teaching career in a one-room schoolhouse. One doesn't accomplish that and get to be 103 years old by being overly delicate." With that much decided we sat in silence, each of us lost in our own thoughts.

"Roy was out early, too," she said at last. "Hard to tell what his problems are at the moment."

I took the opportunity to bring up another part of my morning. "You'll never guess who came by The Lutfisk today." I gave her a second or two to give up. "Rune Gunnarson."

"Okay." She pondered. "This would be …"

"Ex-boyfriend non grata," I stated emphatically.

"Right, I thought you two—"

"Broke up months ago. Sure. But apparently the menace will not stay gone. He and Marsha Ellen got together, you know, started dating."

"No. You didn't tell me."

Her face assumed a slightly pinched concerned-mother look that signaled the need to head her off before we got into a full-blown lecture about my tendencies for secrecy and how I'd promised to reform. Fortunately, I could jump in with the truth. "Too painful to talk about at the time," I said, hoping I wouldn't be asked for more intimate details.

She took the hint and ventured, "So, he came here to …"

"To ask for my help. If you can believe that. Seems he's managed to make Marsha Ellen as mad at him as I am, which I can believe."

"How could he expect you to help with that kind of, um, you know, sensitive situation?" she said, shaking her head.

"I don't know. I shut him down before he could tell me too many details of his pitiful story." I started to steam up all over again and tried to shake off the mounting anger I felt. Unfortunately, my calming breaths turned into a yawn. I made myself focus on the present moment. "Anyway, that's when I started back home. Which reminds me, I have to check my messages. See if someone will do me a favor." I dug my cell phone out of my shoulder bag. I bypassed a couple of recent texts from Marsha Ellen. She would have to wait. I kept scrolling. Sure enough, Lars was willing to help me out. I could take enough to time for a shower and getting myself ready for a day of finding out what exactly Mr. Hemcourt expected of me in my new position as interim director. Teeny Mom shooed me upstairs. I think she was glad to have me leave the room taking my sullen disposition and smelly clothes with me.

I made my way upstairs and found my bed just as I had left it: a mass of twisted sheets, lumped up pillows, and the quilt kicked onto the floor along with my robe. The scene elicited another yawn. I resisted the urge to climb back in by giving myself a sniff test. A hot shower was a must. I placed my cell phone on the nightstand and draped my robe over my arm but paused at the doorway to stare at the collage to my birth mother I had hanging on the opposite wall. I sent her a whispered wish for spiritual guidance and a little more luck. I frowned and stubbornly shook my head. No. I needed more than luck. I needed to prove myself.

CHAPTER 3

The call had me fumbling for my cell phone. By some miracle I got the right buttons pressed without losing the connection. Lars, sounding serious, asked if I was awake. “Getting there,” I mumbled. Then the panic hit me. “*No! No!*” I should not have been asleep. “I’m so sorry!” I shouted that and more apologies into the phone as I sprang off the bed and made a dash for the outfit I’d chosen to wear. At least I’d gotten that far before some insane impulse made me nestle under my quilt and dose off.

Technically, Lars Trollenberg was a Swedish exchange student and part-time summer help for the Nikkerbo Museum & Conference Center. There was a lot more to Lars besides being tall and Nordicly handsome with his blond hair and vivid blue eyes. Now I heard Lars’s musical Swedish accent in my ear giving me instructions on what to do. “Get to Nikkerbo as fast as you can. Call no one. Meet me at the back door.”

Twenty minutes later I pulled into the employee’s parking lot. I dreaded my next meeting with Mr. Curt Hemcourt V, my employer and owner of the brand new Nikkerbo Museum & Conference Center. The one who gave me an outstanding career opportunity, which I may have bungled royally by being late. I met up with an antsy-looking Lars in the employee’s parking lot. He hushed me before I could apologize, yet again, or find out what the super-secret spy routine was all about. He hustled me into the kitchen’s pantry area. Only then did he think it was safe for us to speak.

“What is going on?” I asked, in what I thought was a perfectly acceptable tone and level of voice.

His whole body seemed to shrink, not an easy task for someone so tall and good looking. He waved for me to keep my voice down. "Quiet please. No one needs to know you are here. Not yet."

"Is there a hostage situation in the lobby?" I ventured with a lowered voice. "Or are you having a really boring day?" I was trying to come up with some more caustic humor when he cut me off.

"*Nej*," he said. "It is much worse."

"What could be worse?" I knew I was in trouble, but my brain couldn't pick up on a good excuse for Lars acting so charged up.

"Not a what, but a who," he hissed back in his accented English.

"Please, let's not play any more games," I said. "You've got to be more direct. What's going on?" Lars couldn't answer because he was too busy peering around the corner of the pantry's doorway. "I give up. Who is here?"

Lars quickly drew back and placing a finger to his gorgeous lips shushed me. "Mr. Hemcourt came in this morning in as dark a mood as I have ever seen."

"Okay," I said. "It's a Monday morning after a rather eventful weekend. For goodness' sake, I'd say he's entitled to some grumpiness. He is human after all. We all are."

"Businessmen from Chicago were here before I came in. They have been in Mr. Hemcourt's office all this time." Lars glanced out the pantry doorway again as if checking we were still alone in the kitchen. "I hear shouting sometimes. Loud noises."

"Uh, like things breaking?" I inquired.

"More like pounding a fist on a desk, I think. I recognize two as very important. I don't know about the young assistant. Is that the correct word?"

"That'll do," I answered. "I knew Mr. Hemcourt wanted to see some key people. I just wasn't sure it'd be this soon." I couldn't have picked a worse day to be tardy.

"Mr. Hemcourt called for me to take lunch sandwich orders and I must leave soon to pick them up."

"Okay, but meetings with food are not earthshaking events. We have things like that even out here in the middle of the cornfield triangle." I was trying to sound upbeat and reassuring for his sake, as well as mine.

"*Ja*, *ja*, I know," he said, still obviously on edge. "That was before Mr. Ekollon, the director you are replacing, came. He is the one waiting in the lobby. He has no hostages."

Now, he had my full attention. "That doesn't make sense. Are you sure it is David Ekollon? Middle-aged guy. Not too tall. Not too fit. Distinctive mustache. The sheriff had him in custody as of late Saturday. That's the last I saw of him. He should be in a comfy jail cell up in Cambridge."

Lars looked confused, "They have such things here?"

"No, I was kidding." The confused look didn't go away. However, he wore it well. "I was trying to make a joke. Funny. Ha, ha." That last bit finally connected.

"You must be serious," he admonished. "I fear for your job."

It was my turn to look confused. But he was right about loud voices. I heard two baritones go at a final volley of profanity as the double wooden office doors swung open. We ducked out of sight as Mr. Hemcourt stalked out. Silence descended when the doors closed behind him. Mr. Hemcourt paused a moment seeming to gather his thoughts before walking past the kitchen. The echo of his footsteps faded as he headed toward the lobby.

Lars and I crept closer, remaining out of sight below the counter tops and lower cabinets. I couldn't hear all of the encounter between the agitated museum owner and the disgraced museum director, but I did get a few fragments. Ekollon said: "You need me," "I can help with," and "She can't." Then a final "Not now!" from Mr. Hemcourt.

Lars stood up acting as a protective shield, while shooing me back into the pantry. I caught a glimpse of Ekollon's khaki-clad backside exit by way of the front door.

Mr. Hemcourt didn't seem surprised to see Lars. "Check on our lunch order," he said. "In the meantime, bring us some coffee. The good stuff." He opened his office doors and resumed his part in the meeting.

Lars pointed to the closed doors of Mr. Hemcourt's office and nudged me into motion. "The food is coming from that restaurant north of the park. I'll go get it. You must serve the coffee."

I hesitated too long for his liking. "Do you want your job?"

I stalled for a couple of heartbeats asking myself if I really did. I was so sure yesterday. And this morning. Then, I let myself fall asleep and came in late. Now, it seemed like it might be an impossible stretch of my abilities. Who was I kidding?

Exasperated, Lars said, "Go in there and fight for your position."

"How do you know what I have to do?" It seemed like a stupid question, but I laid it out there anyway.

"I know of these things. Ekollon was here to negotiate for his job." Lars leveled his intense blue eyes at me. "Did you not hear?

One of his demands was to get rid of you. You must show Mr. Hemcourt you belong here. Not him."

"I was only named interim director a few days ago and now I have to fight to stay?"

Lars stared into my eyes. "You can do this. Go in there with strength." He made a fist and commanded "Make your Viking ancestors proud."

I squared my shoulders. Told myself I had to stay. "I deserve this job. I need this raise." I made a fist and added my own "I can do this" to further bolster my resolve.

Lars took off for the parking lot and, I presumed, the borrowed car he'd been using. I set about the task of brewing some fresh coffee from the secret stash of Columbian beans. With that underway I proceeded to prepare an attractive tray for my hostess duties. I had my part done before Lars returned. It was time to launch myself into the choppy waters of corporate politics. I knew Mr. Hemcourt had concerns about the financial future of Nikkerbo, his pride and joy and tribute to his late father. My money problems paled to insignificance when compared to the embezzlement schemes of the former chief financial officer. These rushed meetings had to be about those two topics. I wished I could do more than serve coffee.

My knock on the wooden doors echoed. Mr. Hemcourt yanked the doors open with an irritated "What now?" He had his suit jacket off and his shirt sleeves rolled up, not at all what I'd come to expect. He studied me and the tray, clearly not expecting to find both on his doorstep at the same time. Pulling his composure together, he asked stiffly, "Where is Lars?"

His mind was having a difficult time changing gear. I had to make a little head motion to indicate asking me inside his wood-paneled office would be appropriate. He recovered smoothly. "Ms. Anderson, do come in."

"Thank you, sir," I said. "Lars will return with the lunch order presently. Do you want me to pour the coffee?"

Mr. Hemcourt motioned for me to use an empty side table located very near the seat I had occupied yesterday afternoon when we had our conversation about colony history, artifacts, and my future. "Thank you, but no. We'll serve ourselves."

"Sir," I asked quietly, as he administered to his cup first, "was that David Ekollon leaving the building?"

"Unfortunately, yes." He gave me a strained look that quickly passed, then uttered a hushed, "You're fine. My Galva lawyer, Mr. Patrick, will be joining us later. We need to talk about the specifics of a certain person's contract, among other things." His additional directions followed in a louder voice. "You and Lars can set up the sandwiches on the kitchen's pass-through counter. Please encourage the others to eat in the employee lounge. We must have minimal disturbance for our working lunch." He made sure the others in the room heard the emphasis he placed on "working."

"Yes, sir," I said. I only had the briefest chance to form an impression of a room that held two older business types, roughly Mr. Hemcourt's age, and one younger guy, closer to my age. The young man had stopped in mid-presentation of a projected spreadsheet containing columns of data. He gave me the oddest look, like he recognized me, or maybe he wanted to be rescued. Hard to say. He was instantly reprimanded by one of the older men and quickly returned to his task. I left to get on with my work.

CHAPTER 4

Tuesday, June 10, 2008

The morning crowd at The Lutfisk Café hummed with tension. Someone had seen a Henry County sheriff's department cruiser turn onto a village side street and speculations were running the gamut from mundane to exotic. Perhaps exotic wasn't so far out of the realm of possibility anymore. After all, I'd made the 911 call for Herb Anderson only twelve days ago.

I tried to ignore the buzzing gossip by sitting at the back-corner table. Better to keep to myself as I raked my fingers through my still damp hair, fluffing up my perm. I'd paid good money and endured hours of chemical fumes for volumizing curls. However, the gesture was in danger of becoming a habit whenever I needed something to distance myself from present surroundings and connect with that place that allows new thoughts, new connections to form. I continued to fuss with my hair as I stared at the wall across from me hoping for some kernel of an idea. Inspiration had eluded me in my office space at Nikkerbo yesterday afternoon and at home in the red brick house last night. So why expect something more by placing myself here among the early risers of Bishop Hill? I was desperate, that's why. I felt I couldn't show up at Nikkerbo today without something new, something that held promise.

Old black-and-white photos of long-past baseball teams stared back at me without offering the least bit of illumination. I glanced down at my coffee cup. Empty. Nothing there either. I looked around for Talli Walters, heart and soul of The Lutfisk.

Sure enough, the stout, dark-haired owner was headed toward me with coffee pots in either hand. She was a reliable pro who had a sixth sense about refills. It didn't hurt that it also kept her in the loop on all the important happenings in the village.

"Mornin' there, Ms. Shelley. You look like you could use another shot," Talli said brightly as she came to the table. She eyed my yellow legal pad that held scribbles, doodles, and a partial list of ideas. "Judging by the amount of work you haven't done; I'd say you need the full octane in your cup."

I nudged my cup closer to the pourer, fewer stray drops that way. Not that it mattered, Talli was right about my progress. I hadn't written down anything useful since I'd gotten out of my late meeting with Mr. Hemcourt, owner of Nikkerbo. We had a nice chat about possible future events after his other business meeting ended with sullen suit-types filing out to the parking lot. A few droplets of coffee wouldn't matter in the least.

"I picked out the loudest cup I could find this morning." I held up the purple cup and put on a pleasant face. "Team Lutfisk hasn't given me the morale boost I need to come up with some promotional slogans for a new event at Nikkerbo."

Talli leaned in to take a better look at the pad of paper. Amid some sketchy artwork was a list of slogans for the boss's proposed *Nikkerbo's Olof Krans Arts and Crafts Festival*:

OK Fest in Bishop Hill
Our Fest is Better than the Rest
It's OK to Fest in Bishop Hill
Fest with the rest in Bishop Hill
You don't have to be Swedish to …

"Wow, you need more help than what's in these pots," Talli cooed, setting one down on the table in order to free up a hand. She pointed to each in turn and muttered, "No. No. Yuck. Turn 'rest' into 'best', sounds better. As for that last one, I'm not a full Swede—so when I took over The Lutfisk it took a good while for the thaw to set in. I wouldn't go there if I were you."

I laughed. Swedes had a reputation for being slow to warm up to new people. Or for new ideas. And new museums, like the one I was working for, well, that might take even longer. "Thanks for the input," I said. I crossed out the unusable items and made a note of the suggested correction.

"I'm glad I don't have to do that kind of work for a living. Let me sling a pot of coffee any day." Talli set the other pot down and rummaged through an apron pocket. Her hand came out with two wrapped mints, which she offered to me.

"Maybe you should think about it," I said, and took the candy. A sugar spike might do me good. As I worked a cellophane wrapper open, I added a new thought "How about starting a Lutfisk Festival?"

"Are you kiddin'?" Talli scoffed. "People would pay to stay away."

"See, that rhymes. You have a natural flair for this stuff."

Talli chuckled. "As in, 'Try our lutfisk. It's worth the risk?'"

"Sharing the herring shows you're caring."

"Jeez. Let me outta here." Talli shuddered, but I noticed she struggled and failed to keep a smile from forming as she took her coffee pots to the next table.

I popped the mint into my mouth. Humor aside, I knew I was in big trouble. Mr. Hemcourt needed a way to draw people in and wanted to start a new event. I understood that, but attempting to ride the coattails of a bigger, more well-established festival was going to ruffle some feathers. First and foremost were some important feathers belonging to Christina Colberg, my Teeny Mom. She took my twin brother and me in as four-year-old motherless orphans who were in the protective care of my mother's much older brother, Roy Landers. My uncle was a Viet Nam vet, a struggling artist, and a tender soul in need of a lot of help, too. When they married, she became an aunt first and a mother later after we were legally adopted. To cope with this strange pedigree, I took to calling her Teeny Mom. It seemed natural to extend a nickname a lot of people used anyway because of her name and her slight stature.

Our home, the red brick house on a rise north of Bishop Hill, owed its size to all the additions that were built onto the original post-colony house. The Edwards River separated us from the village proper or provided a cushion, depending on your point of view.

The river also provided a wide, grassy, and relatively flat expanse for the *OK Art Fest in the Meadow*. The original late summer arts and crafts show started out in the park in the center of the village but was discontinued at one point. Teeny Mom started it up again in the converted field and gave it a new name. Her careful planning and clever promotion allowed the show to regain its former glory and then some. Since my plans for grad school were on hold, she had asked for my help this summer.

It wasn't so bad; I would have volunteered to help out anyway. But now Mr. Hemcourt was hot for me to come up with a new show for the same weekend—and for this year, no less. I tried to explain that gathering artists and vendors together for a new show would be difficult and should take far more time than the two months I had to work with. There had to be plenty of advance notice and promotion. When we began discussing the project late yesterday afternoon, I could tell he wasn't impressed with my list of reservations. I felt pressured and ultimately acquiesced to everything he wanted. The guaranteed conflict with Teeny Mom gave me a headache and left me with another sleepless night.

I heard the front door open and close a few times. The café was beginning to fill up with its second round of morning regulars. I decided to call it quits and began to collect my things when I heard the distinctive Texas drawl of Marcella Rice. I had to pay my respects. She was an old friend of Teeny Mom, and I had helped save her life when she had driven her car off the road trying to avoid a deer. Both items had to be acknowledged.

I waited for her to settle into a chair by the front window and stow her quad cane out of the way before I approached. "Good morning, Marcella. Good to see you up and about."

"Why Missy, I thought that was y'all hiding back in the corner. Sit down for a spell."

Michelle was my given name and I wanted to be called Shelley. I didn't care for her choice of Missy, but it was a command I couldn't ignore. My escape plans evaporated like the steam rising from the coffee cups Talli placed on the table in front of us. Talli glanced at me and I knew she would have winked if she thought she could get away with it. I flashed a sarcastic grin at Talli when Marcella wasn't looking and sat down.

"So, how's life out at the new museum? Y'all still director out there?" Marcella asked with an air of feigned innocence that was her trademark.

"I'm still acting as *interim* director," I said with a pleasant smile. "My temporary position is giving me loads of practice at scheduling and employee relations." Getting the hang of the politically correct schmoozing might take longer. I thought it best to keep that thought to myself. "You're looking good. I hope the leg is on the mend."

"Oh, sure. It's doing better. I finished up my physical therapy this morning. I've been cleared to drive again."

"You've got your car back?" I said with surprise. "I figured it would be totaled after its side trip into the ravine out by Red Oak Grove." I looked through the window and didn't see her big Buick parked in one of the preferred spots close to the door.

"No, the old girl was a goner. My son's still driving me around until the insurance money comes through. But at least I can go car shopping. I gotta find something roomy, y'know," Marcella cackled.

I smiled, too. "I'll miss seeing that big boat of a car." I'd discovered the accident before anyone else. I was glad to have helped Marcella, but reliving the rescue began to make me tense up. Sort of like a fight or flight response. She brought me back with a not-so-subtle probe for more information. Gossip was gold in the village.

"I hear you're not going back to school in the fall."

Leave it to Marcella to get to the heart of my problems.

"No. Grad school is on hold. I'll be working out at Nikkerbo and helping Teeny Mom with the *OK Art Fest in the Meadow*. I'm saving up my money."

"I'm surprised Teeny is being so hard on you."

"No," I said cautiously. "She's not being hard on us. My brother and I have always worked and saved for college."

"Surely Teeny could find a way to help you out," Marcella persisted. "She's got all that money."

I'd heard stories about that before. The idea that Teeny Mom had loads of money stashed away went all the way back to her father and the original owners of the red brick house and farm. I didn't have the time to spare for debating or debunking myths. I couldn't help but calculate the closeness of the door and the desired speed to make an exit. I was looking for a tactful way to disengage when the means of another way out arrived with a bang of the screen door.

CHAPTER 5

Deputy Dana Johnson entered the café. She stood scanning the main dining room. Her search stopped the instant her eyes came around to me.

I was certainly glad to see her. I would always be in her debt. However, with her brown hair tightly drawn under her hat and a hard look to her dark eyes I did not get a warm fuzzy feeling.

The deputy took the few steps over to our window table and leaned over to give me a firm order. "I need to speak to you."

"Okay," I answered cautiously.

"Outside, please." She used a lower pitch to her regular voice. I took it to mean "Don't give me any grief, fool."

Hearing that official slant to her request left me mystified. I couldn't image why she'd be pulling the tough deputy act on me. I said a quick goodbye to a surprised Marcella and got myself up and out the door that the deputy politely held open for me. I gave her a puzzled look as I passed in front of her.

"What gives?" I asked when we were safely outside the café. I knew Marcella would be watching intently. And a few others as well. I wondered if their lip-reading skills were up to the challenge.

"Don't panic," Deputy Dana said. "I just need to ask you a couple questions."

"Questions about what?" I had to be wearing my confused face. Again.

"Like, how your business card ended up in the wallet found in the Bishop Hill cemetery this morning."

My confused countenance remained in place. “I didn’t know I had a business card.”

Deputy Dana looked at me like I was a first-class idiot. “Come on, you didn’t know your name was printed on this nice card saying you worked at that Nikkerbo whatsit center?”

“Uh, no.” Then it came to me. “Okay, sure, I was supposed to get business cards. I just haven’t seen them yet.”

“The card they found listed you as ‘director’ and had what looks like your personal cell phone number written in on the back.” She paused to fix me with a look that was meant to convey the serious nature of this discovery.

“Why is it a big deal? Somebody lost a wallet in the cemetery. And they had to call you in? That seems a bit over the top in the drama department.”

“The wallet was found in the cemetery. There were signs of a struggle nearby. Drag marks in the grass and such.” Deputy Dana kept her face blank and let the facts sink in for a few seconds. “Since I had a history with you, they sent me down here to get your statement. Maybe save you a trip up to Cambridge.”

“I appreciate it. Really, I do. But I need more to go on. Can you give me a name?”

She gave me a name. A name that left me totally, utterly dumbstruck. Rune Gunnarson.

Deputy Dana gave me a cool look. “I take it you know this individual.”

I had difficulty finding the right words. “We dated. Ah, in Galesburg. Ages ago.” I got that much out in a somewhat coherent fashion.

“When was the last time you saw him?”

Simple question. Fair enough. But how do I explain the last morning in my Knox campus apartment. My roommate, cousin, and now former best girlfriend had hooked up with my former boyfriend and I couldn't get out of there fast enough. Talk about drama.

"So, when did you last see him?" Deputy Dana rephrased her request.

I struggled with the bare facts: "There was yesterday morning … and then the Friday morning when I left Galesburg … before I drove past Herb Anderson's antique business, the Varnishtree. When I found Herb…." I couldn't go on any further.

"Okay, I got the part about Herb Anderson." Deputy Dana said. She knew that Friday morning almost as well as I did. She had been one of the first responders to show up to the crime scene. Memories of poor Herb dead on the floor of his workshop and a disoriented Great Auntie Pearl next to him came flooding back. "Tell me about Monday morning, yesterday, with Gunnarson," she asked. I caught the sense she was trying to convey something to me. Somehow Rune and Herb were now connected. Something bad had happened to Rune. I was stunned and just couldn't process this new information fast enough. I didn't want to. I rebelled against it. This couldn't be happening. My head began to swirl. My legs felt alarmingly jelly-like. I needed to sit down—fast!

Deputy Dana read the message on my face and guided me over to sit on the edge of the back seat of her cruiser. "If you're going to puke, do it out here," she ordered while holding the door open.

I wished she hadn't said that. I buried my head between my knees and didn't surface until I was quite sure I could retain my breakfast.

After that episode passed, Deputy Dana insisted that I go with her to the sheriff's department to elaborate on my Monday morning scene with Rune at The Lutfisk. I did not have a pleasant ride up to Cambridge. The cemetery must have yielded more than my business card in a lost wallet. I would soon find out if Rune Gunnarson was in a hospital or the morgue.

CHAPTER 6

Two hours later I'd written my statement, endured a grilling by the sheriff's investigators, and was back at my car thanks to Deputy Dana. She drove off to her next assignment. I avoided eye contact with the curious faces at the windows of The Lutfisk Café, while I slid behind the steering wheel. I might have imagined those faces. My brain wasn't exactly hitting on all cylinders after the series of shocks I had to deal with so far. However, I did see Talli hustling out to catch me before I drove away.

"Are you all right?" I'd seen that worried look far too many times on Teeny Mom's face. It didn't look right on Talli either.

"I'm good," I insisted.

"You look too pale to be all that good," she said cautiously. "You goin' home?"

"No, I can't. I'm really late for work at Nikkerbo. They'll be wondering what happened to me." I drew an unsteady breath. "Of course, they might not be wondering."

"Right, the Bishop Hill grapevine works incredibly fast and with great efficiency when you're least likely to want it." Talli gave a slight nod toward the café windows. "Don't you worry about them and what they may say. You take care of yourself now," Talli admonished. "And call Teeny first thing."

I pulled away and watched her grow smaller in my rearview mirror. She disappeared as I crossed the Edwards River going north toward the brand new Nikkerbo Museum and Conference Center.

I resisted the urge to make any phone calls until I got safely stopped in the employee's parking lot. I chose a spot relatively secluded from prying eyes and pulled my cell phone from my shoulder bag. Marsha Ellen's number was still on speed dial. She shouldn't have moved just yet; our lease was good until August. I dreaded hearing her voice again and hoped I might be spared by a busy signal or enough unanswered ring tones to activate voice mail. What kind of message could I leave?

Upsetting images of her sharing our old apartment with Rune crept up on me. Marsha Ellen and I found the apartment together. We decorated it with our odds and ends over the last two years. Our artwork hung on every wall. Then Rune came along and took over. I felt pushed aside. Now he managed to drag me into his latest fiasco in the worst way imaginable. No, I corrected myself, this was his last fiasco. The photos left no mistake.

My voice betrayed my mixture of emotions by the time she picked up the call. "It's me," I said curtly.

"And which 'me' might this be?" came her chilled response.

"Come on Marsha Ellen, we've known each other forever."

"Oh, it's the 'me' who hasn't returned any of my calls or texts. The 'me' who's been acting like a brat since the end of last semester. The one who stood everyone up at the Senior Showcase. The very last college art show for both of us, I might add. And you missed graduation."

Her anger caught me off guard. I kept my temper under control as I countered with the facts. "Look, I've been through a lot since we started working on that show. Finding Herb and all. And, you know, trying to keep people from shooting me. Stuff like that." I omitted the current problem of the cemetery. I'd been warned.

Marsha Ellen sniffed. "So, why are you calling now? You being so busy and all important."

"Because I've spent the last two hours talking to a large part of the sheriff's investigations department about Rune Gunnarson, *your* boyfriend. Haven't they called you?"

"Well, no. Why would they?"

I massaged my left temple and led with the hook that Deputy Dana had used on me. "Because they found his wallet in the Bishop Hill cemetery. You have any idea why he'd be out there?"

"Look," Marsha Ellen said with a cool, crisp huff. "He was in Bishop Hill looking for you. That's why he used that old duct tape thing we were into making ages ago."

Her frank statement left me speechless as my mind went blank until I finally recalled making stuff out of duct tape during a brief high school fad. "Yeah, now I remember, we only made a few of those things before our enthusiasm wore out. You actually kept them."

I had to get back to the current problem. Why had he been looking for me? He and I had worked together on a mixed media project the semester before. The one where he took all the credit when it was finished. We hadn't dated all that long. I certainly never considered it serious. At the time I had my dreams of escaping Bishop Hill with its small-town life and building a shiny new future somewhere else. His ambitions were going to keep him closer to home and the family newspaper business. He wanted Marsha Ellen to be a part of that picture.

Marsha Ellen's wispy voice broke the spell. "Look, Shelley, Rune and I have gotten serious about each other lately. Thinking about, you know, getting married. He wanted to talk to you about us having our wedding and reception in that museum place you're working for. He figured a nice new place like that … and the fact that you could not be a bridesmaid, well, it seemed worth checking into as far as he was concerned. I wasn't on board with that, and it led to a major fight."

It was a good thing I was well away from Marsha Ellen. I sucked in a breath and released it with, "Whoa, back up to the part where I can't be a bridesmaid at your wedding."

"Come on, Shelley," Marsha Ellen said. "You and Rune have too much history as, you know …"

"A couple?" I tried not to sneer but failed.

"Yeah, there's that," she paused, "and you seriously don't like him anymore."

She had a point, however completely useless as it was now. I had to get her back to telling me about Rune's plans. I exhaled slowly and tried a new angle. "So, he was coming to see me at Nikkerbo about wedding stuff. I never saw him there yesterday." That was a truthful statement, if not totally complete. I paused for a deep breath and continued to massage my throbbing brow. "Or this morning."

"It's all been happening kinda fast. Talking about future plans and all. He hasn't even done the formal proposal thing. I don't have a ring. He called late yesterday and asked me to meet him in Bishop Hill this weekend." She paused long enough to make me wonder if she was becoming suspicious. "He was going to stay with his uncle in Galva last night. Rune planned on telling him about me … us. He had an interview lined up. Uh, maybe two. Are you sure you didn't see him?"

He'd gotten my business card somehow. And my cell phone number. The number hadn't changed, so it could have come from any number of friends. Even his uncle, Albin Gunnarson, who had helped me find some writing assignments once upon a time. It was the inked-in title of "director" that threw me a curve. Rune had to have been at Nikkerbo sometime yesterday. Someone there wrote that in.

"Marsha Ellen you've got to work out a timeline for Rune: When you last saw him. When he left for Bishop Hill and Galva. The people he intended to interview. All that stuff."

"He was just going to talk to some old guy and meet up with a frat buddy. She gasped. "Oh, I remember now, that's what he called him, Buddy G." I heard the fear creeping into Marsha Ellen's voice as she began to realize that something bad was happening. It was a feeling I was well acquainted with. "Shelley, tell me what's going on."

"Like I said, someone found Rune's wallet in the Bishop Hill cemetery. My card was in it, so I was questioned."

"What … aren't you … telling me?" she choked out.

"Marsha Ellen," I took another deep breath before continuing, "they're thinking there was some kind of struggle." I'd been sworn to secrecy and shouldn't have called, but Marsha Ellen was probably sitting there all alone. Hearing her voice breaking apart like this, was enough to melt the icy spot in my heart.

"Marsha Ellen," I encouraged, "call someone to come be with you."

I heard sobs catch in her throat as she disconnected. The timing was perfect, I didn't want her to hear me as I cried my first real tears.

CHAPTER 7

I bypassed entering Nikkerbo by the employee's door in the back. Rune would have used the front door and been greeted by Lars, the one most likely on duty at the time, and the few extra steps wouldn't hurt me. I needed to calm down after talking with Marsha Ellen and compose myself as best I could.

As soon as I hit the front door Lars's blond head swiveled around to greet me with a singsong "*God dag*" and a friendly smile. He dropped the smile fast. "Very good to see you." He pointedly stared at his watch. "And in time for lunch."

"I'm sorry to be so late. I've had a busy morning." Busy was an understatement. I had to press on and find out about the business card.

"So much you forgot to call or text? That is two days in a row." His bright blue eyes twinkled as he gave himself away. Giving me a hard time had become a sport to him.

"I said I was sorry." I reminded myself to focus on my goal. "Lars, did anyone come in asking for me yesterday? Someone wanting information about reserving space for a wedding and a reception?" Lars had a blank look on his face until I added, "A guy by himself?"

"Ah, *Ja*, sure," he said. "There was this guy in here much later in the day. You were in a meeting with Mr. Hemcourt. I told him you would be free soon. He said he could not wait. Some other meeting was most important to him. I gave him your new card." He pulled one out to show me. "They came to us yesterday. When he said he was a first-class friend of yours and needed to make sure he could reach you, I wrote down your personal number."

"And you made sure he knew I'd had a promotion."

Lars gave me a pleased-with-himself grin. "Of course, I added your new title."

"Then he didn't come back."

"I did not see him again yesterday and I have been out here all today." He studied me and grew serious. "You look upset. Is this about the strange business in the cemetery? Am I in trouble?"

"You're okay. But please don't give out my personal number again," I looked him in the eyes, "because I haven't been so lucky." I shouldn't have said that. I didn't want to discuss the details of my morning at the sheriff's department. "Um, by the way, what have you heard about the cemetery?"

Lars needed no further prompting. "A woman was walking her dog along that narrow street by the cemetery early this morning. The dog started acting crazy-like. Pulled her along and won't stop until they got up to an old tree, they said. She found the ground torn up and saw a wallet. She called 911 because it looked like a body was dragged off." Lars barely stopped for a breath. "You know, just like on one of your American crime shows, where there is fight, someone is dragged to a car, and there is a big getaway chase." His paced slowed as his energy level dropped sharply. "Except there was no hostage, I think. Or no chase, perhaps."

Still, Lars looked pleased enough with his action-packed rendition. I'm sure he was about to add some further comments about our taste in television programming when I cut him off. "Okay, that's about enough with the storytelling."

"This man from yesterday. It was his wallet?"

"Yeah, we were both students at Knox, in Galesburg. But we had different majors. His was journalism and pre-law, while mine was museum studies and art."

"Ah, you dated this man," he said, with a self-satisfied know-it-all nod.

"How could you have guessed that?"

"*Ja*, I can see it in your eyes. He was special to you?"

"Right, I'm going to do a tell-all confession." I gave him a weary sigh. "You're not getting any details from me."

"Just one small piece." Lars could be very charming when he was pleading like a little boy. He earned my best you've-got-to-be-kidding stare. "It's been so dull today," he said, with a mock whimper.

That made me snap, "Oh, stop it. Get a life." I felt my cheeks warming up. This wasn't getting me anywhere, so I blurted out, "This interview is over."

Lars perked up at that, then snapped his fingers in my direction. "*Ja*, now I remember. That is what the man said, interview. He had to get to his interview on time. With someone who liked to say, 'time was money.' You know such a person?"

"Nothing comes to mind right now, but it gives me something to go on. I think."

"You are going to do this yourself? Like before. Not tell the police. Find out what happened to him, this special friend."

Lars left me flustered and unsure of what to say. I chose to correct a small logistical fact. "Sheriff. We have a sheriff here. And sheriff's deputies." I added, "But you're wrong. I don't need to get involved in this." No matter what else happened, I had to keep my distance. I'd been warned that it would be in my best interest to stay away. I left Lars to his imagination and walked off in the direction of my office space.

The rest of the day kept me busy, but not enough to keep away the nagging sensation that I was missing something. A part of my phone call to Marsha Ellen kept coming back like an echo that needed an answer. Her list of complaints about me mentioned the Senior Showcase, which had been the last chance for us graduating art students to get together and show off our artwork. I came to realize my reason for missing the show wasn't exactly what I had told her. I had missed it because of Rune. I was angry at him and it had carried over into the Monday morning scene at The Lutfisk. I was at a loss as to how I could make right letting my friends down, and Marsha Ellen, who, as my cousin, was more than just a friend.

Thankfully, Mr. Hemcourt spent the day in meetings with the same people he had on hand yesterday. They were again joined by Les Patrick, a lawyer well-known to our family. Whatever was going on kept Mr. Hemcourt from asking me about my progress on starting a new festival or event or a whatever something that would increase the museum's visitation numbers. I had little more to offer than the flimsy list of doodled notes I'd shared with Talli at The Lutfisk, before Deputy Dana showed up and turned everything upside down with the news of finding Rune's body in the cemetery.

CHAPTER 8

After work, when I was about to turn my Chevy Prizm into the driveway of the red brick house, I realized I faced two important dilemmas: I hadn't checked in with Teeny Mom about my morning in Cambridge as Talli had ordered me to do, and the Anderson Brothers's largest towing vehicle took up most of the available parking space. If there was a tow truck, my primary high school antagonist would not be far away. I couldn't honestly say I was looking forward to either conversation.

Teeny Mom and Michael J. Anderson sat at the kitchen table. Michael was in the process of polishing off a good-sized piece of pie or he might have said hello. As it were, he waved a fork at me and nodded a welcome. Marsha Ellen, Michael, and I were unrelated Andersons, but were always lumped together in roll calls and lineups all during our school years. I didn't say anything about the pie. I had promised myself I'd cut out the J jokes I'd started back then. However, if he didn't watch his food intake, the J for his middle name might someday stand for Jelly Belly. I would like to think we'd all grown up since high school graduation, but, in reality, he was way ahead of me in that department. Military service in Iraq matured a person.

Teeny Mom said, "Shelley, sit down. We have some news for you."

"What's up? You having car trouble again?" I asked hopefully. I looked into her eyes trying to get a reading on the seriousness of the potential news and saw the obvious. "You know about Rune." I steadied myself with a gulp of air and spoke the words I'd been dreading all day. Words I hadn't said aloud to anyone else. "That he's dead."

"Oh, Honey. It's been all over the news. Finding a body. They haven't officially released the name yet, notifying the family and all. Michael knew who it was and told me. Come on and sit down," she said, as she applied a soothing caress across my shoulders. I melted into a chair. "Tell me what happened to you this morning."

She sat close by as I gave a blow-by-blow replay of Deputy Dana finding me at The Lutfisk. Getting grilled by investigators in Cambridge. Looking guilty because of the things I said to Rune at The Lutfisk Monday morning, but not guilty enough to be arrested. Being told not to reveal any details pertinent to the ongoing investigation or to leave town.

"I had to talk to Marsha Ellen, of course. I was careful. I just didn't want her to be alone when the investigators called." I took a moment to gather myself together before I asked, "Have they called here?" Teeny Mom nodded. "And?" I asked.

"Oh, you know Talli, she gave me a heads up that you might be in trouble." She supplied another comforting rub to my back. "I told them the truth; you had a restless night, but you never left the house after dark."

Michael spoke up for the first time. "The sheriff's department called into the garage for a tow and I volunteered for the job. Rune's sports car was parked over by the B&B, the one with a good view of the park. They wanted it, the car, up in Cambridge, so their forensic team could go over it. I guess they got permission for the tow from his parents." He shrugged. "If they needed it."

He tried to brush away some crumbs from his place at the table, but Teeny Mom got up to do it for him. "Tell her what you found inside," she prompted.

I held my breath and silently waited all of three seconds, tops. "So, tell me already."

"Flowers," he said. "Well, actually, one flower." He paused. "A handmade rose with a note to you."

"Oh, great. That means another visit by a sheriff's deputy. Hopefully, it will be Deputy Dana again. We're starting to bond over the misadventures of Rune." I wanted to pull those words back as soon as they left my mouth. I moaned, "I'm so sorry." I wiped my eyes dry. Then the obvious thought came to me. "Did you unlock that car? I thought your ethical code prevented, what did you call it, committing a breaking and entering?"

I could tell he wanted to argue the point, but he glanced at Teeny Mom and changed his mind. "The car wasn't locked. I guess he didn't expect to be away too long. Anyway, all I had to do was look through the window. It was sitting in plain sight on the front seat. Nice ride by the way. He must have some bucks."

"His dad has some bucks. Rune is still trying to find his own way."

"A rose was kinda nice," Michael said. "Were you two an item again." He stalled, as if unsure if he should wait for an answer.

"No way. Not. Any. More." I answered slowly and with maybe too much force. "To be sure, if I were getting one rose, Marsha Ellen would have gotten a dozen. They are the item, the serious couple, and have been since the senior art show last month. At least that's when I found out about it, them, their involvement." I got up and went to the fridge to pour a glass of milk. I did not want to lose my voice.

“Well,” he said, “I hope she got some real flowers because this one looks like it was made by seven-year-old kid.” Michael produced a truly sad looking creation from his pocket and handed it to me. It was red, all right, but the sorriest excuse for a rose I’d ever seen.

“Why do you suppose he was staying at the B&B,” Teeny Mom said.

“Doesn’t his uncle work for the Galva newspaper?” Michael asked.

“He used to. He’s retired now. Nice guy. He had me write up some feature-like profiles for some high school seniors. It was good practice writing practical stuff fast and making deadlines. I got to see my name in print, too.” I absentmindedly poked at the crinkled petals, then attempted to press them out and fluff them up a bit. I wasn’t having much luck. The whole thing was just too lumpy. Did Rune think he could bribe me with this?

“I remember reading those stories. They—”

“They were just fine,” Teeny Mom said, sidetracking Michael before he could add any remarks meant to annoy me.

I appreciated her efforts. I doubted if it would have bothered me much at this point. But it got me to wondering if old Mr. Gunnarson might have given his nephew a story to chase down. Something juicy enough to capture the attention of a hot shot journalist wannabe like Rune. A good enough reason to get him out in the Bishop Hill cemetery at night to meet with someone who thought “time was money.” It would take a lot to gain points with his dad. That had to have been the ultimate goal. Impress his dad. Impress Marsha Ellen, too. I couldn’t imagine what there would be around here that could be that tempting and bring the kind of danger that would get him killed. But he had checked into the B&B instead of using his uncle's place. I had to ask myself a chilling question: Was he afraid of something?

"Albin Gunnarson still writes for the paper. I see his name on the occasional feature story," Teeny Mom said. "Comes into Bishop Hill to join a group of his old cronies at the bakery most mornings," she added.

"What, not a fan of The Lutfisk Café?" I said, still fussing with the flower.

"The man likes his cinnamon rolls," Teeny Mom informed us. "You guys could, maybe, accidentally run into him, oh say, tomorrow morning around seven."

"Not me," said Michael. "Still working the night shift. I'll be on my way home to crash."

"I doubt if I'll be up that early," I said. "Today has been exciting enough for me." I shook my head. "Well, dreadful would be a better word for my morning in Cambridge. I still can't believe I was a real suspect for a while. Of course, it probably had a lot to do with my big mouth and how I shouted at Rune 'You're gonna die' loud enough for the whole world to hear." It made me miserable all over again. "I can't blame anyone but me. Good thing I don't have any immediate travel plans because I've once again been instructed to stay put and out of trouble." I shook away a clammy feeling that made my skin crawl. "I'm not going down that road again."

"What road is that?" Teeny Mom asked with pretend innocence.

"The one that gets me tangled up in solving a crime."

Michael gave me a know-it-all look. He was envisioning me turning up at the bakery tomorrow morning. I would show him. "Look, I just want to keep my job at Nikkerbo. Leave it to the deputies to find the clues. Catch the bad guy. I don't need any more guns pointed at me."

Michael added a thoughtful, "No. You don't get used to that."

I was surprised. He rarely revealed anything of this personal side since coming back from Iraq. I'd heard others of his Army National Guard unit were like that.

Michael realized he needed a diversionary tactic to camouflage the shift in his mood. "Come on, now, Rune left you that nice flower thingy."

I fingered the paper rose. "It's going to take more than this."

CHAPTER 9

Wednesday, June 11, 2008

I found myself wide awake at six o'clock the next morning. I stared at the ceiling with my thoughts revolving around Rune. Why the cemetery? What could have gotten him there? What made it dangerous? The dilemma of Rune faded as thoughts of fresh, warm cinnamon rolls betrayed me. My mouth watered. My stomach growled. So, why not stop in at the bakery? It couldn't hurt. It would just be me and a couple of early-rising farmers. I'd sample Talli's competition. Mr. Gunnarson would be a no-show, and, presto, I'd be morally off the hook with Teeny Mom for making the suggestion in the first place. No pain at all.

Wrong. I walked in and guess who was already there? Michael J. Anderson with a substantial looking cinnamon roll slathered with icing and swimming in a pool of melted butter. This time the J probably stood for Just Had to Have One.

I uttered a polite, "Mind if I join you?" before sitting down. He smirked like he knew all along that I'd show up. I scanned the room while I waited for the waitress to notice me. "I'm getting an early start this morning, so I thought I'd just drop by and see if the cinnamon rolls were really as good as advertised. You know, worth the trip."

"Well," he said, "so far, so good." He leaned in and whispered, "I'm hoping Talli doesn't see me down here or she'll dish out an extra big helping of grief next time I'm at The Lutfisk."

"Oh sure, she's not going to notice the giant tow truck. Like she's suddenly gone blind." But I hadn't seen it out front, so he had put a little effort into being inconspicuous. "Where does one hide a monster like that?" I asked.

"I got it stashed down past the park, behind the state site workshop."

"Right, like that's going to fool her." My turn to smirk. "She's got special radar fine-tuned for sniffing out that sort of thing."

We could have kept that banter up forever thanks to lots of practice from our school days, but the front door opened and Mr. Albin Gunnarson came in by himself. He had the haggard look of someone with too little sleep and too much sorrow. Michael sawed off a bite of his roll. I smiled at Mr. Gunnarson and wished him a pleasant good morning. He gave me a stiff nod and sought out his usual morning companions. I returned to my study of the menu.

As luck would have it, Mr. Gunnarson's group sat well within hearing range. All had heard the sad news about his nephew, Rune. The eldest farmer expressed his condolences and asked how he was holding up. Mr. Gunnarson's face clouded over and remained silent. The others filled in with their own words of sympathy. Reluctant at first, he slowly opened up as he fondly recalled his nephew. Eventually, he got around to their last conversation.

"I'd been expecting him to call, or to just show up sometime. We'd talked a few times in the last month about his career plans. He'd have his journalism degree and was looking for freelance ideas for articles that would look good on his resume, maybe bring in some cash." He paused. "That's when I found out about Marsha Ellen Anderson. Rune was set on getting himself engaged." Mr. Gunnarson made no pretense of being happy at the news, but it sparked a round of discussion between the men at the table about which Anderson clan she belonged to. In due time everyone on hand indicated their approval.

"Thanks guys," Mr. Gunnarson said. "But Rune needed more than my blessings. I gave him my ideas for stories. I thought the best potential was with Oliver Carlson and his Galva coin business. You all know how he is about gold coins and obsolete currency, especially that of the Bishop Hill Colony." There was another round of knowing head shaking and more general discussion about Carlson.

Gold coins were easy to figure out. I've seen photos of gold eagles and double eagles. Personally, I'd always liked the graceful flowing lines of the silver liberty coins from an artistic point of view. But when I silently mouthed a query about "obsolete currency" to Michael, all I got back was him shrugging his shoulders just enough to convey that he hadn't known that currency could become obsolete either.

At least I had a name, Oliver Carlson. Nice, but if I had it so did the sheriff's department and, therefore, the end of the line for me and my amateur sleuthing. Time for me to go to work at Nikkerbo and continue to pretend to fill in for David Ekollon as interim director. I had reports to work on and some interesting new research to start.

Monday's meeting with Mr. Hemcourt, the one that resulted in me missing Rune, hadn't been all about the potential for a new arts and crafts show. David "The Dragon" Ekollon might indeed be coming back to resume his position as director. It seemed that a lot of lawyerly negotiations had gotten him out on bail and were close to getting him back into his old position thanks to a clause in his employment contract. Judging by Mr. Curt Hemcourt V's cool reporting of these events, I took it to mean that all was not amicable between the museum owner and his not-so-trustworthy director.

I pulled into Nikkerbo's employee's parking lot. Both spots earmarked for "Director" were filled, one with Mr. Hemcourt's black BMW and Ekollon's ancient Mercedes in the other. I stared in disbelief. I could feel my jaw tense as I gritted my teeth. Mr. Hemcourt never mentioned Ekollon would be here today. The surprise did not sit well at all. This meant I'd be passing the directorship's torch back sooner rather than later. The immediate upshot for me was I'd have to vacate the director's spacious office for much smaller digs, most likely in the storage area down by the archives room. Hopefully, I'd have a computer station up and running on my new desk sometime soon. It might ease the pain of losing my raise, a window to the outside world, and ready access to a great personal library focused on Bishop Hill history.

When all this interim director business began, I was so nervous about taking on the extra work, the additional responsibility, and the peer pressure from rising too fast. At the time the most pressing need had been to keep the museum open, and the staff organized. Mr. Hemcourt declared Ekollon unavailable due to an emergency leave of absence. I was the only one with any formal education in museum studies. My new college degree gave me certification potential. Then I realized I kind of liked it. All but the grumbling and dark looks I got from nearly everyone I worked with. After all, I had started out as a summer hire. Now, I had transitioned to permanent employee with a lot of benefits. Only Lars Trollenberg genuinely appreciated my rise in status. Too bad he would only be here for the short term as a foreign exchange student, or at least that was his official designation. I'd already figured out he was more than what he appeared to be. The tip off came when an angry Ekollon let slip a comment about Lars having diplomatic immunity. That was unusual even for Bishop Hill, a place where Swedish royalty did show up from time to time.

I entered through the back door and paused to consider where to go first. The employee break room could wait; I had bakery coffee with me. Dropping by Mr. Hemcourt's office had no appeal, as it probably held the triumphant Ekollon. I might as well go and see how things were shaping up down by the archives room. Former storerooms can have some ambient charm with the right accessories. My collection of Bishop Hill memorabilia didn't have the scope of Ekollon's, but I had a good start.

Luck was with me when I opened the most likely looking storeroom door and encountered James Viklund, the younger half of the two local tech experts I knew I could trust.

"Shelley, *mon cher*, welcome to your new abode. Be patient, I just need to finish up this last connection."

"You saw David 'The Dragon' for instructions?" I inquired, trying to dampen my surprise.

"What? Ah, no, I mean *non*. His presence was felt all the same."

"Then who?"

James straightened up and said, "*Monsieur* Hemcourt asked for my best efforts." He produced a sweeping arm gesture ending with an enthusiastic bow, pointing toward the desk that held a flat screen monitor and a laptop computer. "*Voila! Mademoiselle*, allow me to familiarize you with the wonders of your new two-screen workstation."

His French accent needed some work, but I gasped in admiration and suppressed a giggle as I sat down in my new chair. “I’m glad you’re hanging on to some of your French vocab words. I hope this means you got all your language credits in for graduation.”

He sniffed indignantly. “Fire and torment upon the souls of all those who impose foreign language requirements on us poor engineering majors.”

“Well, here’s to graduation and your freedom from old world languages.” I raised my coffee cup in a salute.

“Indeed. It shall be so.” James set about guiding me through the basics of my new setup: finding the on/off switches, using the correct connecting cables, a lecture on setting secure passwords, how to initiate secret searches, and many other things I hoped to remember someday. He tried to interest me in some hot game he and his brother, Alan, had recently discovered. I declined. However, he made sure I at least knew how to get some good background music. I must have looked totally pathetic to him.

“But how did all this get here?”

“As I said, *Monsieur* Hemcourt asked for my best efforts. He called last night with his request for your new office setup. I must humbly admit that these items,” he indicated the entire desktop, “are from my collection. But have no fear, my old laptop and monitor are superior to what you’ll find elsewhere in this building. Should you change your mind about gaming, let me know.”

“Thank you so much for everything. I was interim director for only five days, and I came in late for two of those days, so I’d better pass on playing games at work.”

After James left, I settled into the comfy office chair and began some web surfing. I had to remember to thank Mr. Hemcourt for smoothing my transition back to regular employee. I hoped for a half an hour of internet time before having to surface for instructions about the new order of things here at Nikkerbo.

All too soon my desk phone rang, and I had to venture down to Mr. Hemcourt's office. I entered to find David Ekollon just where I expected him to be. However, neither he nor Mr. Hemcourt appeared at ease. I guessed we all wanted this awkward meeting to be over with as quickly and as painlessly as possible.

Everyone said the right words, and all was pretty much as it was before with Ekollon issuing the daily marching orders to me and the rest of the staff. The exception was my new title of assistant director. Mr. Hemcourt apologized for having to dismiss us rather abruptly by saying he was late. He was scheduled to lead a group tour for his visiting executives and not to expect him back until well after lunch.

On our way out of the office, Ekollon handed me a printed list of upcoming events. A list I had prepared three days ago. He passed me a second list in his own distinctive handwriting. It held the names, contact information, and personal data for potential customers who had expressed interest in Nikkerbo's services. I was told to contact each one. Then he left me to go to his office. I scanned the events list first as I walked back to my windowless space, making sure there hadn't been any last-minute changes. I wouldn't put it past Ekollon to try something sneaky, something to undermine my performance.

Everything appeared to be in order. After reading through the list of potential clients, all was better than being in order, there was the personal contact information for the Galva coin dealer that Mr. Gunnarson had mentioned at the bakery. The additional notes made it seem like Ekollon considered him an old friend. If Rune had connected with Oliver Carlson for an interview on Monday, he may well have been one of the last people to see Rune before whatever happened in the cemetery … happened. Perhaps, they even agreed to meet in the cemetery, and, therefore, he was an eyewitness.

Or maybe this contact held another possibility, a much more sinister one.

I told myself not to get worked up. If I was thinking of this, then so was the sheriff.

Back in my new office, I punched Carlson's phone number on my cell phone and then thought better of it. I should use Nikkerbo's phone system. The number would look familiar to Carlson and I was following up on his original contact. I checked the list again. He had inquired about the possibility of booking space for a coin show. Perfect. We'd get to talking about all things coin and money related, which would include the mysterious world of obsolete currency. My morning's research garnered some barebone facts about the general nature of printing private money in the 1800s. The high spot in all this activity was how nicely it overlapped with the Bishop Hill Colony era. I might get some traction there to keep the guy talking to me. People around here loved to talk about Bishop Hill's old colony days.

While I listened to unanswered ring tones, Ekollon slid into my line of sight. He carried a box that held the few personal items I'd brought in during my short stay in his office as interim director. I hung on for a few more sounds of not available before disconnecting and acknowledging his presence.

"Thank you so much for walking those down. You shouldn't have. Just sit them anywhere."

Anywhere turned out to be on the desk, evenly spaced between us.

"I'm glad to see you tackling the contact list first," he said, pointing to his handwritten list and my pile of scratchy notes. I took a moment to neaten the pile and slid it out of the way. "You know, Mr. Hemcourt wasn't very impressed with your lack of enthusiasm for his idea for *Nikkerbo's Olof Krans Arts and Crafts Festival*. I thought of it as a wonderful opportunity. But then," his tone acquired added sarcasm, "I don't have the potential conflict of interest you have."

"Right, and how do you propose to get artists and vendors, most of whom are booked up for a year ahead, at minimum, to come here for an untried event?" I leaned over my desk, tented my fingers, and waited. I wasn't totally new at this.

"True, it will be a challenge. I assured Mr. Hemcourt that I could find a way to produce results." He leaned over the opposite side of my desk, balancing his fleshy hands on the edge. "And I will."

I nodded in agreement. He certainly needed to go big to earn back Mr. Hemcourt's trust. After all, he had tried to sneak off with Hemcourt family property and got caught. He must have one amazing contract to pull off this second chance.

"What's your plan?" I asked. A good assistant would have offered more at this point, but I held back. He had made a feeble attempt to frame me for his so-called misplacement of the family's painting.

"Among your contacts there, is one Oliver Carlson, a coin dealer from Galva. That's his personal cell number."

"Is that so," I said, trying to belie any prior knowledge on my part.

"Well, we're good friends and have had several occasions where we discussed potential plans for having a show for premier numismatists, you know, coin dealers. He was most keen about it and assured me he had a great many contacts at the top levels in the field. Now is a perfect time to discuss it further." Ekollon looked extremely pleased with himself.

"As a matter of fact, I've just tried to call him," I said. "No answer. I'll try again later."

"When you do get him on a line, transfer the call to me, if you please." He gave me a smug smile. "You do remember how to do that don't you?"

I didn't bat an eye. "Yes, sir."

CHAPTER 10

I had no luck getting Galva coin dealer Oliver Carlson to answer my second call. I wondered what I could do to speed things along, not for Ekollon's sake, or for the general good of Nikkerbo, but for Marsha Ellen. And yes, out of regret for treating Rune so harshly on what would become his last day. I owed it to them to find out more about Rune's interview with Carlson last Monday. If Carlson hadn't been Rune's last stop, he might be able to steer me in the direction of where Rune was off to next. Rune had mentioned that he had more than one interview in the works. Plus, I wanted to hear Carlson's own words. Any kind of a hint would help. Some little thing that I would find significant that a sheriff's deputy or investigator might miss. I could very well be over-estimating myself here, but I too needed to hope. I cautioned myself to not trust him completely.

After my third attempt I figured that if Oliver Carlson wasn't answering his calls, I knew someone else who might be in and willing to talk. Albin Gunnarson, Rune's uncle, was the one who hooked those two up for the interview in the first place. I placed the call and crossed my fingers.

Mr. Gunnarson answered right away and sounded annoyed when he realized mine wasn't the voice he wanted to hear. "I'm expecting a call from my brother, Rune's father," he said. "I can't stay on the line for too long. I'm sure you understand."

"I'm so sorry to bother you, sir, but have you heard from Oliver Carlson today?"

His silence provided the answer—no.

I spoke with a near-breathless urgency, "I promise I won't take up too much of your time. I'm trying to get hold of Oliver Carlson, actually, to return his call, and I wondered if you've seen him today? Or heard something about him recently?"

"No. I haven't seen him. I've tried to call him, too. No luck. It's like he dropped off the edge of the earth last Monday." He paused to suck in an anxious breath. I could make out the nervous clicking of his fingernails on his desk. "It makes no sense. It was just an interview about the obsolete currency from the Bishop Hill Colony."

"I don't recall the Colonists printing their own money."

"No, not directly. A couple of Colonists brought the currency in from Nebraska. Bad timing, though," he said.

"Why say that?"

"It was just in time for the Panic of 1857. They lost their colony shirts over that deal." He followed the joke with a single dry laugh.

"And Oliver Carlson knows about this?" I asked.

"Of course."

His answers were getting shorter and so was my time. "So, if this currency didn't have any value back then, why would anyone be interested in it now?"

"Scarcity and rareness are a collector's friend. Young lady, you should know this. I'm sorry, but I need to go now."

"Did he have a good source or supply of this currency?"

"Not enough to suit him. He was always looking for more. Now I really must go."

"Thank you for your—" He disconnected before I could finish. I couldn't blame him.

I thought about driving by Oliver Carlson's Galva home. I also thought about how one might go about looking for obsolete money, especially the Bishop Hill kind. Teeny Mom and her shopping expertise came to mind.

When I got back to the red brick house after work, I found the kitchen deserted except for a slow cooker simmering full of what smelled like vegetable stew. I went outside to see if I could find her. It would not necessarily be an easy task; there was a barn, the six visitor cabins plus a restroom/shower building for the Ox-Boy Campground, and lots and lots of flower beds. I found her in the barn surrounded by kittens.

"Looks like a momma cat has brought her babies out of hiding," I said. "How are they doing?"

"They look healthy, but they're not used to people. We've got to get them tame enough to catch and get them to the vet."

"Have we reached our quota for barn cats for this year?" I asked.

"I think we can handle two out of his litter, but no more, and I can't think who might want our overflow. Barn cats are always plentiful this time of year."

I sat down on a bale of straw and tried to coax the multicolored mob over to me by daggling a long stalk of hay in what I thought was an enticing way. They showed some interest but stayed well out of petting reach.

"They're getting big enough to use the dry food. Of course, everything loves cat food," Teeny Mom reminded me.

Right on cue, Flicka, the neighbor's black lab, showed up expecting her regular hand out. The momma cat arched her back and hissed at the large dog. One of her babies imitated her. The rest ran for cover. Flicka appeared unperturbed.

"Go on home, girl," I said and shooed Flicka out the door. "You'll have to try again later."

Teeny Mom brought me up to speed on all the local news: A car crash with a gasoline spill had occurred up by the northern turn off to the Bishop Hill road. No new information on what happened out in the cemetery. Then she proceeded to report on the host of wild theories that were beginning to float around, including the one that hauled out the old legend of the Hound of Bishop Hill.

Uncle Roy had gotten us started on that nonsense. He used to make up all kinds of stories when my brother John and I were young and impressionable. I think he was trying to instill some moral lessons, but I couldn't honestly remember anything of significance. I just recalled the part about the big, mean dog carrying off misbehaving little kids to be raised as, well, wild dogs. Scary stuff at one time, especially around Halloween, certainly not now. I wondered who would have thought of that angle. A certain Michael J for Joker Anderson might be a good candidate.

When I finally had my chance to talk about other topics, I asked Teeny Mom if she knew about the Bishop Hill money, the obsolete currency from the 1800s.

"Sure, I do. I even have some."

"Really?" I was astonished. "I don't remember seeing anything that looked like money."

"I keep it in my bedroom."

"You do?"

"Shelley, you've seen it. You always liked looking at the horses. I used it to help you learn your numbers. At least for 1, 2, 3, and 5. They didn't make a four dollar note." She gave me a quizzical look. "You really don't remember?"

What she described didn't ring a bell for me. I could only think of the framed art prints she had hung on the walls in between family photos and flowery wreaths in nearly every room of the house.

"Oh, come on I'll have to show you."

We went upstairs and she pointed to what I thought was a nicely segmented art print, an engraving on ecru-colored paper with a heavily mottled visual texture. So yes, she was correct, I'd seen this piece countless times since I was young. I'd forgotten that it was something once meant to be so very utilitarian: money.

"See, this is a whole sheet as it was printed. It was meant to be cut apart. I liked how it looked and left it whole. I've been told that it might be worth more cut apart and each one sold separately." She gazed at the stylized scenes of the old west and sighed. "But I'd never do that."

"Who tried to talk you into cutting them up?" I asked. "Would it have been Oliver Carlson?"

"Yes, he thinks he's a big expert on this type of money. He's always looking for more to add to his collection and, of course, anything he can sell for a profit. Like these, because they are dated and have two signatures. I always turned him down when he asked if I was ready to part with mine."

"You're the second person to mention he was always searching for more of this obsolete currency. Where would he go for more?"

"I search for it on eBay every once in a while. They have a category for it."

"Obsolete currency? You're kidding."

"No, it's there. Go look for yourself sometime. Search for 'Bishop Hill obsolete currency'."

"I've never been on eBay. I figured I didn't have enough money or trust in how the site worked." It was more than a little irritating to realize that in some respects my Teeny Mom was more up to date on the modern tech world than I was. And to think I've been known to make fun of her computer skills.

"Okay," I said. "Oliver Carlson has his coin business, he has a network of other dealers, and he can shop on eBay. Any other places he might go?"

"Well, there might be one more thing …"

I waited. She looked embarrassed. Before I could prod her, she started, "You know how the Hound of Bishop Hill legend came up earlier."

I nodded.

"You know how there are a few other Bishop Hill legends out there."

I nodded again. "Seems like there are plenty of legends to go around. Something for every occasion and season."

"Do you know about the buried treasure one?" she asked.

"I guess so. I always thought of it as a box of gold nuggets that prospectors brought back from the California gold rush."

"That's a nice take on it. But I'm more in favor of the old colony trustee who took the useless Nebraska bank notes and buried them."

"Okay, so let's say there is in fact a box of old money in the ground somewhere—so what?" I shrugged.

"So, occasionally, some fool decides to go out and look for it. A lot of fools over the years have dug up their own yards and fields." She stopped for effect. "And sometimes … those of others."

"You're suggesting that Oliver Carlson might be one of those fools?"

“I’m afraid so.” She looked sad. “I’ve had people tell me they’ve seen him walk by their houses with a shovel over his shoulder on his way to dig where he shouldn’t be digging.”

“Would he dig in the cemetery?” I asked, aghast at the gruesome image.

“No. He’d get into too much trouble for that. I’m certain he’d have the good sense to leave the cemetery alone.”

“But he could certainly walk by the cemetery on his way somewhere else, oh say, down by the Edwards River?”

“Now, I could see that,” she said. “There used to be storage sheds for the broomcorn crops down by the river past the cemetery.”

“Was there a full moon Monday night?” I inquired.

I could tell she was busy calculating the moon’s phases and probably wondering how to explain it to someone, like me, who took those natural cycles for granted to the point of being oblivious to the details. “No, the moon will be full closer to midsummer, sometime next week. Last Monday night would have been more of a waxing gibbous moon that would have set around midnight.”

“Leaving darkness,” I said.

“That’s right," she nodded.

CHAPTER 11

After such an enlightening conversation about Bishop Hill legends and Oliver Carlson's penchant for nocturnal expeditions with his trusty shovel, I took the opportunity to drive into Galva by way of the backroads and search out Carlson's house.

I found the two-story wood-framed house with the wide front porch near Wiley Park. I pulled into a parking spot nearby and waited for lights to go on. Nothing happened as the evening's darkness deepened. No car in the driveway, either. I wasn't about to get out and peek into the windows. I tried to maintain a few standards of conduct. So, I allowed myself sufficient time for boredom to set in before deciding to leave well enough alone, for now, and go downtown to McKane's bar and restaurant. I'd drive by the house again later as I left town.

As I prepared to leave my parking spot, a dark two-door car passed me. It slowed down long enough for a better look at me before it accelerated to the corner, where the driver touched the brake pedal for a brief flash of red before disappearing beyond the reach of Galva's streetlights. Someone sure was in a hurry to get their Toyota Scion out of town.

McKane's was doing a good business for that time of the night. I got the last empty booth and settled in with the menu. I felt slightly bad about taking up a whole booth myself, but I had no intention of being here long. I wanted something fast and couldn't decide between an appetizer or the salad bar. I hadn't made up my mind about food by the time the waitress came along to take my order, so I stalled for time by ordering a cup of decaf coffee.

Michael J for Joker Anderson and Deputy Dana Johnson seemed to materialize out of thin air. I was taken aback when Michael slid into the booth without any "May we join you." Deputy Dana, not in uniform, looked hesitant before she slid in beside him.

Michael didn't bother to suppress the grin on his face. "So, how's your investigation going?"

The deputy's expression went from hesitant to ruffled.

"I'm not investigating anything," I insisted casually.

"Oh, yeah. Then why were you parked near Oliver Carlson's house."

I took a beat to process the scene where any number of people may have been intently watching one house in Galva. "I've been trying to reach Mr. Carlson all day. He called Nikkerbo about renting space or something, and Ekollon was on my case about getting results," I said. It was a mostly true story. "Why were you two there?"

"Well, we—" he started to say.

Deputy Dana cut him off. "She doesn't need to know."

"Trust me, she knows," he said, grinning at me.

"Okay, I might have wanted to ask him about his interview with Rune. How it went." I stalled for effect. "And, maybe, see if he'd been near the cemetery, you know, recently. Like, really recently."

"See, I told you," Michael said, practically beaming.

I could tell that off-duty Deputy Dana was beginning to shift into full deputy mode. Like I was still a potential suspect for the odd goings on in the cemetery. "And that's why you were in front of his house after office hours?" she inquired.

Michael could not restrain himself. "Come on, she's heard the same story we have."

"I may have heard," I admitted, "a little something about Mr. Carlson being interested enough in old Bishop Hill buried treasure stories to actually try digging in, shall we say, likely spots around the village."

"Ah ha!" Michael pointed a triumphant finger at Deputy Dana, "Told you."

She swatted the offending digit away from her face. "Michael, please keep your voice down," she admonished, in what was a quiet tone for her, "and your hands. We don't need to broadcast." She turned to me. "Did you get a good look at the car that passed by just before you left? We were too far back."

"It was a dark, probably black, two-door Toyota Scion. Illinois plates with three very memorable letters MAD. You're going to ask how I know that much. Well, it's my dream car. Except for the MAD part.

"You know," I said, after my little report, "I can figure out what she was doing there," I nodded toward Deputy Dana, "but what about you, Mr. Civilian?"

"I wanted to talk with Dana about applying to be a deputy." He shrugged his shoulders. "I got invited to ride along on this stakeout."

"Well, it wasn't what you could call an official stakeout," Deputy Dana demurred.

"Oliver Carlson's car was seen in the vicinity of the cemetery late last Monday. It wasn't hard to put two and two together," he said.

"Michael," Deputy Dana cautioned.

"Does that mean someone found the shovel?" I ventured.

"How'd you know about a shovel?" Michael asked.

“Come on, Michael. She’s just guessing,” Deputy Dana said, aggravated enough to start chewing on the silverware. “Am I correct?” she turned to ask me.

“You sure are. But people do tend to dig with shovels, you know,” I said, with a great deal of satisfaction.

“I can’t say … officially, but you probably made a correct assumption.”

“Was there blood on it?”

Dana’s silence and the thin, pinched line of her lips told me what I wanted to know.

“Was it Rune’s blood?” I asked.

“The lab results are not in.” She gave Michael a cold stare that cut off any further discussion about crime scenes. I took it as my cue to pay for my coffee and leave.

I had no other reason to stay in Galva and needed to get back to Bishop Hill anyway. Michael and the off-duty deputy remained at McKane’s to ostensibly discuss the finer points of the upcoming testing process for new deputy candidates. If this was his night off tow truck duty, he could do what he wanted. Deputy Dana must have had the night off, too. It wasn’t any of my business to know any more than that. It was just beginning to rain when I swung back by Oliver Carlson’s darkened house by the park on my way out of town.

CHAPTER 12

Thursday, June 12, 2008

The weekly newspaper, the *Galva Prairie Pioneer*, came out on Thursday mornings to a collective yawn of predictability. The usual fare consisted of newsy items about school children, local sports teams, and family reunions. It was topped off with the personal comings and goings of the average citizenry—i.e., births and deaths.

This Thursday morning's edition was nowhere near typical. The bold headline announced a startling find near the Bishop Hill cemetery, the body of a young man, one Rune A. Gunnarson, a recent graduate of Knox college. The victim's name was familiar to many by way of his uncle's work with Galva's newspaper. Sheriff Henry declined to make any specific details known for the sake of the ongoing investigation, but he did ask for anyone with information about this young man's recent activities to please come forward. He praised his staff of criminal investigators and insisted that all available resources would be used to maintain public safety.

Despite the sheriff's best efforts, the most asked questions over morning coffee cups in the small towns around the area were: How could this happen here? First, it was Herb Anderson, unassuming woodworker, found dead on the premises of his antique business. Now, this poor young man in the cemetery. Was no one safe? Was a serial killer on a crime spree? Who would be next?

I knew nothing of this commotion as I started my day by way of an early morning cell phone call that jolted me out of an ominous dream of dark cars, empty houses, and shadowy figures skulking around with equally shadowy shovels. I groped for my cell phone, nearly knocking it to the floor before connecting to the caller. Marsha Ellen's frantic voice called my name. "Shelley! Thank God you're there."

I fell back onto my pillow with my cell phone to my ear. "Where else would I be at this hour?" I strained to see the time on my bedside alarm clock and gasped. "It's 5 AM! Are you CRAZY?!" I shouted before regaining enough control to muffle my voice and ask a more relevant question through gritted teeth, "What's going on?"

"Oh, Shelley," Marsha Ellen whimpered. "I have to drive up to the sheriff's department in Cambridge. They want me back for another interview. Can you meet me there? Pleeease."

She used all her breath to draw out the final part of her plea as long as possible. I imagined it was to help get me over the shock of the early hour and her urgent request. I closed my eyes, relaxed my jaw, and said yes.

Under normal circumstances it would take Marsha Ellen over an hour to drive from Galesburg. More if she had to find a nice outfit and apply full makeup first. That would hardly happen today. She'd probably be flying up Interstate 74 to Cambridge within minutes. I threw the quilt back and swung my feet over the side of the bed. I stood up as Teeny Mom opened the door and asked, "Who was that? What's going on?"

"Marsha Ellen is needed in Cambridge. She has to talk to the sheriff's investigators again." I paused to clear the last few cobwebs from my sleepy brain with a long stretch and a yawn. I needed time to take in the enormity of situation. "She asked me to meet her up there." I yawned again.

"I'll make some coffee. You go shower." Before closing the door, she said, "I don't like the sound of this." Then she left me to the grim business of pulling myself together.

Marsha Ellen hadn't made it to Cambridge by the time I arrived at the imposing brick annex to the Henry County courthouse that housed the sheriff's department and jail. I entered the main door and ran into a surprised Deputy Dana.

"What are you doing here?" she asked. "How'd you know I wanted to talk to you?"

Her sudden appearance took me by surprise. "Ah, I'm here because Marsha Ellen, my cousin, asked me to meet her. What are you doing here?" After getting a better look at the deputy I added, "You look, um, like you didn't get much sleep either."

"I got the call to come in shortly after Michael went back to his place. So, no to any sleep." She tensed her muscles, gave herself a loose shake, and declared, "Must have coffee. How about you?"

"Lead the way," I replied, and followed her through unfamiliar hallways that seemed to turn too many times. If they wanted to disorient people on purpose, they had certainly succeeded with me.

"This stuff isn't great, but it will do the trick." Deputy Dana pointed to the coffee pots in what had to be their break room. She filled a cup and waited for me to do the same. We made our way to a vacant table.

"I'm glad you're here. It saved me a drive," she said, in a sheepish way that wasn't keeping with the rigid and sometimes confrontational character I'd come to expect from her.

“Is there something else?” I asked.

“Yeah,” she said. “I was told to bring you back in today for more questions. Now that we have a suspect.” She paused as she took a long pull from her cup, grimacing as she forced it down.

“Come on,” I exclaimed, “why would I have to come in again? I explained about what I said at The Lutfisk the other day.” I recalled all too vividly my ill-fated outburst about Rune being dead. “I was kidding,” I said. I thought about it for a second and added, “Okay, look, I was still sore at Rune for getting together with Marsha Ellen and being all serious about her. It was too sudden, and I was being a total jerk.” I stared at my coffee cup and debated if it was safe to drink. “I didn’t want him to, like, actually die.”

She thoughtfully studied me for a longer moment than was necessary and finally said, “Relax, I believe you. You’re not the suspect. I have to follow procedure here.”

I took a drink of the dark, silty brew and forced it down like she had done. I would never make fun of Talli’s coffee ever again. “Okay, now what?”

“Since it’s painfully obvious,” she cleared her throat, “you knew Rune rather well, and, obviously, Marsha Ellen, too, I’ve got to ask you about Oliver Carlson.” She led me off into the same interrogation room I’d been in the other day.

“Oliver Carlson is your suspect? That seems to be a stretch,” I said, before checking myself. They may have found something, some new evidence.

I braced myself as she laid a folder on the table in front of me. I placed a hand on it. I wasn’t about to let her open it yet. She said, “Yesterday was my day off, so I didn’t know anything about this last night when I saw you at McKane’s.”

“And Michael?”

"No, Michael had last night off, too." I'd swear the deputy was starting to add some color to her cheeks before she got back to business. "So, no, Michael slept through everything yesterday with the wreck and the fuel spill clean-up out on the Page Street Extension. And he missed out on all the other details."

"All the details about what exactly? Sounds like you're leaving something out here. A whole lot of something," I said.

Deputy Dana drummed her fingers on the table. "It seems that Sheriff Henry thought the wreck might provide a nice diversionary cover for the forensic crew to do more work in and around the cemetery. It appeared to have worked with everyone … except a certain reporter."

"That might be Albin Gunnarson, Rune's uncle. And a good friend of Oliver Carlson," I added.

"That's what I hear," she said. She pulled a photo from the folder in front of me.

"Do I have to do this again? Look at these pictures?" I asked. The answer was yes.

This would not be easy. I averted my eyes as I steeled myself, willed myself to be strong, then slowly cast my gaze down to the table. Thankfully, this photo was not quite so graphic as some of the others I'd been shown on Tuesday.

"The wound was not caused by a shovel."

"And the blood that was found on the shovel?" I asked.

"Was not Rune's blood type. That's as far as I can go."

"Then how does this involve Oliver Carlson?"

"He's our main suspect right now. At least until we find him and get his side of the story. If you are in contact with him in any way, or at any time, you must tell us—right away." I nodded. "Shelley, you have to say it."

"Yes, I'll tell you. Call you." Not that I ever expected to see Oliver Carlson, given all the official interest in him.

I was given her card, thanked, and freed to go. She cautioned me not to leave the area. I gave her an exasperated look. "Procedure," she said.

CHAPTER 13

I wasn't late to work yet, but I had to get to Nikkerbo. I waited for Marsha Ellen just outside the front door, leaning against the solid mass of Henry county's judicial might. I mentally issued her a two-minute warning when Deputy Dana caught up with me once more.

"Shelley, I'm glad I caught you. I just got some preliminary search results in for the license plate ID info you gave us last night. Some very interesting results."

She had my attention. "Now, remember it was only a partial so we can't verify a hundred percent positive hit on any one person, but the list of potentials has a car registered to a man with some very shady connections in Chicago. He's someone you've got to steer clear of if your paths should ever cross again."

"Why should our paths meet again? We were just two cars passing in the night." I gave her a shrug and a small smile. I was all out of cleverness.

She didn't bother to return my smile. "The situation was strange enough for you to pay attention to him. You noticed enough about his car to help us make the tentative ID. So, it's very likely he got a good look at your car as well. It's possible that he could track your identity down as easily as we've done with his." She made a point of looking all stern and deputy-like. "You've got to consider him armed and dangerous."

"That's hard to believe," I said. "It was just a car on a dark street in Galva."

"This isn't the kind of guy to fool around with. Him, you, me, Michael we were all there scoping out the Carlson house. That can't be a coincidence."

"Let me guess, you don't believe in coincidences."

"Well, they're always telling us not to. My sergeant especially." She gave me a light, make-believe fist bump to the upper arm. "You be careful."

I gave her a smartly firm salute. "Yes, ma'am." That made her smile.

She walked away and so did I. Time to get back to our jobs.

I had to hustle, too. I was late due to the precious minutes I spent on the phone explaining to Marsha Ellen why I couldn't wait any longer. Ekollon was bound to notice I wasn't making yet another call to the phantom-like Mr. Carlson, to see if I could get them connected, so they could pull off a miracle and save Mr. Hemcourt's pet project—a brand new arts and crafts show to be held a mere two months away. It suddenly struck me as odd that these guys were making all the plans and I was the one expected to carry through with the grunt work that would make their dreams come true. Could this be a slice of the real-world gender inequality I'd heard so much about? My first thought was yes.

And speaking of a dose of real life, what if Mr. Oliver Carlson surfaced from wherever he was hiding, and tried to explain about what he had been doing by the cemetery last Monday? I was willing to take bets that he'd have something remarkably stupid to say about carrying a shovel around Bishop Hill at night. And how does one lose a bloody shovel?

I was spot-on about Ekollon being on my case. I had no more than sat down at my new desk when he came slithering in, pretending to be all polite and concerned. "Are we having another difficult morning, Ms. Anderson?"

"Sort of, sir. I did have to speak to a Henry County deputy again. In a way it was work related."

"How could that be?" he asked with suspicion.

"Well, I happened to be in Galva last night—"

He cut in. "What you do on your own time is of no importance to me or to the business operations of Nikkerbo—"

"Sir, if I might finish." He didn't seem at all pleased by my interruption. "You should know that I took the opportunity to drive past Mr. Carlson's house. No one appeared to be home."

Momentarily mollified, he maneuvered the conversation in a different direction. "Commendable, to a point, but an activity that I should think hardly needs the involvement of a deputy."

"Well, it did in this instance. I noticed—" This time his loud harrumph made me lose my train of thought for a moment. With a moderate amount of personal control, I continued, "I noticed an odd-looking car go by. I gave my information to a nearby deputy." He remained silent. "This morning the deputy gave me some words of caution should I encounter that car again."

"Not relevant, Ms. Anderson," he said, with a sniff. "Do get on with your work."

As he turned to leave, I asked, "Sir, were you aware of Mr. Carlson's keen interest in an old story about a sum of Bishop Hill's obsolete currency being buried and lost?" That made him freeze in place. "Interested enough that it had him going around and actually digging holes looking for it?"

He turned back to me. "Variations of that old legend surface every now and again. Someone always goes off the deep end. It never amounts to anything." He paused to glare at me hard enough to make his point. "I've never known Oliver to be that suggestible. And I wouldn't mention that when you get him on the phone." He turned to leave again but hesitated. "Speaking of legends involving buried money and such, you should be talking to members of your own family. Christina and Roy. What do you call them? Oh, yes, Teeny Mom and Uncle Roy. They may have closer ties to the proverbial buried treasure than anyone else around here." With that, he exited my humble office.

That was the second time this week that someone dropped snarky hints about large amounts of money and a tie to my folks. My Uncle Roy didn't seem to care for money, and I had my doubts about his ability to handle large quantities of it. However, Teeny Mom was an efficient manager and more than capable of taking care of the farm, the Ox-Boy Campground, and the family's finances. I would have to find out more and not take an easy brush-off.

All that would have to wait for tonight. I got out my list of Nikkerbo's potential business contacts, supplied by Ekollon, and started making a fresh round of calls. Of course, my first call was to Oliver Carlson. I tapped in his number not really expecting an answer. Still, I harbored some small hope of hearing from an officious-sounding man with some big ideas for a coin show, and who might have a perfectly logical reason for his strange hobby. My hope dimmed as I counted the ring tones. I let it go until his prerecorded instructions about leaving a message came on. I repeated what I did yesterday, I hung up.

I continued working my way through the list with my calls but was bothered by the growing suspicion of something not being right. The feeling nagged at me until Deputy Dana's warning about the Chicago connection for the MAD license plate surfaced. Of course, Chicago was the clue that led me to what was missing from my list of call backs—it held no names or numbers of Hemcourt's corporate managers. A few high-ranking ones had already shown up for those heated meetings of the past week. If others were supposed to show up for, say, a working retreat over the upcoming Midsummer weekend I, the lowly flunky, would have to be making the arrangements, oh say, like, right now. That had to be Ekollon's scheme to discredit me. I had to get on this.

Something else bothered me about those meetings, especially that first one I brought the coffee into. There were the older men, corporate types to be sure, but there was a younger one, a guy more my age, or rather Rune's. I was in and out quickly, but I remembered this look he gave me, like we knew each other. Could I have met him through Rune?

Talking to Deputy Dana seemed like the right thing to do. I fished in my bag for her card and naturally couldn't find it. I'd have to dump the whole bag out for a thorough search. That gave me second thoughts about making the call. It didn't seem remotely possible that any executive-type connected with Nikkerbo would know Rune, or Oliver Carlson, or have any reason to be out and about the Bishop Hill cemetery last Monday night. Still, I might bring it up the next time I saw her. For now, I had work to do.

Later in the morning I had a couple of people interested in reserving space for family reunions; one for a retirement party; a meeting of a local historical group, if the price was approved by the committee in charge; and maybe a wedding reception, again, if the price was right. The talk of wedding plans made me wonder if I should give Marsha Ellen a call. I had been tying up Nikkerbo's phone lines for quite a while and I might have missed her. I got my cell phone out of my bag and checked it. I hadn't missed anything there. It made me wish I knew what was going on. So much for not wanting to get more deeply involved.

I could have, and should have, emailed my results to Ekollon but a deliciously wicked thought had me scuttle that option. I would print out my results and hand deliver them to his office, his inner sanctum, the very one I used in his absence. The annoyance factor was appropriately high. It would bother him, break his routine, possibly take vital time away from his security observations. So much drama to joyfully disrupt.

I ran through his possible reactions as I prepared to knock on his door: not there, too busy, or perhaps using his ample body to physically bar admittance. Well, I thought, I'd pass on my report and say at least I tried. Any inhospitality would be squarely on his shoulders, delivering, by omission, a few points for me.

I knocked on the door and heard a very clear "Come in." I checked the door just to be certain I was in the right place. I entered with a fair amount of caution. This wasn't a thug from Chicago but someone almost as dangerous. He still held a good amount of influence over my career, and he knew it.

"Ah, Ms. Anderson. I had hoped I might see you yet again this morning."

I was not going to let him get to me that easily. I handed over my report, which made a prominent point of Mr. Carlson not responding to calls, or messages I'd already left, and today's lack of success. I figured I'd be dismissed and took a step toward the door without his encouragement.

"Wait a moment if you will," he said, in what passed as a warm and friendly tone for him. "Your comments about obsolete currency and buried treasure piqued my curiosity and I looked up some reference material for you. On top is an old article written by George Swank for Galvaland. There's an image of the notes in the text but I'm afraid it's not of very good quality. I have a framed set of the actual bills, uncut, but I keep that at home. You understand."

"Of course. I found out that Teeny Mom, excuse me, Christina, has something similar in her bedroom." I felt embarrassed about mentioning her bedroom and wished I hadn't. Too late, I could tell that he was winding up for a lecture about some pertinent fact I needed to be informed about. No doubt crucial to him and only him.

"I'm glad you mentioned Christina. As I hinted at earlier today, she, or more rightly, her father, when he was quite young, and old Nils Westbloom may have happened upon some very interesting treasure, as it were. Do have a seat."

I made sure there was a clear path to the door in case I needed to sprint. Six steps maybe. Four steps if I had to move fast. Three if I had to fly to safety. No steps at all if I had to use some of my self-defensive moves on him. I didn't study Tae Kwon Do for three years for nothing. I was confident my old black belts wouldn't let me down in a pinch. I took a seat.

"Now, of course you know all about how Nils and Cilla Westbloom built the red brick house on their joint allotments of property after the dissolution of the Bishop Hill Colony." He paused to make sure I nodded. "And you know how they, being orphans themselves, always made their home open and available to any child in need."

This time I added a "Yes, sir" to my nod. While it was difficult to hold my tongue, I thought it best for him to tell the story in his own way.

He carried on about Christina's father, my Grandpa Colberg, being one of those orphans and how he stayed on to "help out" when the Westblooms got on in years. I certainly knew how he inherited the property. My Teeny Mom, Christina, had maintained her own version of taking in orphans. That's how my twin brother John and I came to the red brick house on the hill. That's ultimately how Uncle Roy and Christina got together and finally married. They wanted to gain total custody and protect us. There wasn't any new information here and nothing that could translate into any kind of treasure, buried or otherwise. I was starting to get bored, but I kept on nodding.

Ekollon assumed a sly smile. "You know all this, correct."

"Yes, sir," I said dutifully.

"Did anyone tell you about the night the Smoketree got its name?"

"There was a car accident. The car hit the tree, and both caught fire." I shrugged. "The smoke could be seen from the village."

"Not really," came his cool answer.

"But—"

"There, there. Be patient. Don't get upset and I'll tell you what my father told me. He was one of the volunteer firemen who responded."

I never liked the condescending tone of a "there, there" or a "don't get upset." This double teaming of clichés had to be a harbinger of a story I wasn't going to like. I squirmed a bit and remained silent.

"There was a car crash that night and the tree caught fire. No one from the village knew about it though until the fire department was called in. This was at the height of the roaring 20s. Can you imagine what kind of people would be racing along our county backroads in the dead of night?" he asked.

"I don't know," I ventured. "Probably something to do with bootlegged alcohol."

"Yes, quite correct. Those nice old folks up there on the hill were up to here," Ekollon waved a hand over his head, "in the bootlegging business that ran between the Quad Cities and Peoria. You get the picture?"

How could I not? He continued with his story. "They had a lot of illegal cash to conceal, so they took to burying most of it. They had to spread it around, you know, not keep it all in one place. Some of it is still out there. That's the buried treasure Mr. Carlson and some others keep looking for."

"I find it hard to believe I've not heard of this before," I said. It came out far more stiffly than I wanted.

"Your 'Teeny Mom' has a lot of practice keeping secrets. I suggest you try to pry some of them out of her." With that he gathered up some papers off his desk and handed them to me. "Read these and get yourself familiar with obsolete currency. You'll need to be up to speed when you get Oliver on the phone."

I was dismissed and glad of it. I took the research materials he handed me and left. I looked back at him as I closed the door. He seemed quite contented with himself.

Of course, Teeny Mom was good at keeping secrets. We all were. Even though the air was cleared between us on a lot of matters, why shouldn't there be more. And with things that happened so long ago with Grandpa Colberg I could certainly see why no one wanted to bring up every little detail. Ekollon's intent struck me as a devious ploy to drive a wedge between Teeny Mom and me. I pitied him for having such a jealous mind and vindictive soul. Such a waste of energy. However, it was good to be reminded to be wary around him.

CHAPTER 14

"Will you be eating with us tonight?" Teeny Mom called out as I came in through the back door loaded down with the stuff Ekollon had given me to read on top of my own late-night study material on the history of obsolete currency. "Is that work or recreational reading you've got there?"

"A little of both," I said. "They overlap, so some of it is duplicate material. I'll have to sift through." I looked around for a convenient place to unburden some of the load. "I still haven't connected with Oliver Carlson, our errant coin dealer, so in the meantime Ekollon wants me to be better versed on obsolete currency." I noticed that the quantity of food Teeny Mom was preparing seemed more than for just the three of us. "Are you expecting company tonight?"

"Yes, as a matter of fact."

I saw a self-satisfied smirk on her face. There was scheming going on.

"Okay, give it up," I demanded. "You look way too pleased with yourself."

"I've had pretty good luck with renting out cabins this week. There was this nice family from Rockford. Some businessmen came in from the Chicago area. And I have a few more reservations for Midsummer. I thought I'd celebrate with an invitation to supper."

"You invited all of them?" I couldn't believe she'd really do that. Uncle Roy would probably have a fit and refuse show up at all.

"No, no. Just the one," she said, with a soothing lilt. "Most of the businessmen checked out early this morning. They had a tour planned and were heading back to the big city after lunch. One of them, however, wanted to stay another night. The Rockford family had plans for the evening before they leave tomorrow, which helps to open up enough space for that group coming in for Midsummer."

"What group?" I asked, wondering if the group she referred to might be an entourage of Mr. Hemcourt's Chicago executives. Could I possibly get that lucky? "Who made the reservations? Were any references made about Nikkerbo?"

"One of the businessmen who checked out this morning, a Mr. Hanson, said he'd be coming back and needed the space for a group. He was lucky I had a cancellation on top of the other free cabins." She thought for a moment and nodded, "Sure, he made it sound like they needed to be close to Nikkerbo."

I heaved a sigh of relief. "It's good to know that Mr. Hemcourt's returning executives are booked into a reputable establishment." She looked at me quizzically. "Plus," I said, "you're a life saver! I was out of the loop for that one, but you've got it covered." Much more like I dodged a bullet. The little kid inside me did a happy dance. When it was over it was time for the next important question. "Okay, who's unaccounted for since you said 'most' of the business types checked out?" I was past suspicious by this time. "Am I supposed to know this person?"

"I imagine you do," she said, with a beaming smile. She obviously thought she'd preformed some amazing coup.

"This would be a youngish guy?" I couldn't honestly remember more than stylish clothes, nice haircut, and the strange look when he turned away from his presentation to see me deliver the coffee. The brief encounter had left me with a disembodied feeling of déjà vu.

"Honey, at my age everyone looks young to me. This one's name is Charles Guyer. He said he went to Knox, so you might know him from there."

I didn't know what to make of that. Process of elimination said no to an art student. More likely, a business major. Probably a fraternity brother for Rune. Marsha Ellen had mentioned a name, but Charles didn't seem a good fit.

"Well, we'll have to wait and see if he shows up for supper. You need me to do anything?" I asked.

She gave me some small jobs to do. I stowed my homework out of the way and got busy.

While I helped Teeny Mom set the dining room table with the good china, I broached another topic that needed further exploration. "You know, lately, people have been dropping hints that you know more about this buried treasure business than I do. Marcella, for one, alluded to it the other day. I never took it seriously. Then Ekollon did a similar thing today."

"Oh, you know how it goes. There are still a few people who wonder how my father, an orphan, managed to inherit all this land and these buildings from the Westblooms," Teeny Mom said.

"Still? After all these years?"

"Honey, when people live as close to a place such as this for over a hundred years, give or take a few, the past can seem pretty much like the present to them."

I let out a sound of discontent. She paused before continuing.

"I've told you before, don't let those things bother you. Just go on."

"And what about the Westblooms being bootlegging outlaws? That's a tiny bit bigger deal," I said, holding up thumb and index finger to approximate the pinch that expanded to represent the higher degree of my concern.

This time the pause stretched out and I noticed she hadn't moved. I wasn't sure what to expect. Teeny Mom usually kept her emotions in check. I assumed that came from years of dealing with Uncle Roy and his drinking problems and other misadventures. She never had a bad thing to say about Grandpa Colberg. In fact, she often held him up as a model for charitable living. Same with the Westblooms.

"Where exactly did that come from? This fiction about bootlegging outlaws?" she asked at last.

"Ekollon told me he got it from his father. He said the buried treasure people try to dig up, every now and again, is actually illegal cash from selling, what was it called anyway?"

"Moonshine, bathtub gin, and a lot of other unsavory names. It was all alcohol that was made cheap and in a hurry. Some of it was quite unsafe to drink." Teeny Mom pulled out a chair and sat down. "People did those things for a lot of reasons. I want to assure you that my dad, your grandpa Colberg, never did anything that involved making or selling that stuff during Prohibition. And certainly not the Westblooms, either."

"I sense a but coming up here," I said.

"The 'but' here is that those people, who might have been considered outlaws in their time, occasionally did stay in our Ox-Boy cabins. They paid cash after all. It was sorely needed at the time."

"Wow, that's major," I practically squealed.

"Shelley—"

"Which cabins? Can we put up some plaques? I'm already composing copy for a new brochure." I fluttered my hands in the air like I was directing a symphony. "This will be so much fun."

"You have to calm down if you want to hear the whole story."

"Okay, I know, focus." I settled myself as best as I could. "I'm good. So, go on."

Teeny Mom recited the parts of the Nils and Cilla Westbloom story that I knew well. How they were orphaned by a Cholera outbreak shortly after their arrival from Sweden in the early days of the Bishop Hill Colony. They were taken in by the communal society and cared for like the other orphans. They studied in the local one-room schoolhouse to learn to read and write in English. They learned useful trades at the hands of their elders. The Civil War disrupted their lives with men and boys marching off to fight. Nils came back needing care. Cilla's beau did not return. Brother and sister never married but always kept their door open to children in need.

"I love that part of their story: orphans disappointed in love helping out other orphans. It's so tragically romantic. And I know Grandpa Colberg was one of the orphans they took in. And that he never left. But how does that become, you know," I wrinkled my nose, "even slightly criminal." I winced at the distasteful thought. "My memories of Grandpa Colberg are of a really gentle white-haired old man who never had a bad word to say about anyone. How could he...." I couldn't finish. The notion was inconceivable.

"By the 1920s, when Prohibition came around, the Westblooms were in their 80s. My dad, your Grandpa Colberg, was one of young men helping them out. And as I said, sometimes they rented cabins out for cash without asking too many questions. One night a crash woke everyone up. A car had hit the Smoketree. Of course, it wasn't called the Smoketree at the time because the fire hadn't really started."

"But it would soon?" I interrupted.

"Yes, Shelley. The car hit the tree because the man driving it had been injured. He had lost enough blood to make him too weak to see where he was going. Those old cars weren't made with all the safety features of today's cars. The gas tank started leaking soon after impact. They were lucky to get the man and a woman out before the fire took hold."

"That's when the Smoketree got its name," I said with a satisfied nod and a barely suppressed grin. "There was just more to the story than I knew about."

"Yes, dear," Teeny Mom said patiently. "Nils and the boys had the couple out of sight before calling the volunteer firefighters from the village, who showed up in time to help put out the fire and save the tree. Nils told them the driver had escaped in another vehicle. Which is probably where the bootlegger story came from."

"So, no bootlegging stills in the barn," I said.

"You sound disappointed."

"Sorry, a fiery car crash is pretty dramatic," I said. "But it isn't quite at the same level as what? A federal crime spree."

"Will you rein in your imagination and let me finish the story."

"Yes, ma'am," I said, placing my hands in my lap and waiting.

"The man and his female companion had bullet wounds—"

I sucked in a breath then blurted, "Like Bonnie and Clyde!"

"Stop it," Teeny Mom said. I knew she wanted to throw her hands up. Or maybe do something else with them. I was too excited to tell which way she wanted to go.

"Like I said," she cleared her throat and continued, "they were wounded and eventually helped to a cabin. They were cared for until well enough to leave. It took weeks. The sheriff came around looking and asking questions. As did some other men. Nils and the boys didn't let on to anyone what really happened. They just helped two people hide from the revenuers and the other gang."

"The other gang, just like West Side Story?"

"Shelley, there was no singing and dancing going on here. There were guns and it was dangerous."

"Got it," I said, and settled myself again. "So, why did they take dangerous chances for outsiders?"

"Prohibition laws weren't universally liked around here. Germans like their beer. Swedes took to making near beer. Plus, some of those people had a reputation for helping out poor people."

"Like Robin Hood?"

"Of a sort. Anyway, when it was time for the couple to go, they asked to use Nils's truck. It was an old flatbed Ford with a lot of miles on it, but it was all they had on the farm. To let it go on a promise that they would return it was an immense leap of faith for him."

"But he did it anyway," I added softly.

"Yes, he never fully expected to see the truck or them again. He had no idea how he could ever replace it. He figured he'd have to go back to using a team of horses for farming and getting around."

"There's another 'but' coming up here, isn't there."

"That man came back with a new truck and a generous reward for helping him out when he needed it the most."

"Like Robin Hood."

Teeny Mom nodded. “So, Nils coming up with a new truck and extra cash probably added to the bootlegging story the village was inventing.”

“What happened to the money? Is that what was buried and lost? The treasure folks like Mr. Carlson are so hot to find,” I said.

“Give your Grandpa Colberg some credit. The stock market was the place to invest money in at the time.”

“Oh, that would be just before the crash in 1929.” I began preparing myself for a sad ending to the story. “All the money from the unexpected windfall would have been lost in one day of panic on Wall Street.” I sighed. “The little guy never wins.”

“Some stocks fared better than others, and your Grandpa Colberg was a rather progressive young man for the time. He persuaded Nils to invest the bulk of the money in what today you’d call the latest hot new technology.”

It was too painful to consider what she meant by “new technology” in the 1920s. I couldn’t say anything until I thought of airplanes. “Grandpa Colberg used to build model airplanes with John and me. Mostly John.” I held onto a sliver of hope than he had bought into one of the airline companies that hadn’t folded or gotten bought out. “Did he…?”

“Remember that I said he ‘called’ the fire department. He bought into a little company that eventually became better known by its initials: AT&T.”

My jaw dropped. All I said was, “Way to go Grandpa!”

I helped get the rest of the food ready for our supper, still in the afterglow of my grandfather’s triumph. I knew he wasn’t a blood relative, but in my humble opinion, he was so much better. He and Teeny Mom were the ones I most wanted to emulate. Someday, I might measure up.

CHAPTER 15

The red brick house built during Bishop Hill's post-colony years by Nils Westbloom and whoever lived on the premises at the time had developed into an odd assortment of rooms that made entertaining difficult. Teeny Mom planned to seat our guest, Charles Guyer, in what she considered our formal dining room. A room bursting at the seams with mementos of the past alongside the living present. It suited her. I thought it reflected her personality perfectly: strong, confident, and solidly rooted to the earth but soft and approachable when necessary.

Our mystery guest arrived and knocked softly. If I hadn't been expecting company, I might have missed it. I opened the door to a smartly dressed young man with dark hair, a pale complexion, and dark shadows under intense blue eyes. He introduced himself as Charles Guyer. "Welcome and do come in." I lead him into the front parlor. "Charles, I'm glad you could join us this evening. I don't know if you remember, but we met for one fleeting moment last Monday."

"Yes, I do remember," he said. "You brought in coffee." That was all I got out of him before Teeny Mom popped out of the kitchen to greet him with a warm welcome that left him inexplicably mute.

I did my best to be the helpful hostess by giving him his seat choice at the table and observed that he opted to face the doorway. No one would sneak up on him tonight. Uncle Roy, as expected, was a no-show, who left us ladies to create polite conversation during the course of our meal. Our guest's replies were short and to the point. He remained quietly self-absorbed, reflective about something he wasn't ready to share.

Frankly, his early departure wouldn't have bothered me in the least. I had things to do. He probably had things to do. In order to move the evening along I had to speak up and find a conversational topic. Nothing came to me, except the truth.

"Charles, I'm wondering if staying in one of our cabins is a new experience for you. Not that we don't have a certain degree of piney charm. Perhaps it presents too much of a shift away from the usual B&B or hotel room loaded with amenities and creature comforts. One has to be used to hiking trails and camping out to fully appreciate the kind of closeness to real nature that staying in one of our rustic cabins presents." I took the opportunity to casually add a name that might strike a nerve. "I'm reminded of a friend of mine from Knox, Rune Gunnarson. Now there was someone who always remained a city boy through and through."

His head drifted down. He cast his eyes up under a creased brow. "I thought you might have known Rune."

I looked at Charles Guyer and failed to figure out how or where I might have met him. I shed the layer of false politeness and blurted out an impatient demand. "Tell me what you know about Rune. And why are you acting so … so guilty?"

Teeny Mom stared at me in disbelief at my rudeness and was about to say something when he began. "Yes," he admitted, "I knew Rune. We met up last Monday." I turned a questioning look to Teeny Mom. She gave a slight nod to Charles who took that as his cue to tell his side of the story. "It'll be best if I just start talking so I can get it all out. If I stop … I, I might lose my nerve." We waited in silence for more.

"Well, I'd driven my own car down here the night before. I wanted to get checked in and be ready for my part in Monday's meeting. I stopped for morning coffee at your little café. I was supposed to meet Rune there. Rune and I were in the same fraternity at Knox. I was a couple of years ahead of him, but we got close. I didn't have enough time to spare right then and neither did he, so we arranged to meet later in the day. Back at the café.

"You see, I had to give a financial presentation to Mr. Hemcourt. I'd been rushed in my preparations by my boss, Mr. Kleinmann, and wasn't sure how it would go over. I had my doubts about a lot of things." His cheeks flushed. "I saw you bring the coffee in and I recognized you. Though I doubted if you remembered me."

I acknowledged his grim smile in a way that urged him on. Teeny Mom gave me a suspicious look but didn't say anything.

"So, when we met up again, Rune was quite excited about a freelance story his uncle Albin had given him a lead on. It was about an old, outdated type of money. He was going on about the overall historical angle, and the direct connection with this Bishop Hill Colony you have here. How stuff like that would find a market, give him some cash, and make a nice entry for his resume. He told me all about Marsha Ellen. I was happy for him and his plans."

Charles paused to moisten his mouth with a sip of coffee. He held up the cup to examine it. "This is what got me in trouble." He looked at us over the rim. "Not this exact cup. It was the one from the café." He cradled the cup in his hands as if it were a prayerful offering.

I started to lift my hand like I wanted permission to speak, but he waved me off with a shake of his head.

"Our friendly reunion didn't stay happy for very long. When it was my turn to get him caught up on my life, I started on a long list of gripes about how toxic my job had gotten over the past year. Yeah, toxic was the word I used. I think I wanted to test him. See how he'd react. When he didn't, I got into some technical terminology for the new financial transactions Kleinmann wanted to propose—or rather, wanted to push onto Mr. Hemcourt. I saw Rune's growing confusion and apologized for sounding like a dreary accountant. We finished our coffee and the food we'd ordered when I asked him to walk with me for a bit. I wanted to see a little more of the town. I was curious. And frankly I needed time to de-stress. He said okay. We crossed the street and headed toward the cemetery. Not much out that way except trees, bushes, grass … and more grass. I relaxed some, you know, became quiet, thoughtful, weighing my options. When we got to the edge of the cemetery, I turned to him and asked for a favor. He said sure. I was a frat brother after all."

Charles stopped to look at me. "He was using the duct-tape wallet you and Marsha Ellen made years ago. Rune gave me one, you know." He shook his head. "Nah, you wouldn't know." He became lost in his thoughts for a moment. "God, we were so innocent back then." A bemused smile crossed his lips. "We stood there looking at our matching wallets and started laughing like a couple of idiots. That's when I pulled out a USB flash drive and asked him to keep it for me. I told him it had important research on it and to meet me at that same spot at midnight so he could give it back. It didn't seem like a big deal. We both thought I was overreacting." He heaved a heavy sigh. "Or so I thought then."

He appeared to be drifting off again, so I cut in. "And you did, didn't you? Went to meet him at midnight."

"Yeah, I missed the turn for the cemetery. I found my way back and parked across the street in the church parking lot. Figured it would be okay. I didn't expect to be long. Anyway, I found the main entrance and walked down the lane with all the trees. It was dark with spooky shadows everywhere. I regretted the whole thing more and more with each step I took."

"Was he there?" I asked.

"No," he said. "I couldn't find him. He didn't answer my calls. I started to panic a little. Then I got angry. Even though I needed my flash drive back, I left without it. I wasn't worried when I didn't hear from him the next day. I figured he was busy on one of his writing projects. I gave him some time. Then I read about him in today's paper, and it hit me—I'd left him out there all alone." His face crumbled. With extreme effort he regained control. "Okay, I'm sorry. I'm sorry for everything."

He seemed unable to find his way back into his story. "But you were in the cemetery," I prompted. "Did you notice anything strange?"

"Like I said," he began once again, "I left my car and walked to the cemetery. Rune had talked about how safe it was walking around the village even at night. I passed under the big trees, reached the first headstones, and stopped to call out. I got no answer. I only heard the creaks and moans of the trees. I kept walking and getting really bugged that I was getting jerked around like it was a prank. I got to tell you the darkness and the shadows were bad enough, but when the howling started, well, that was just way too much wildlife for me. I couldn't gauge how far away they were, or what they were, just that they were getting closer. So, yes to 'strange.' I was more than ready to get out of there."

He tilted his head as if trying to concentrate, to remember something. "An out-of-place movement caught my eye." He performed a slow-motion wave with his left hand. "A shape emerged from the shadows. It morphed into a silhouette of a guy who disappeared into some trees. I headed in that direction. I came within range of calling out again. I figured it was Rune and I really wanted to give him a blast of what I thought about this infantile hide-and-seek game he was playing, when what I thought I saw turned into something else entirely … some old guy with a shovel. I'd had enough. I just turned around and walked back to my car. Figured I needed to chill out and I'd catch up with Rune in the morning. We'd share a good laugh about the ghost story over coffee." Another heavy sigh, "Of course, that didn't happen."

I gave him time to compose himself before asking for more information, a better description, anything. "Charles, I need to understand exactly what you did and where you went." He gave me a quizzical look. "You entered the cemetery by the main entrance lane and walked under the big trees." He nodded. "You stayed on that lane while you called out for Rune to show himself." Again, a nod. "You're still walking along the lane when something caught your attention. Was it to your right or left?"

"It was to my left," he said.

"Then you started walking that way toward this shadowy figure, this something."

"Yes."

"Were you on grass or gravel? Was it still the lane?"

He thought a minute. "It was grass. But solid underneath."

"Okay, the main lane bends to the left and connects with the street. The place where you were supposed to be. You would have had to leave the cemetery to find a clump of bushes large enough for someone to hide in."

He shrugged. "If you say so."

"Thank you, this helps me know where to look when I go out there."

"Okay," he said. "But what do you hope to find?"

"I don't know, Charles. The place has been searched already. I just feel that I have to go out there, see it for myself. Maybe, find a way to understand it all."

"Shelley," he said calmly. "You might as well use my nickname like Rune did. I am, I was, his Buddy G."

The sound of a car in the driveway made us freeze in place. "Who could that be?" I quickly got up to look out the window. "It's Marsha Ellen."

"I've got to go. I can't see her right now."

"Why?" I asked.

"Because I am guilty." He sucked in a ragged breath. "And a complete failure."

CHAPTER 16

Charles Guyer rushed out the front door and made his way across the road to his cabin. Marsha Ellen pulled her car around to the far side of the house and parked close to the barn. She was closer to the kitchen door that way and I got there in time to open it for her.

"Oh, my," she said, with a start, "that was fast."

"By any chance did you see the guy who just left?"

"Kind of," she said.

"Did you recognize him?"

"I don't know," she said hesitantly. "Should I have?"

"That was Charles Guyer." Her face didn't register a response that would count as recognition. "Otherwise known as Buddy G."

She gasped, "Him? That was Buddy G? What? Why?"

She started to sputter and turn crimson. I ushered her inside and toward the dining room table. Teeny Mom quickly cleared a place for her to sit and got her a glass of water.

"We've just heard an amazing story. I'll fill you in," I said, "just don't faint on me."

She inhaled, held it for a beat, then exhaled slowly. She gave me a nasty look. "I don't faint." She brushed a strand of blond hair aside. Took a long sip of water. "You, of all people, should know me better than that."

"Good," I said, and proceeded to relate Buddy G's story about meeting Rune Monday morning at The Lutfisk Café and returning there later in the day to connect with him again. How they ended up near the cemetery not once, but twice. After she had some time to digest the new information, I asked, "Do you know anything about a USB flash drive that would have been in Rune's possession?"

"Uh, no," she said.

"It might have been in his wallet. One of those duct tape things we made once upon a time," I said.

"I couldn't believe he got that old thing out and started using it again." A sob rose in her throat that she choked back with a swallow of water. "I thought he was trying to impress someone. It certainly wasn't me."

"Marsha Ellen," Teeny Mom asked, switching into her super-mothering mode, "are you hungry?"

"Thanks, Teeny, but no. I drove back to Galesburg after my interview with the investigators this morning. I ate supper with Rune's parents near campus before I drove up here. I had to be with my mom after getting a full dose of Rune's mother."

"They were in Galesburg?" I was puzzled enough to ask, "Why were they in Galesburg?"

"They wanted to start packing up Rune's apartment. They made a side trip over to my place." She gave me a guilty look through puffy eyes. "Sorry, our apartment." She realized that still didn't come out right and added, "It was yours and mine first. Rune and his stuff came later. Anyway, that's what they wanted to pick up … Rune's stuff. Just odds and ends, really." She dabbed a tissue to her eyes. "We got it all sorted out and boxed up." She snorted, "They came prepared." After a brief pause, she continued, "We made it through the meal. And for dessert I got an ultimatum."

"Rune and I weren't together long enough," I said, "or close enough for me to have met his folks."

"Lucky you," she said. "Rune and I had a fight last weekend. A big one. He was trying to make up with me and wrote down some mushy stuff, you know, sloppy sweetness. He slipped it under my bedroom door. I was still in a mean mood and rejected him. But we made up later. Turns out that his folks were shown that note by the investigators up in Cambridge. It really set his mother off. She doesn't believe Rune was going to propose to me. Doesn't care that I would have accepted. And to top it off—she demanded I give her mother's wedding ring back."

"I saw that note. And what you wrote. I can see why that would upset future in-laws. But he told me how badly he wanted you back. He was going to propose and did mention a ring to me. He called it his Gran's ring."

"Right," she said, "We talked late Monday." Her composure began to slip away. She found it again and went on. "We made up over the phone. He proposed and I accepted. I know it was sudden, but it just felt so right. Of course, there was no ring. Though he said he was working on a big surprise for me." Her face crumpled and the tears flowed.

Teeny Mom hugged her and offered a napkin to wipe away the tears. I wiped mine away with the back of my hand. Great, I thought, now there are two things to find: a USB flash drive and an antique ring.

While I waited for Marsha Ellen's tears to ebb, I had a brilliant idea. "Hang on a second."

I ran to the catch-all drawer at the far end of the kitchen. I pawed through until I found the right something. "Here, wear this on your ring finger." I handed her an elastic hair band that was only slightly used. I could tell she wanted to go eww, yuck, and drop it. "Look," I said, with all earnestness, "it has to be something that comes from me. I'm the witness to Rune's true intentions. That will have to make do for the short term with Rune's parents … and for you. I'm going to find that ring. I promise."

She slowly looped the elastic around the ring finger of her left hand and stared at it. "Thanks, Shelley," she said. "You are my best friend forever." She moved in for a hug.

I shrank away from her embrace. "No hugs if you're going to start crying again."

She socked me in the upper arm. "Ow! That's going to leave a bruise."

"You so deserve it," she sniffed back. "You can be so darn annoying sometimes."

"You're right," I said, as I surrendered to my best friend. We hugged as I whispered, "I'm sorry."

She whispered "I'm sorry" back to me.

Teeny Mom had to turn away. She still had the remnants of a teary smile as she swung back around to face us. "Marsha Ellen, if you don't think you can make it home tonight you can stay here."

"Thanks, Teeny, but I can get there on my own. I must thank my mom for being so normal. I never fully appreciated her until now." Marsha Ellen turned to me. "Shelley, do you think this Buddy G will be at Nikkerbo tomorrow?"

"I don't know." I thought a moment. "He read about Rune in the newspaper. So that kept him here today. It might make him stay longer. If he wants to help Rune. Get his flash drive back. Yeah, sure, there's a good chance."

"Okay," Marsha Ellen said, "I'm going to show up for a tour tomorrow morning. That's what Rune and I decided on. Had decided on." She stopped to take a deep breath with eyes tightly closed then released it slowly. "We will see what we'll see. You'll have to drive me, though."

Her eyes were mostly dry. Mine weren't at all.

CHAPTER 17

Friday, June 13, 2008

I could have driven to Marsha Ellen's house with my eyes closed. Which wasn't too far off the case today. My mind was pondering so many things that my body was on autopilot until I was there. She appeared next to my car and seemed vastly more put together and upbeat than last night in our dining room. We left on our mission of visiting Nikkerbo for the grand tour.

Not overseeing the employee's morning review of assignments worked to my advantage for once. I shepherded the smartly dressed Marsha Ellen in and introduced her as a prospective customer who needed a tour of the facility, and Ekollon had no choice but to approve with a curt nod. It felt so good.

When we were out of Ekollon's line of sight and sound I gave Marsha Ellen a giant squeeze and squealed, "Thank you, that was so great. Almost as good as the time we ditched last period gym class for our own early out. Do you remember?"

"I sure I do. We went to Galesburg and almost got caught by a mall cop. That's when I realized just how resourceful you could be."

"Oh, come on," I said. "I was more afraid of Teeny Mom's wrath than the security guard grabbing us during school hours. And we got lucky."

"It wasn't just luck, Shelley," Marsha Ellen said, suddenly serious. "You have devious talents. That's why I know you can help."

"What? Does this mean you don't want the tour?"

"Yes, I want the tour, but you don't have to try too hard to sell me." She took my hand. "Shell, if I ever have a wedding, you're the only one I'd ever trust to make it perfect."

"Well then, let's start with the nerve center of Nikkerbo," I said.

"You mean your office," Marsha Ellen said.

"Ack, no. Much too dungeon-like. The kitchen. Then we'll end in the lobby. I'm saving the best for last. You can meet Lars."

"Lars? Am I going to like this Lars?"

I flashed her a coy grin. "I imagine you will. You along with every other woman with a breath in her body." She gave me another fist to the arm that landed in the same spot as before. "Ouch! Will you stop that! I need this arm."

I was winding down on the tourism spiel as we approached the imposing desk centered in the front lobby. We caught Lars intently studying the video screens for the security camera system. He waved us over.

"What's so interesting, Lars? Other than watching us walking around," I asked.

"*Ja*, I could see you two ladies. I was more curious about this young man." He pointed to Charles Guyer, also known as Buddy G, who appeared to be idly perusing exhibits.

"How long has he been here?" I didn't wait for his answer. I made hasty introductions: "Marsha Ellen Anderson, meet Lars Trollenberg. Lars, meet my best friend, Marsha Ellen. Please take care of her for a few minutes." I started running to catch up to Buddy G. I was quite winded by the time I found him studying the portrait of the first Curt Hemcourt.

"Is this the painting I've heard so much about?" He waited politely for me to catch enough breath to answer with more than a positive head motion.

"I don't know what you've heard," I answered, "but this one's back on display after it's little side trip, shall we say, into someone's personal collection. It still has the original label information. There's an ongoing discussion about how to handle the new background material in the description of provenance."

"Are you involved?"

"No, not really. It's up to my uncle and Mr. Hemcourt."

"Do you have an opinion?"

I answered without hesitation. "Yes, call me naive but I want truth. I want honesty. I want an acceptance of a less than perfect past that allows us to move on." I shrugged. "Just a few little things like that."

"Not so 'little,' these things," he said.

"That I am learning," I said. "And what about you? What are you learning?"

"That honesty has a high price. So do morals. That I'm not as brave in a pinch as I'd hoped I'd be. I wanted to talk to Mr. Hemcourt this morning, and … I just ended up walking around." His head sunk so low his chin nearly met his shirt. Then he lifted his gaze to the ceiling as if he alone could find some image there. "Rune—"

"Rune needs you to talk to the sheriff's investigators about what happened Monday night."

"I know."

"I can make the call for you if you like."

He uttered a quiet, "Yes, I think I'm ready."

Buddy G and I rejoined Marsha Ellen and Lars out front. I gave the briefest of introductions before pulling Marsha Ellen to the side and informing her that Deputy Dana Johnson was on the way to escort Buddy G to Cambridge for an overdue interview. She stared at me, deliberately avoiding the sullen Buddy G, and forced a buoyant attitude. "Look, Shelley, don't worry about giving me a ride back. I called Michael Anderson and he'll be here soon."

"You do know that you've committed yourself to riding in a rather large tow truck. With a very friendly dog," I said.

"I can't think of a good J joke for this occasion," Marsha Ellen said. "You know, like you used to do back in school. I wanted to call him and see how he's doing. Maybe that's the J—as in Just Had to Call." A satisfied look crept across her face. She was making an effort to connect with her Galva school buddies. That made it good for me, too.

"So, you got Michael to pick you up after his night shift. Have you got something on him that I don't know about?"

A deep blast from an air horn interrupted us as Marsha Ellen took off for the front doors. "See you tonight after you get off," she called out. And she was gone.

That left a startled Buddy G, a mystified Lars, and me standing at the front desk when an irascible Ekollon came charging in. "What was the meaning of having that … that monstrosity blocking the front entrance … and the noise!" He hissed out the last word.

"Not my doing, sir," I said. "My potential customer made her transportation arrangements without my knowledge."

Lars interjected. "And very inventive, if I might say so."

"Well, you don't have to say anything," Ekollon said, loudly enough to make his words echo through the lobby. He turned to Buddy G. "I thought you were finished here."

"Yeah, 'finished' is a good word." He rocked on his feet a bit before he added, "I'm waiting for my ride, too."

"And you need Ms. Anderson's help with this?" Ekollon growled.

Buddy G and I looked at each other and nodded in unison. Lars also nodded. At that Ekollon stomped away. No doubt to take refuge in the sanctuary of his office.

Those of us who remained in the dust of Ekollon's passing exchanged knowing looks of recognition. "He reminds me of my boss, *Herr* Kleinmann," Buddy G said, with undisguised contempt.

"Your boss is, ah, German?" I asked, trying to be politically correct.

"*Nein*," he answered, "just a wannabe—"

Lars chimed in. "Germans don't own all the *päm'päsətē* in the world. Self-importance, I think. I have a few in my family."

By the time Deputy Dana Johnson pulled up in front of Nikkerbo, Buddy G had become the most relaxed and natural I'd ever seen him in our short period of acquaintance. I walked outside with him and pressed one of my new business cards into his hand. "My number is on the back. Call if there's anything us rural types can do to help you."

Back inside, Lars appeared to have a few ruffled feathers. "You gave him your personal number didn't you."

"Yes." He appeared to be ready with a comeback remark. "Look, it's my number to give out, not yours." I started to walk away but turned back. "By the way, thank you for staying with Marsha Ellen while I was chasing down Buddy G. I appreciate it."

"Not a problem," he said. "She was delightful company."

I blew off the goofy grin spreading over Lars's face as an aberration. I had more important things on my mind. I knew what I needed to do next. Talk to the person who might provide more information about *Herr* Kleinmann and the other executive suit-types who had been here earlier this week: my own Teeny Mom.

CHAPTER 18

It hadn't been lost on me that Deputy Dana looked steamed when she drove up to Nikkerbo. I'd interrupted her morning routine, whatever that was, but she'd hidden the brunt of her anger under the veil of professionalism. Until she realized what I'd given her, a first-class witness as Lars would probably say. That might have accounted for the fact that I hadn't been asked to join Buddy G on the ride to the Sheriff's Department in Cambridge. That amounted to my only break in the routine of the rest of the day.

When I got back to the red brick house after work, I encountered Teeny Mom sitting alone in the kitchen, taking a break with a cup of coffee.

"I need your help," I said, as I took the closest chair. "The name Kleinmann keeps coming up. That would be Buddy G's boss. Since he stayed here, could you show me his registration card? He stayed here with all the others gathered for the meetings at Nikkerbo. And what can you tell me about him? How did he act around you? Did he get along with the others in his group?"

"Sure," she said, "give me a minute." She rose and walked the few steps to her designated office space.

I knew Teeny Mom's index card system for cabin registrations had all the information about each rental and each guest; she would enter those facts onto a computer spreadsheet once a month, so she didn't need to keep the physical cards. But she liked having the paper cards around because that's how she had started and that's what she was most comfortable with. I waited as she thumbed through them concentrating and softly muttering to herself, like she was trying to remember something.

"I was talking to you the other day about the recent tally: a family, our surprise young man, and the rest of the businessmen from Chicago." She collected all the cards she needed and brought them back to the table.

The first one she handed to me was for Walter Kleinmann. She thought it a proper sounding German name. I suppressed my urge to giggle. He had an address in one of the nicer suburbs of Chicago and an Illinois license plate number. The next card held similar data on Charles Guyer, who I now knew as Buddy G. The exception was an apartment number added to the address line. He also had an Illinois license plate number.

She held out a third card. "This one guy, this William Hanson, was something of a puzzle. I thought I might have made a mistake with this one."

"What? You make a mistake. I find that hard to believe."

She showed me the card. Like the others it held Hanson's name, address, and license plate number. Only this time there was a notation in pencil with a question mark beside it. "See, I wasn't sure if I entered the correct plate number for this car because there was another one, car, that is. At the time, I couldn't tell if the other car was a temporary visitor, or an additional guest, or even if it could have belonged to another cabin. People do take liberties with parking sometimes. I wanted to make sure I remembered to come back to the problem."

At this point I was silent, which encouraged Teeny Mom to keep talking.

"When this man, Hanson, checked out yesterday he told me there was another person who was his guest and needed to stay a few more days. I said that would be fine, but I'd need the cabin free for Midsummer weekend. No need to worry, he said, he was the one who made the reservations for this past week and was also in charge of reserving space for the returning group for Midsummer. He told me to just keep the cabin registered to him and use the same credit card information to pay for it. I noticed a while ago that the guest's car was parked by the correct cabin, but off to the side. Makes it difficult to see. I'll have to get in there to clean sometime and get a proper name for my records."

I had been staring at the card in a kind of numb shock, tuning out most of what Teeny Mom said. The penciled-in plate number on the card started with MAD. This had to be the mystery man who'd passed by Mr. Carlson's house. No wonder he had slowed down to scope me out. He'd been right here the whole time. I asked for a closer look at the cards. Teeny Mom handed them over. I shuffled through them, concentrating on keeping my hands steady, trying my best not to let my rising panic show. I didn't want to alarm Teeny Mom unnecessarily.

"I see what you mean," I said, stalling for time. "Kleinmann checked out Thursday. Guyer still occupies his cabin for the time being. Hanson checked out on Thursday. While he isn't physically here, his guest, the owner of this MAD car, is most definitely still here."

Yesterday, Deputy Dana used my partial ID for a search and came up with a list of potential owners. One in particular worried her enough that she had warned me to stay away from him if our paths should ever cross again. I hadn't taken her seriously. Today was a different story.

I made myself appear calm, somewhat disengaged, and not at all anxious. I figured my next move had to be contacting Michael—somehow. His night shift would be starting soon, and I might get him to swing by here before he had any calls to answer. In the meantime, I tried to get more information from her. "What do you remember about these guys? How did they look? How did they act?"

"Okay, these two, Kleinmann and Guyer, were definitely working together even if they weren't sharing a cabin." She held up their cards. "Boss and assistant, though I got the impression that they didn't have the best working relationship. The other one, the older guy, Hanson, I took him to be the one really in charge. Like I said, he came in and handled all the paperwork." She held up a card. "You know, this one, our young Mr. Guyer, struck me as a bit odd from the first time I saw him."

"What makes you say that?"

"The whole time I was checking him in he never looked me in the face. Seemed overly nervous, antsy, like he was expecting trouble. But I only saw him a couple of times. That is, before I invited him to supper and found out he had found his share of trouble. Or trouble had found him." She gave the card a little wave. "But I may be using hindsight to read too much into his actions."

"What about this other one, Hanson's visitor who turned into an extra guest? You ever see much of him?" I thought about Deputy Dana's warning again. Surely a bad guy, with a MAD car, licensed in Chicago, wouldn't be able to blend in around here.

"Just from a distance," she said.

"What did he look like?" I asked.

"He seemed fairly tall to me. Sturdy, but not over-weight. Dark hair. Needed a haircut. Nice clothes, though on the dull side. But that's the big city for you, wearing a black leather jacket is the thing to do. Seems rather boring if you ask my opinion."

My attention drifted as I tried to picture what that would look like. By the time I swung my attention back to Teeny Mom she was waiting for me to say something.

I had to scramble. "I bet he stood out like a sore thumb around here."

That weak cliché satisfied her for the time being. I endured her stock answer before excusing myself to go outside and look for a place to make my call to Michael. I had to talk to someone and, as a friend and a deputy wannabe, I trusted him the most.

Michael and I hadn't always gotten along in our past lives in school. We often went out of our way to irritate each other, but it was never mean-spirited. Well, mostly. He was more like an extra brother and a pest than anything else. At least, that was then. This was now, and sometimes I wondered about my true feelings toward him. Especially, with Deputy Dana coming into the picture now. And with Lars out of it.

Michael J for Joker answered on the fourth ring, just before I started panicking. "Yo, Shelley, speak to me," came his cocky reply.

I didn't know how to take the sudden recognition. Did it mean he had my number saved to his contact list? It left me momentarily flustered and all I could get out was a faint, "Um."

"Hello. I can't hear you," he called into the phone, sounding like he could start laughing at any minute.

"Michael, I'm so glad I got you."

He answered with a drawn out, "Yeah."

"Am I calling at a bad time?" I asked.

"Yeah," he repeated.

My panic shifted into embarrassment until I remembered who I was talking to. Or rather, who I was trying to talk to. "I know this is inconvenient, but I have to talk to you in person, soon."

"Why the urgent need?" His voice drifted off. He must be reaching for Sadie, his dog, and leaning away from his cell phone.

"Remember the other night in Galva when we sort of all met up by the park near Mr. Carlson's house? You, me, and Deputy Dana?"

"It was a strange evening for sure. Dana's been standoffish about it ever since. You know something that I don't?" A wary edge entered his voice.

"Yeah, I'd say so. I can explain everything to you when we talk."

"You can tell me now," he said, with his customary directness.

"No. I'm in the barn and Teeny Mom mustn't know about this thing just yet."

"These mystery things are getting worrisome but suit yourself. I can swing by to pick you up in thirty minutes. Meet me out in front."

"Okay, thanks."

"Better not thank me yet," he answered.

His time estimate was very close. Flicka, the neighbor's dog, followed me out of the barn and kept me company while I waited, pacing along the side of the road. I think she looked disappointed when the big tow truck pulled up and I got ready to leave without giving her anything to eat. Like she needed anything to top off the dry cat food she'd already helped herself to. Sadie, Michael's dog, hung over the edge of the window like she wanted to take off after Flicka. Michael had a tight hold on her collar.

"So," he said, as he got Sadie settled down, the tow truck into gear and headed down the road away from the Edwards River, "you don't think Teeny is going to notice I picked you up? It's never easy to sneak around in this beast."

"I'll have to deal with the fallout from this sneaking around later."

"Whatever. So, what's up?"

"The other night in Galva a black Toyota passed me. Slow, like it was scoping me out."

Michael groaned.

"Hear me out, okay?"

"Sure, but this had better be good. And not some kind of I-had-a-bad-date story, either."

"Oh no, nothing like that. I got a partial plate ID and Deputy Dana ran it through the system."

"Yeah, I remember. Deputies can do that. She did you a favor. So, what?"

"She didn't say anything to you? Give you a heads up or anything?"

"No. But then she was off duty the other night and just there to help me with my job application," he said.

"Right, she had to keep a low profile." I paused to gather some nerve. "She came to me, later, and filled me in on what she found out about this one guy who owned a Toyota just like that one. With a similar plate." Michael kept his eyes on the road like he was encouraging me to keep talking. "She found out he had a record of doing some heavy, nasty stuff and warned me to stay away from him if we should ever cross paths again."

"Okay, so …"

"So, this car with a similar plate spent some time in one of our cabins."

"So," he repeated.

"That might include Monday night. He's seen me. He's seen Teeny Mom. He knows she's got his license plate number."

"Okay, definitely sounding more serious, but—"

"Michael, he's still there. This is probably the type of guy who doesn't like to have witnesses, you know, people who can identify him and all."

"What?"

"This is a seriously bad dude. He knows too much about me and my family. And he was in front of Mr. Carlson's house."

"This is important because?"

"I haven't been able to reach Mr. Carlson for days."

"Not necessarily bad," he offered with a hopeful slant.

"Mr. Carlson was seen in or around the cemetery on the night they found Rune's body."

"You've lost me there." He shot me an irritated look. "Wait a minute. I towed Rune's car from the B&B, sure, but that's all. I don't know anything about his business. And certainly nothing about Carlson's."

"I'm not saying that you do."

He groaned, "Okay, there's an evil dude from Chicago camping out in rural Henry County. So what?"

"There's more. Turns out that Rune was in the cemetery trying to make a connection with some guy he knew from Knox."

Michael groaned again. "That idiot." He shook his head. "You know, Marsha Ellen called me this morning begging for a ride because you'd driven her in to Nikkerbo, had to work late, and could I give her a ride home." He paused long enough for a disgruntled cough to clear his throat. "She talked about how she and Rune were engaged. Had been…." He grumbled and studiously stared out his driver's side window so I couldn't see his face. After a minute he cleared his throat. "And she was all worried about his folks and some ring she never got."

"Yeah, she told me about that," I said.

"So, how are we supposed to help her? What can we do?" He used the fingers of his right hand to tick off the pertinent points. "Rune is gone. Carlson's a no show. Bad guy from Chicago needs to be left alone. Who does that leave?"

"Funny you should mention that."

Michael gave me a sideways glare under furrowed eyebrows.

"He got picked up this morning from Nikkerbo."

"Who got picked up?"

"Charles 'Buddy G' Guyer. Rune's friend and former frat brother. A second witness to what happened in the cemetery last Monday night." I used my left hand to register those points. Then added two more. "Deputy Dana drove him in for questioning this morning after you left with Marsha Ellen. I haven't heard if he's been arrested or anything like that."

Michael put a heavy foot on the brakes. Not such a good thing to do with a heavy vehicle on a gravel road. He gouged out some new grooves before coming to a full stop. By that time, I don't think he had it in him to yell at me about Buddy G or anything else.

CHAPTER 19

Michael J for nothing-I-could-think-of-just-then Anderson and I basically drove around in circles while we, mostly me, talked about a potential bad guy residing in one of the Ox-Boy Cabins, Marsha Ellen's lovely experience with her not-to-be in-laws, and Buddy G's potential troubles with the law. Talking it out with him helped me calm down enough that I began to ponder possible ways to be helpful, as opposed to just staying put and avoiding trouble.

Michael must have noticed the change in me. "I don't know what kind of scheme you've got cooking in that brain of yours," he said, "but don't expect me to participate. Like you and me are going to catch this nasty dude from Chicago in some act of," he couldn't find the right word, "well, nastiness, all by ourselves." His exasperation hit a record high level. "That'll never happen."

"Why not?" I asked. "Come on, together we could manage something."

He started to speak when his radio began squawking at him in ten codes. "I have to turn around and take you back. I'm needed."

"Look, we're close to Bishop Hill anyway. Just drop me off in front of The Lutfisk. I can walk through the field." He gave me a skeptical look like he was judging my fitness to cross over ground I've walked alone for years. "Honestly, I'll be home before you know it."

"What about the coyotes? Don't they spook you?"

"They're shy animals. You know that." As long as they were coyotes and not a pack of wild dogs that weren't afraid of humans. Those really could be dangerous for livestock and such. For now, I was in a hurry to get out of the truck and out of range should his temper flair up again.

"I was more thinking about the two-legged kind of creeps that come out of the shadows when you least expect them."

"There's still daylight," I started to say, before looking around and realizing I'd totally spaced out about how long I'd been in the tow truck. "Uh, what time is it anyway?"

"Seven," came his short reply.

"Oh my gosh, Michael, I'm *so* sorry. Marsha Ellen and I have taken up too much of your day. I feel so bad." There wasn't anything to do besides apologize and feel terrible for being so insensitive.

"Yeah, well, you guys owe me big time."

He dropped me off with a warning. "Be careful. It looks like we're in for more rain. Promise you'll get someone to pick you up if you don't think you can make it, you know, safe-like."

"I promise."

Michael J for Just Be Careful drove off, leaving me standing by the porch of the closed Lutfisk and wondering about my sanity. What was I thinking? I sat down at an empty picnic table and studied my cell phone weighing my choices, do I or do I not call Teeny Mom for a ride. I couldn't decide, so I tucked my phone away and stood up. I thought about Buddy G's story. He and Rune, his friend from the fraternity, would have been standing right about here when they decided to take that walk around the village. The one that ended up with the transfer of the computer memory stick and the promise to meet up again later.

From where I stood it was a straight shot to the cemetery. Well, almost straight; Bergland Street was just off to my right.

It led into the rear section of the cemetery, by far the oldest. I began moving before I'd decided how far I'd go.

I walked past the last house on my left. It was a pleasant looking, well-kept two-story dwelling with a set of windows softly illuminated with light cast from an unseen television set. The sound was muffled, and I quickened my pace to get past before I gave myself away to people or pets. The house on my right stood in stark contrast. It hadn't seen a coat of paint in ages. It was dark, quiet. Old Mrs. Holder used to live there by herself. Not much in the way of family to take care of things after she'd died. I guessed it would be sold at some point, but for now it had an abandoned stagnant air about it. I pushed on. Soon I had nothing underfoot but grass with clumps of bushes and small trees ahead of me closing in on what used to be a street in some distant past.

I tried to imagine Rune and Buddy G walking and talking as I neared the intersection of Bergland and Cemetery Streets. I slowed down and studied the ground with a small flashlight Teeny Mom made me carry. It wasn't really going to help me find much. I wanted to know where the wallet was found. Maybe get really lucky and find Marsha Ellen's engagement ring. So far, it was difficult to even see the signs of the struggle Deputy Dana had mentioned. There were too many footprints mixed in. It had rained Wednesday night. Tattered strands of yellow crime scene tape hung here and there. Try as I might, I couldn't make out what I was looking at.

A nearby voice called out, "What are you doing here?"

Deputy Dana stepped out of the shadows and into my line of sight to find me doubled over, trying to catch my breath, with my hands clutching my racing heart. There was no way I could respond to her challenge. Not that it mattered. It didn't stop her.

“Are you out of your mind? You shouldn’t be walking around here. It’ll be raining soon. Getting dark.” She was clearly exasperated. “Getting darker. You could get hurt by slipping on wet grass or falling into a hole.” She chose her next words carefully. “Or come across some sort of pervert.”

I recovered enough to stammer a protest. “This is Bishop Hill. It’s as safe as—”

“As finding the occasional dead body.” She had her hands on her hips and was clearly in no mood for backtalk.

I wanted to come up with a clever comeback, but nothing came out of my mouth. Speechless in the eyes of the law. Very classy.

“I suppose you want to see where we found Rune’s wallet?”

I nodded, then figured she might not see my head clearly enough. “Yes, ma’am.”

“Don’t ‘yes ma’am’ me. We’re nearly the same age.”

“But you have the badge,” I managed to say.

“True,” she admitted. “Well, since you’re here, I’ll show you around. The crime scene team is finished. Since I had to drop Guyer back at his Ox-Boy cabin, I was assigned to clean up over here. Taking the tape down and whatnot.”

She held wad of yellow tape balled up in one hand. She held her own flashlight at the ready in the other. It was the nice sturdy number I’d seen her with before. I had flashlight envy until I gauged the impossibility of ever fitting it into my shoulder bag.

I followed her as she pointed out where the wallet was found. Where the signs of the struggle could be sort of made out. The tangled area of footprints was so large that I had to take her word for some of what she was saying. What was clear, though, were the gouges that had to be the drag marks of shoe heels digging into the ground. They led to a clump of trees.

“Is that where …” I started to ask, unsure if I wanted an answer.

“Yes, that’s where we found him.”

“Rune,” I said. “He walked here since his car was at the B&B. Buddy G said—”

“I might have known that Guyer talked to you before I got to him this morning.”

I wanted to let it slide. No sense antagonizing her, but I had to add what I knew. “Buddy G told me about Rune being an old friend from college, fraternity brothers. They came back here to meet up again. To help each other.”

Deputy Dana hadn’t made a move that might acknowledge the information. She continued with her own line of thought. “Guyer probably parked beside the Methodist church like I did. He’d have no problem walking to here to meet up with Rune.”

While she talked, I studied the ground some more. The waxing gibbous moon was being helpful at this point, and my flashlight beam crossed what looked to be tire tracks taking off toward the river.

“Anyone follow these?” I asked. “They look fresher than the other tire tracks and footprints.”

“I don’t know for certain,” she said. “As you know, Mr. Carlson has been seen in this area.” She gave a disgruntled snort. “Him and his quest for buried treasure—” She would have said more but I dared to interrupt.

“Him and his shovel.” I wanted it to sound funny. Add some comic relief. It didn’t fly.

Deputy Dana, unamused, continued. “Turns out all of us were wasting our time parked outside of Carlson’s Galva house the other night,” she said. “I found out that he was on the outs with his wife.”

I nodded and said, “Ekollon told me he traveled a lot.” I paused as a vague thought began to surface. “Wait a minute, what do you mean by his ‘Galva’ house? Does that mean … he owns more than one home?”

“I was told that he was probably staying in his Bishop Hill house while things cooled down at home, in Galva.”

“Okay, and that other house would be where exactly?” I asked.

“It’s back behind the Bishop Hill fire station. It’s an older house and isn’t much to look at. It’s been years since anyone took time to fix it up. I hear he’s using it for storage. Like a warehouse. Can’t image it would be fit to live in for long. We checked it out anyway.”

An obvious fact registered with me. “But why would he drive to the cemetery when he was staying so close? I walked by it on my way here. You could see it from here if the leaves were off the trees.”

She looked at me. I looked at her.

Together we said, “Good question. You don’t suppose ...”

We walked down the unused section of Cemetery Street until our flashlights reflected off the car hidden in a dense patch of brushy overgrowth at the end of the grassy lane, almost all the way down to the Edwards riverbank.

CHAPTER 20

Deputy Dana and I retraced our steps away from the abandoned vehicle we discovered hidden down past the cemetery. I couldn't help listening in as she made her report. When she was finished, she turned her attention to me. "Shelley, I appreciate you getting Charles Nobody's Buddy Guyer to turn himself in this morning. He'll be a valuable witness. Unless, of course, we uncover some incriminating evidence that convinces us he had a motive to harm Rune." I started to protest but was cut off. "I get that you have developed a certain rapport with him. Just remember you don't really know much about him, and it would be safer to keep him at arm's length until we wrap up the investigation. Now, let me get you home."

"Thanks. I appreciate the ride. But speaking of investigations. Remember when you told me about the preliminary results you had for the MAD car from Galva?"

"Yeah, my license plate search came up with a list of possible matches that included a guy from Chicago I thought you should steer clear of. So?"

I took a breath and pushed on. "Well, it turns out that we've had someone like that show up at one of our Ox-Boy cabins. In fact, he's still there, occupying a cabin."

She stopped in her tracks. "Are you serious!"

I tried to head off an impending indignant retort. "Yes. But wait a minute. At least I can give you the full license plate and a name this time."

We resumed walking as she asked me to repeat the description of the car, its correct tag number, and the rest of the information I'd gathered from Teeny Mom. We rode in silence while she thought.

She stopped the cruiser in front of the red brick house and started issuing orders. "Don't do anything," she directed. "I've reported the hidden car and we'll run those plates. As for this other guy, your Mr. MAD Man, I'll run the new information and get back to you as soon as I can. It might be a wait-and-see game on how things match up." She lingered long enough for another warning. "Shelley, stay clear of him. And that goes for that so-called friend of Rune's. He has problems that are all his own, you do not need to share."

"But they both have cabins with us," I said.

"I know it's a difficult situation, but Nobody's Buddy can't leave."

"What?"

"It's like they say on those cop shows," she affected a deep voice as she repeated the well-known lines 'Person of interest. Don't leave town.'"

"And you can't tell me why," I said.

"Nope. Makes them easier to watch though." Her radio came alive. "Now, I gotta go."

I climbed out and she left, going North toward Cambridge. She had a real call to answer along with everything else.

I made sure we had each other's personal phone numbers. I looked over to the cabin of the mystery MAD Man. It was completely dark, and his car was missing, making me wonder what he might be up to. Dim light filtered through Buddy G's windows. That just made me feel sorry for him.

I crossed under the yard light and almost went all the way up to the front door. I thought better of it and circled around to the back door. The only thing I disturbed was a cat making its way to the barn. Then I got inside and found Teeny Mom waiting for me.

"It's about time you showed up, young lady," she snapped. "You are not too old for me to punish."

"Uh, yes I am," I answered sweetly.

That got me a serious frown and that pre-lecture look of a ticked-off Teeny Mom. I tried to head her off. "Please don't be angry. I can explain. Well, most of it anyway."

She motioned for me to sit down and waited in her Teeny Mom way.

I had to start somewhere. "Well, I wanted to get in touch with Mr. Carlson for work. I had no luck calling him. So, the other night I drove by his house, his Galva house, a couple of times. Even parked out front for a while."

"He probably never was there at all."

"Yeah, that would be right. I didn't know he'd bought a house here in Bishop Hill." My turn to frown. "I wasted my time. Anyway, while I was watching for lights inside the house, this car drove by all slow and strange-like. It was spooky enough that I memorized part of the license plate, the MAD part. Deputy Dana did some checking, and it turns out that she thought the car might be registered to someone scary. She will find out for certain with the info I gave her from your cabin card." I reached out to hold her hand and felt her tense up. I kept going.

"And we, Deputy Dana and I, just a while ago, found a car hidden in a pile of brush on the far end of Cemetery Street. The part that hasn't been kept up as well. You know, down by the riverbank."

"Really," she said.

"Deputy Dana has reported it. We'll find out who it belongs to." I gave her hand a warming rub. "I'm just worried that our Ox-Boy cabins have become the common denominator for all of this."

"You mean this terrible business with Rune being found out by the cemetery," she added.

"Yes." I hesitated. "Those two guys, Buddy G and Mr. MAD Man, were possibly here at the same time, you know, Monday night. And, well, they are still here."

The worry lines on her face deepened as she clung to my hand, signs that our closeness to danger were beginning to sink in.

CHAPTER 21

Saturday, June 14, 2008

I tried extra hard to be the first one in at work. I made it by ten minutes. Time enough to put on the coffee pot in the employee's break room. Ekollon entered, glowering disdainfully at me before retreating to his inner sanctum of security and comfort. Yesterday, I had dared to skip the morning meeting of employees when I took Marsha Ellen on an impromptu tour. I assumed he'd wait for an audience before taking action for the breach of protocol. So much the better for him to set an example and remind all underlings who's the boss.

I likewise adjourned to my modest office to check for new emails and changes to the schedules. Still nothing listed about any upcoming meetings with executives or board members related to Hemcourt's emergency meetings from last week. William Hanson had made reservations at our Ox-Boy Campground before returning to Chicago. A lapse in scheduling could have been easily blamed on me by Ekollon. The problem never developed because it had been covered without my help, but I still found it annoying that Ekollon had tried to slip this by me and distressing because it might have worked.

Nothing new about Mr. Oliver Carlson. No surprise there. Deputy Dana informed me that we had indeed found Carlson's vehicle hidden near the crime scene. Evidence that couldn't help but aim more suspicion in his direction. How long Carlson could stay out of sight was debatable. Rune's name had been revealed in the current edition of our weekly local paper by his uncle,

Albin Gunnarson. The larger daily papers would be picking the story up now that the body had been officially identified. Sooner or later the connection between Rune and Oliver Carlson would be revealed in greater detail. I wondered how Sheriff Henry would handle it. After all, he had kept a tight lid on the publicity for days.

I couldn't hide forever. When I judged my time was up, I put my computer to sleep and left for the employee break room to check the coffee situation and to see who else was there. I hoped to find Lars before the morning staff meeting started. I halfway expected him to announce plans for flying back to Stockholm to be with his family for the upcoming Swedish Midsommar observance.

I filled my coffee cup, found a place at the large table, and sat down. The morning staff meeting and the ritual of assigning the day's stations would soon begin. There were only five of us. So, surprises were hardly in store. I knew a disgruntled Ekollon would not spare me an embarrassing moment. I only had to wait for whatever he had in mind.

Ekollon opened the door and the background chatter dropped to zero. All our eyes were on him, until they turned to Mr. Hemcourt who came in next. I couldn't think of a time Mr. Hemcourt attended a morning staff meeting. Even for the brief period when I was acting director, he left me to run things as I wanted. I looked to Lars for a clue if Mr. I-have-diplomatic-immunity might have had some influence over this kind of situation and only got an enigmatic shrug in return.

Ekollon cleared his throat and proceeded to list the day's assignments. My name was conspicuous by its absence. He turned to Mr. Hemcourt and indicated it was his turn to speak. He pointed to me and said, "I need to see you in my office."

I replied with a subdued, "Yes, sir," and followed him out of the room. Leaving in our wake puzzled looks and, I'm sure, fodder for gossip.

We reached Mr. Hemcourt's office, I sat down in the chair nearest his desk. The other chairs I'd seen on Monday had been moved back against the wall and out of the main traffic flow of the room. Someone had made an attempt to tidy up the place. But there were still all the indications that Mr. Hemcourt had to hastily clear his personal effects out of the way because some were still stacked in messy piles by the large window. Extra power cords were nudged up and out of the way underneath his desk. I took this in as I waited for him to begin to tell me the bad news: I was fired—again. Last time it was Ekollon who'd made the decision, made the pronouncement, only to have Mr. Hemcourt hand out a reprieve. It certainly didn't look promising that I'd have a repeat performance.

"Ms. Anderson," he began, "I want to hear from you about next weekend's activities for Midsummer. What will Nikkerbo provide for our visitors?"

Okay, I thought, this is potentially good. "Well, first of all, we are using Midsommar, the Swedish spelling for Midsummer, for all our posters and such. We had the folk music group booked well in advance. No problems there. Same with the make-and-take crafts for children. Two Pippi Longstocking movies are scheduled, one in English, one in Swedish. A speaker from the genealogical society will do a presentation on the Bishop Hill Colony outposts. It will tie into the original Nikkerbo and give some context for the choice of using the Swedish name. Those have been in place for months now. Press releases have been sent out. All we, the staff, have to do to prepare for the weekend is make room for tables, chairs, and get the movie screen set up."

"Yes, but are any of these uniquely different from what everyone else is doing? This is the first time for me, for Nikkerbo, to participate in a village-wide festival event here in Bishop Hill."

I had to pause and judge how truthful I should be and decided to forge ahead with my own opinions. "Honestly, sir, most of this is pretty standard fare for Bishop Hill. The speaker from the genealogical society promised a new slant on the information about the original Nikkerbo, which will make it specific for us and therefore special."

"I like that. What else can we do?"

"Of course, your family's display of artifacts will be a potential draw now that your painting has been returned to the exhibit. The people who have heard about it in the news will naturally be curious. I think it will be very popular."

"Ah, yes. That painting…." He left his thought hanging.

"Sir?" I ventured. "How is work going on the provenance?" I couldn't make out where he wanted to go with this talk of "that" painting. Was it the involvement of Uncle Roy in creating a Krans-style painting so good that it fooled many folk-art experts, or was it Ekollon's unsuccessful attempt at, shall we say, relocation because of its possible resemblance to the colony's founder? The negotiations for Ekollon's return to Nikkerbo and his old job must have been quite interesting. I could sense his reticence to reveal his opinions.

"We can come back to that. How are the preparations going for…?" He didn't finish that thought either. "Well, I'm calling together some of my corporate department heads and I might as well call it what it is, another emergency planning session. I want them comfortable … but not too much so."

“Sir,” I said, greatly relieved for the change to a subject I definitely wanted to discuss. “I have not been assigned any specific tasks for any upcoming planning session. I’ve only worked on a callback list for prospective clients, future customers of Nikkerbo’s hospitality services, and have been given a few other minor jobs. Which is going well. But Mr. Ekollon—”

“Has kept you in the dark.” He filled in the blanks like my answer was not unexpected. “I assume you knew he was ready to fire you this morning for coming in late and insubordination having to do with some disturbance yesterday morning.” He glanced at a sheet of paper that looked like a printout of an email message.

I didn’t hesitate. “Yes, I thought that might be a possibility. Sir, I can explain what happened yesterday. You see—”

“There’s no need to explain. I’ve heard that you’re closely related to the situation in the cemetery. A cousin of yours is involved. And you two were students together with the victim at the college in Galesburg.”

I wondered where he got his information, but so far it seemed reliable. “Yes, my cousin and I knew Rune Gunnarson quite well from Knox College. But I do need to tell you about William Hanson,” I said.

“How would Bill Hanson have anything to do with this?”

“He was here earlier for the meetings you, um, started the week with. I brought in the coffee on Monday.”

“Right, yes, go on.”

“He was staying in one of the Ox-Boy cabins. When he left, checked out that is, he made arrangements for his return and Teeny Mom, excuse me, that would be my mother, Christina, she found enough space for the group that was returning for

Midsummer. I naturally assumed it was for more business meetings."

Mr. Hemcourt looked thoughtful, and his brow began to furrow. "So, you're saying that my people will be taken care of, housed, but without your prior knowledge."

"Yes, sir," I said, "I had no clue." I wondered if my warming cheeks might indicate a corresponding rise in color I couldn't control.

"This will become another item I will want to discuss with David." He sighed. "The list is getting quite lengthy."

"So, William Hanson was staying with us, as was Charles Guyer. I wanted to ask if Guyer was an assistant to Mr. Hanson?"

"I don't believe so. Let me look it up." He turned to his computer and typed in the name. "No, Bill is my interim chief financial officer and a strong contender to replace Thomas Gubben as my next CFO. Guyer is in a different department and was here with Walter Kleinmann, who is more closely associated with our overseas banking interests. And...," he entered more keystrokes, "he's looking into a new avenue of investment opportunities." Mr. Hemcourt studied me for a minute before asking, "Why the interest in young Guyer? Do you know him from Knox?"

"No, sir. Not directly. He was more of a friend to Rune Gunnarson."

Mr. Hemcourt leaned across the desk with an intense look. "Where is this going?"

"I really shouldn't say," I stammered.

"But this has something to do with the young man, your friend, they found in the cemetery."

"Buddy G, that's Guyer's nickname, stayed behind when the other's checked out of their cabins on Thursday." I hesitated. "You see, he and Rune met up a couple of times on Monday. Before … you know…." I was trying to choose my words carefully and faltering. "He was the one who left Nikkerbo with a deputy yesterday morning to give a statement about his contacts with Rune. I haven't had a chance to talk to him since then."

"It's amazing. So much activity for such a small place." He stared as if measuring me for something. "Should I be concerned about any of this?"

"Too soon to tell, sir. I don't have enough information." He nodded and murmured assent. I pointed to the doors. "I should go." But before I made it out of his office, I thought to ask, "Ah, sir, I still have a job here, don't I?"

"Yes, you're fine. Don't let David tell you differently." He grew thoughtful for a long moment before announcing his decision. "In fact, go back to whatever you were doing for David, but consider yourself a personal assistant to me. You, as a local, are better connected around here than I am, as a newer resident, even if I, too, am a Colony descendant. Please let me know when you have more information about Mr. Guyer's situation. And especially if anything pertinent comes up that may impact Nikkerbo. I'll get started on a list of items I need you to do for the upcoming planning sessions. I'll deal with David and the paperwork. I'll make sure your salary will reflect your additional duties."

"Yes, sir. Thank you, sir." I'd no sooner closed the doors when the smile I could no longer contain broke out. I strode down the corridor to my office, my computer, my callback list, and whatever else I could think of to be productive.

CHAPTER 22

I returned to my office in a state of elation that kept me grinning and hopelessly unable to concentrate on anything other than my good fortune. I had things to do, but I kept bouncing from one idea to another without really settling on any one thing. I could read some more George Swank articles on Bishop Hill history. I could work on Ekollon's list and make a few more phone calls to potential clients. I could write up my own list of pie-in-the-sky ideas. I felt a surge of boundless energy to spend wherever I wanted. Then there was the briefest knock on my door before Ekollon poked his head in and asked for a moment of my time. I smiled at the old fox. He could not diminish my lighter-than-air mood. I nodded and motioned to the one and only extra chair I had. I guess it wasn't inviting enough. He stood eyeing the piles of paper on my desk before he spoke.

"Ms. Anderson, would you be so kind as to cover for the other staff members for their breaks and lunches."

"Yes, sir," I replied, and waited to find out what was really on his mind.

"I will be gone the rest of the day. Oh, and you have tomorrow and Monday off. I've cleared it with Mr. Hemcourt. The upcoming week shall be quite busy, and you won't get another day off until the following week." He paused before adding, "But then again, your schedule never seems to mesh with mine." He turned to leave but turned back to ask, "Did you ever make contact with Oliver Carlson?"

"No, sir," I said. I thought it tactful not to mention the main reason I wasn't able to make any progress—because Carlson wanted to avoid talking to the sheriff. “Have you known him to be this difficult to contact?”

“This isn’t like him at all,” he said with a peevish tone and turned to leave.

I interrupted his planned departure with another question. “Do you know William Hanson?”

His mustache waggled as he pursed his lips in deep thought. Probably weighing how much to tell me. He finally answered, “I know the name from corporate reports.”

“And what about Walter Kleinmann, or perhaps Charles Guyer?” I gave him time to draw a blank look on his face. It was an improvement over the mountain range of wrinkles inadequately disguised by his mustache. “They were here for meetings earlier in the week.”

His blank expression turned into one of mild irritation. “Ah, yes, now I remember. Hanson and Kleinmann were here to discuss some financial matters with Mr. Hemcourt.” He studied me and added, “The meetings were private. I didn’t attend in any official capacity.”

“You don’t remember Guyer? He would have been younger than the other two.”

“Yes, one of them was quite a bit their junior. I took him to be an assistant to Mr. Kleinmann.”

“Why is that?” I asked.

“I was called in to the office at one point and the younger one appeared to be busy interpreting the importance of a lot of charts and graphs. It all seemed to be money related: income, expenses, foreign and domestic investments, and the bond market. He and Kleinmann were throwing around some terms I was unfamiliar with. Why the interest?”

"Because they were staying out at our Ox-Boy cabins," I said, and waited for a cue on how to proceed. I wanted more information, but none came, and he started for the door again. "Before Mr. Hanson left, he made reservations for another group to return for Midsummer." Ekollon froze in midstride for the briefest of moments before exiting. I had to give him points for not slamming the door.

I occupied myself at my computer until it was time to start the round of covering for other people's breaks. Lars would be last because I wanted to see what his lunch plans were, among other things.

As I walked through the halls linking the museum exhibits, I could tell that Nikkerbo was having a good day for visitation. I cycled through the employees in an orderly fashion until I got to Lars. We made plans to meet up later.

I was already in the breakroom opening my carton of yogurt when Lars came in to retrieve his brown bag from the refrigerator. When I was sure we had the place to ourselves I asked, "Will you be going back to Stockholm for Midsummer?"

"We call it *Midsommar*," he said.

"Of course," I said. "My apologies, I forgot my *svenska* lessons for a moment there."

"*Ja*," he chuckled, "I can understand. But to answer your question, *nej*, I am staying here."

"Would that involve the business planning sessions coming up?"

"Ah, clever way to put it. That would be a *Ja*. It would be in my family's interest to be close by," he paused, "in case I am needed."

"But of course."

"You know, I was thinking about asking you if you would like to visit Sweden some time. Perhaps you and a friend. Or even a cousin, perhaps," he added with a disarming smile.

I gave him a look. "You were spying on me, on us, the other day, weren't you?"

He laughed a delightful laugh, musical and exotic. "You two," he shook his head. "You and she were impossible to miss."

"Okay by me," I said, "as long as there's a castle in there somewhere. But Lars, just to be clear, Marsha Ellen should not be considered available right now."

"Because the future Mister Marsha Ellen was the unfortunate soul found in the cemetery?"

That left me with an unattractively open mouth. I recovered enough to ask, "How do you know they were engaged to be married?"

"It is, how you say it, my superpower." He flashed a silly smirk. "I know lots of things."

I looked around to make sure we were still alone. "Then what can your superpowers tell me about the big executive business types who were here this last week? Their names were William Hanson, Walter Kleinmann, and Charles Guyer."

"*Ja*, I knew Hanson by reputation only until I met him this week. He is an honorable man and quite interesting. Kleinmann does not merit the same respect. At least not with my uncle. I thought it odd that he would not talk to me at all."

"And Charles Guyer? He was the youngest of the team."

"His manner was very strained, very ill at ease. I tried to speak with him. Perhaps find out what was troubling him. He gave his financial report on Monday and left shortly after. I rarely saw him on the other days. He seemed very …" Lars paused to think of his next word. “I would say *nervös*.” He repeated with the English word, “Nervous.”

“Those guys were staying at the Ox-Boy cabins,” I said. He nodded. “So,” I continued, “if Kleinmann was not in your words ‘respectable’ or ‘honorable,’ would it be possible that he might have some, shall we say, unsavory connections?”

After a moment’s thought he proceeded cautiously. “*Ja*, it would not surprise me. Hanson has family troubles. Kleinmann’s troubles involve owing money to the wrong people.”

The mysterious MAD license plate sprang to mind with a cold chill. I needed to talk to Teeny Mom. I thanked Lars and excused myself to make a phone call that couldn’t wait. I had to make sure Teeny Mom stayed away from Mr. MAD Man’s cabin. The afternoon went at an agonizingly slow crawl.

CHAPTER 23

In my rush that morning I had given Buddy G's cabin nothing more than a passing glance. The curtained windows registered darkness and I hoped he was sleeping. Likewise with the cabin of Mr. MAD Man. I wished him safely asleep. Either of them not being on the premises was a problem I didn't have time to deal with.

Now, after five o'clock, I was free from work and almost back to the red brick house. Questions swirled in my mind from the list I had been building all afternoon. I had to make sure Teeny Mom stayed away from Mr. MAD Man's cabin. I wanted to see the file cards again and make sure I knew exactly who-was-who with respect to the cabin registrations. Make another attempt to find out what else I could get Buddy G to remember about his time in the cemetery.

And what about afterwards? Did I dare knock on Mr. MAD Man's cabin door myself? Did Deputy Dana have the information she promised to share with me? And what about coin-dealer-at-large Oliver Carlson? Those were the many high points for the time being.

Teeny Mom met me at the back door. "I'm so glad to see you're home. Marsha Ellen has been waiting for you."

"She's here? I didn't see her car in the driveway."

"No. The last time she called she said she'd stop by before heading back to Galesburg. She asked for you to wait for her."

"Do I dare hope for good news?"

"I don't think so. She said Rune's mom is blaming her for everything that's happened ever since the alleged engagement. Poor thing could barely keep from crying."

"You know, I suspected Rune's mom might be trouble. She held a tight hold on the apron strings connecting her to her little boy," I said, placing my hand on her shoulder. "Not at all the world-class Teeny Mom you are." She reciprocated by setting her hand on mine and giving it a tender squeeze. "Well, I guess we should be prepared to feed Marsha Ellen whenever she shows up."

"Already on it," Teeny Mom said. She dabbed at an eye as she turned away.

I sniffed the air and asked, "Do I smell barbecue?" I inhaled again. "Per chance is it using Uncle Roy's special bourbon sauce?"

"Close. I'm trying out a new sauce recipe that should have a lower alcoholic content. Got the inspiration from a magazine."

"Let me guess," I said, "Uncle Roy is miffed."

She nodded and said, "It's a toss-up if he'll even show up to do a taste test."

"Well, while that's cooking and Marsha Ellen isn't here yet, may I see the cabin cards we looked at yesterday? The three for the business-man types."

Teeny Mom looked puzzled, then concerned, "Is there something else I need to worry about?"

"I don't know for sure. I got some more information out of Ekollon and Lars today and I wanted to read them over again." I reached for my shoulder bag and pulled out some computer printouts. "And I located some photos from one of Mr. Hemcourt's websites that I wanted to show you. You know, to match faces to names."

"The cards you want are on top of the box on my desk. I thought they might be needed again." She went back to her cooking.

I sat down at her desk and took a closer look at the card for each name I had. Kleinmann's registration information didn't appear to be out of the ordinary. Same with Charles Guyer. I went on to the next card, William Hanson's, which held what little there was to know about our mysterious Mr. MAD Man. I read over Teeny Mom's penciled-in note about the license plates and felt the renewed sense of creepiness of being in such close proximity to potential evil. The guy still hadn't checked out, but the name Bill Smith had been added.

I went back into the kitchen and found a clean spot to spread out the cards and the photos. "I need you to look at these when you've got a minute."

"Sure," she said, as she wiped her hands dry.

"Okay, this is the website photo of this guy. We'll call him Mr. Big Shot #1." I laid down the picture of William Hanson and placed his cabin card upside down next to it.

"This is the other one I want you to see. Mr. Big Shot #2." I placed the printout photo of Walter Kleinmann on the table with his cabin card upside down next to it.

"Tell me who is who?" Formal poses in nice suits might present problems with making an ID of someone presenting themselves in casual-wear mode, but Teeny Mom hardly hesitated. She pointed to Mr. Big Shot #1 and named him as William Hanson. She followed up with identifying Walter Kleinmann as Mr. Big Shot #2. No surprises. I didn't bother showing the photo for Charles Guyer.

"I see here that you've got Bill Smith written in on Hanson's card." I tapped on the card. "I don't remember that being there before."

"I know you asked me not to go over there, but it's been a week since I'd been around to clean. He never answers when I knock on the door anyway. So, this time I taped up a note with some possible times I could come by to do the basic housekeeping things, change the sheets, empty the trash, and dust. When I got back from my barn chores, I found the note slid under the front door with the best time circled and signed 'Bill Smith'. That's all I know."

"It's got to be a false name," I said.

"Quite likely, but we really don't know all the facts about him. I have learned that one should not pass judgment on the private affairs of other folks. Whatever those affairs might be." I caught the knowing look she gave me. She added, "As long as there's no trouble, no noise after 10 pm, or property damage."

I was preparing to raise a point about that last part when Marsha Ellen burst through the back door. "You would not believe the phone calls I've had to put up with today," she said as she collapsed onto a kitchen chair. She took a deep breath as if to steady herself but instead blurted out, "Oh my god, that smells divine." She tried to waft more of the aroma toward her nostrils. "What is that?"

"It's barbecue," I said. "Teeny Mom is trying out a new recipe for the sauce. It does smell good. Not sure I'd go as far as divine." I avoided Teeny Mom's piercing stare beamed in my direction.

Marsha Ellen declared, "No need to try any longer. You've got it." She inhaled again. "I promise not to tell Roy I may have a new love."

"You must really be starving," Teeny Mom said. She got up and began preparing plates of food. She stopped halfway into the sandwich she had started and, with a slice of homemade bread in hand, inquired, "You say you've been talking with the Gunnarsons today?"

"Unfortunately, yes. I wanted to spend a quiet day with my folks. Helping them move furniture around before I went back to Galesburg, but Mrs. Gunnarson kept calling about all these annoying little things. Where's this. Where's that. Then the last call was a replay of our conversation about the grandmother's wedding ring. I told her it still hadn't been found. The news didn't go over any better than the first time I told her. I swear she thinks I'm deliberately holding out on her. I'd be angry if it weren't for my mom talking me down. She reminded me that Rune was her little boy." Marsha Ellen fell silent.

"How are they doing? Your folks, I mean." Teeny Mom put the bread down to finish the sandwich.

"Oh, they're good." Marsha Ellen began fussing with her purse. There was definitely more on her mind than what was lurking in the depths of her handbag.

"Okay, I can tell there's something else bothering you," I said. "Out with it."

"Well, as you might guess the apartment is looking pretty hollowed out. You removed your stuff last month. Rune's things are now gone." She heaved a wistful sigh. "Even if I wanted to stay there, which I don't, I can't afford it by myself." She looked at me. "You can't live there and work here."

"You're right about that," I said softly.

"And I wouldn't want anyone else for a roommate anyway."

"Thanks," I said. "Same here."

"I've talked it out with my folks, and they are okay with me coming back home. I'll find a temp job. Send out resumes. You know, the usual stuff."

There would be no "usual" for Marsha Ellen. She'd be starting her new adult life without Rune. I rose up to give her a totally inadequate hug.

CHAPTER 24

Marsha Ellen ate and described how she planned to redecorate her old room. She cajoled a late arriving Uncle Roy into admitting the barbecue was passable before he adjourned to the local bar for the declared purpose of remediating the loss of his favorite ingredient: bourbon.

We helped Teeny Mom clear the table, took the dishes to the sink, and returned to the kitchen table to share freshly brewed coffee.

"Are you girls sure you want to drink regular coffee this late in the day?" Teeny Mom asked. "I'm used to it. But how about you two?"

"I'm driving. So, I'm good," Marsha Ellen said.

While they fussed back and forth about coffee and sleeping well, I gathered the photo printouts and cabin cards to take back to Teeny Mom's office area. I scanned the card with Bill Smith written in on the bottom thinking it looked like I'd have to knock on the door and see for myself. However, it would have to wait.

Marsha Ellen noticed I hadn't joined in on the banter. "Shelley, I can tell there's something bothering you," she said. "So, it's your turn. Out with it."

"Well, I got more information today about these guys." I held up the cabin cards. "Tidbits about everyone, but nothing for Oliver Carlson," I said. "I sure wish something new would surface about him."

"What have you got there?" Marsha Ellen asked.

I showed her the photos of Hanson, Kleinmann, and the properly corporate looking Charles Guyer. Then I showed her the card with the name of Bill Smith. “I just found out this Bill Smith is staying in one of our cabins right now. It’s troubling that we don’t know anything about him other than his name and that he has some kind of relationship with William Hanson, the guy who originally rented the cabin. Hanson seems to have the strongest connection to Nikkerbo.”

“So, you have a Bill and a Buddy G staying over there,” Marsha Ellen motioned in the direction of the cabins across the Smoketree road. “Either of them acting up?”

“No. Not that I know of,” I said. “But it bugs me. If we know where they are, Oliver Carlson shouldn’t be so hard to find?”

“What are you getting at?” asked Teeny Mom.

“Deputy Dana told me he had a house here in Bishop Hill. Said it’d been searched. I’ve walked right by it on the way to the cemetery more than once and haven’t noticed any activity.”

“I sense a but coming up,” Marsha Ellen added.

“Right,” I said. “But I wasn’t always paying close attention. And … I sure wish I could get inside.”

“It’s going to be a big mess in the old Holder place. Lydia lived there alone for years, and really couldn’t keep it up,” Teeny Mom pointed out. “Oliver does travel a lot.”

“Everyone keeps reminding me of that,” I said. “And you didn’t tell me Oliver Carlson, what, inherited that house somehow?”

“No, Oliver only recently bought it from Lydia Holder’s estate,” Teeny Mom replied. “In fact, I’m pretty sure that’s what he and Kathy disagreed on.”

“And now,” Marsha Ellen interjected, “you want to pay the old place a visit?”

“Yeah,” I nodded. “I do.”

“So where exactly is it?” Marsha Ellen asked.

"Right behind the fire station," I answered.

"All righty," Marsha Ellen said as she took a last sip of coffee. "Let's do this thing before it gets any darker."

"What?" gasped Teeny Mom. "You can't—"

I interrupted her. "Relax, I'm not planning on breaking in. I just want to take a closer look around, you know, for tracks, and whatnot." I shuffled my papers together and got ready to go. Marsha Ellen was ahead of me going out the door.

Marsha Ellen insisted on driving and I agreed to just taking one car, hers. Two cars would attract too much attention. "Thanks," I said as I slid in. "But why are you so keen on doing this? You don't have to, you know."

"Lots of reasons. I want to help. I'm curious. I was afraid your next move might involve talking to Buddy G and I'm still not ready for that," she said.

"Oliver Carlson has potential as a witness." I said and paused. "Buddy G has said all along that he didn't connect with Rune in the cemetery. Unless you can think of a motive for him to—"

She chased the thought away with a firm, "No. Now where to?"

"We need to park behind the Bishop Hill fire station on Erickson street," I replied. "There aren't many occupied houses along that section, so we should be okay."

"What about overflow from the bar? Maybe we should go up by the cemetery and walk back down."

"No offense, but your shoes."

"What about my shoes?" she asked.

"City shoes might not be up to hiking over rough ground and grassy lanes," I said.

"My shoes are just fine."

By the time we came to terms about the suitability of her shoes we had crossed the bridge over the Edwards River and were approaching the intersection with Bergland street.

"Should I turn here?" she asked.

"No. Let's go past and get an idea of how many folks are out and about, as Teeny Mom would say."

We passed The Lutfisk Café, the Colony Church, and the state park on our right. The large colony-era brick and stucco buildings that made up the heart of Bishop Hill stood out on our left. I instructed her to make a left turn onto Main Street followed by an immediate left turn onto Erickson Street. We slowly made our way toward our destination. It appeared we were the only ones present as we pulled over to park in front of the desolate house in serious need of repairs and paint. We exchanged nervous looks but remained determined.

"Here we go," I said.

The subdued palette of shabby grays and browns of Carlson's house suddenly lit up with flashes of red and blue. A Henry County cruiser pulled up behind us and let the light bar grab our attention. I was envisioning yet another trip up to Cambridge when Deputy Dana exited the vehicle. We'd built a kind of rapport over the last few weeks so I thought it best if I got out first, slowly and carefully, with hands where she could see them.

Deputy Dana checked me out, peered into the car at Marsha Ellen, and relaxed enough to take her hand off her gun. "Ladies, what do you think you are doing?"

"Uh, nice night. We decided to take a drive," I said. "What are you doing here?"

The deputy summarized the obvious. "Badge. Uniform. I'm on duty surveilling the residence of a person of interest while patrolling my zone. The Ox-Boy cabins were up next."

"So, you haven't been here the whole time," I said.

"We don't have the resources to devote around-the-clock stakeouts unless there's an urgent need," the deputy replied.

"Then you haven't checked the doors lately," I said. "You know, to see if they're still locked."

"Look, they're closed aren't they," the deputy muttered. When we turned to look at the front door, we saw Marsha Ellen already there, trying to peer through the old wavy glass.

"What is she doing?" said the exasperated deputy. "Get back from there."

"Is this an active crime scene?" I inquired.

"Not yet," Deputy Dana said through clenched teeth. She shook her head and made an attempt to loosen up. "Okay, no, it isn't."

"Then we're here to pay a neighborly visit to Mr. Carlson. Ask him how he is. You know, stuff like that." I edged around so I faced the house, and the deputy didn't.

"And ask what he was doing last week," Deputy Dana added with a huff.

"Maybe," I said. "I really have been trying to get a hold of him for business reasons."

"With you? I find that hard to believe."

"With Nikkerbo," I reassured her. "He's interested in arranging something to go along with his coin business."

"Look, we don't need a crowd here," Deputy Dana exclaimed, as she turned back toward the house. "Where did she go?"

I trailed after Deputy Dana as she stomped along the side of the house. "She'd better not be inside," she said.

We caught up with Marsha Ellen by the back door, which was standing ajar. “Did you open that door?” Deputy Dana demanded.

“No ma’am,” Marsha Ellen said, and bent her head to listen. “I think I hear something.”

“Oh, come on,” the deputy snorted, “that is so old, so lame.”

“She’s right,” I said. “I do hear something. Someone’s in there.” I started for the door and was roughly pulled back.

“Deputy first,” Deputy Dana said as she reached for her weapon. “And stay behind me.”

She must have guessed that there was no way we would stay outside by ourselves.

CHAPTER 25

Marsha Ellen and I hung back in order to give Deputy Dana adequate room to move forward unencumbered as she probed deeper into the house. We had time for the ambient light filtering in from the street to illuminate what had become of the simple lean-to structure added to the back of the house years ago. The enclosed space held tattered plastic bags of old trash, some newish looking grocery bags, and piles of old newspapers and books—lots and lots of books of all shapes and sizes. I picked one up and was amazed at how old it was. I used my little flashlight to inspect it closer.

Marsha Ellen did the same but used her cell phone for a flashlight. "I can't read this," she said.

I flipped through a few pages of the book I held. "Well, this appears to be a ledger handwritten with nineteenth-century penmanship and iron gall ink. Let me see yours." She held out her find so I could study it. "Same thing, but the ink is smeared. Water damage. The roof has been leaking." I surveyed the scene with a heavy heart. "Or it has rained in. It's possible that all of this has been damaged."

A light came on in a far room and we heard Deputy Dana's voice. Marsha Ellen and I froze until we knew for certain that she was speaking to someone in a soothing, caring way. We rushed into what at one time might have been a front parlor but was now a makeshift bedroom. A man lay on an iron frame bed with the deputy hovering over him.

Oliver Carlson had been found and, by the looks of his pale face and labored breathing, none too soon. Deputy Dana motioned to us. "Stay with him. Talk to him calmly. Keep him awake. I'll make the ambulance call from my car."

I stepped forward as Deputy Dana left. "Hi, Mr. Carlson, I'm Shelley Anderson. I've been trying to get in touch with you for days. Glad to meet you at last." I kept an even, soothing banter up as I took stock of my surroundings. With the lights on I was awestruck with what I saw. Piles of stuff everywhere. Mountains of paper, books, and old newspapers leaning against the walls, leaving the dilapidated bed in the only clear floor space. After the initial shock wore off, I became aware that everywhere I looked I saw priceless history being stored in haphazard, uncontrolled disorder. I've never felt so overwhelmed with elation and sadness at the same time.

Marsha Ellen stood close by and distracted herself by picking up another book to flip through. She stopped to unfold some larger sheets of paper that had been stuffed between the pages. "Um, Shelley, this is a ledger of long-ago meetings, business transactions, and such." She gingerly held out the type-written papers. "And this could be the original charter for the town of Bishop Hill. I recognize the names of Colonists."

I took Mr. Carlson's hand in mine. "There's certainly a lot to treasure here." The man struggled to form a lopsided smile. "There, there," I said. "Help will get here soon. You'll be okay. You'll see. Just take it easy." He drew me closer with a feeble hand and tried with the last of his strength to utter a few words.

Deputy Dana returned with reassuring news. "Mr. Carlson. The ambulance is on its way. We'll get you to the hospital. Stay with us." She turned to me and asked, "Has he said anything?"

"He tried," I said. The distant wail of sirens canceled out what I was about to say.

Marsha Ellen and I kept ourselves well out of the way of the ambulance crew. After Mr. Carlson was safely on his way, I noticed a change in Deputy Dana. Subdued and restrained was totally out of character for her.

"Look," she said, "I have to thank you guys."

"Does this mean you're not going to arrest us?" I said hopefully.

"Be serious." Just like that the old Deputy Dana was back.

"We're the ones who should apologize to you," I said. Marsha Ellen nodded in agreement.

"Let me finish," Deputy Dana said impatiently. "If you guys hadn't been here. Made me stop. I might have just done a drive-by check and not seen that the back door was open. The EMTs think we may have gotten to him in time. It'll make all the difference for his recovery. You two deserve the credit for the save."

"There are grocery bags by the back door. I bet his stroke happened as he was bringing them in. We all got lucky." My turn to look a little subdued. "Dana, may I call you Dana?"

"Only if I'm off duty or no one else can hear."

"Got it," I said. "You asked me before the ambulance came if he said anything."

"Yeah, I remember."

"Well, he tried so hard to speak, to make me understand. He looked up at me and said something that sounded like 'kinda smell horse'."

"You sure about that?" she asked.

Marsha Ellen gave me a look and said, "What kind of clue is that?"

"Okay," Deputy Dana said. "I'll put it in my report." She shrugged. "Maybe we can figure it out. In the meantime, we, that is us, have to clear out so the lab crew can do their work in here." She looked at me and added, "We already have your fingerprints." She turned to Marsha Ellen. "We'll be needing yours."

She gasped. "You've got to be kidding?"

"Oh, it won't hurt," I said.

"But it's gross. Inky, smudgy stuff all over my hands. Eww."

Deputy Dana escorted us out the way we came, with Marsha Ellen grumbling all the way. That's how Michael J for Just Dropped By Anderson found us being herded like squawking chickens by a stoic Deputy Dana.

"I heard the ambulance call and came by to see if I was needed," he explained to Dana. He looked over to us and asked, "What did they do now?"

We all tried to tell our own stories at once. Deputy Dana called a halt and took Michael aside for the official version. I was more than relieved when he received another call and had to leave. Deputy Dana walked him back to his truck.

We waited by Marsha Ellen's car. "You should call your mom," I said.

"After you," she said, "my battery is almost gone."

I handed her my cell phone, "You first." I walked a short distance away to give her some privacy.

Pacing back and forth gave me some time to think about Mr. Carlson's words of the "kinda smell horse" message. Those words seemed so important to him. His eyes were beseeching. Like the old treasure hunter wanted me to find something. I began by thinking of his words as more likely garbled rather than cryptic. That didn't get me very far. Too many of my friends had horses, just as I did. I thought I had it when I went with a different, more logical approach—a basic word ladder where you substitute one letter for another, one word at a time, in order to solve the puzzle. My best solution turned into something that was relatively easy to check out. I preferred to be on my own in case I was wrong, but I hadn't the patience to wait.

CHAPTER 26

Marsha Ellen finished her call and asked if I wanted a ride back. I hesitated. She studied my face for a whole five seconds before growing quite suspicious and challenged me. "You've got it, don't you?"

Deputy Dana returned in time to see Marsha Ellen maneuvering me away for a private word. It didn't work. She walked over to us. "All right, what's up with you two?" she asked with her don't-give-me-any-grief tone of voice.

Marsha Ellen started out with an apology. "Sorry, as bad as I need to get back to Galesburg, I just know that Shelley here has a different reason to be anxious to stay." She stared at me as if daring me to fib to her and a deputy.

"Okay, I have to admit that I first thought something in Carlson's house would be the key to his 'kinda smell horse' message," I said. "But I've changed my mind—"

An impatient Deputy Dana interrupted me. "Whatever you've got, it has to be better than searching every barn in Henry County for smelly horses. I'm totally on board with you, now get on with it."

"My plan B," I said simply, "is right over there." I pointed up Bergland street to the cemetery.

"I'm in," declared Marsha Ellen. She glowered at me and said, "Remember, I drove us here and that's that, and no snarky comments about my shoes."

We turned to stare at Deputy Dana who threw her hands up and said, "My shoes are perfect for any situation."

"Then I suggest we take a little stroll this way." I motioned to the grassy path leading toward the back of the Bishop Hill cemetery.

Our destination wasn't actually in the cemetery. We would find it partway down the equally grassy expanse at the end of Cemetery street. I followed the same path Deputy Dana and I walked when we came upon the hidden car. I had noted the weed-covered abandoned trailer in the neighboring field. Since it was protected by a barbed wire fence, I didn't give it a serious thought. Not on my radar at the time. Now it was.

To Carlson's damaged brain, "kinda smell horse" could mean "find a small house." A small travel trailer just might do. Worth checking out. And now I had company. Company was welcome. Deputy Dana had a badge, a gun, and a stupendous flashlight. On the other hand, Marsha Ellen had patent leather flats, light weight slacks, and her best sweater set. She had probably dressed to please Rune's mother. I didn't expect that part of her return to Galesburg would go well. To make matters worse, we'd be walking past the very spot Rune had been attacked and murdered. Looking for clues in Marsha Ellen's presence.

I was sure our treasure was a small computer device that probably held megabytes of information. Financial information important to only highly placed wheeler-dealers of the corporate world inhabited by one Curt Hemcourt V and elites of a similar level. I kept reminding myself to be sensitive to Marsha Ellen's mental welfare as we neared the spot that had previously been cordoned off by the yellow crime scene tape. I anxiously glanced over to Deputy Dana. She strode a few steps ahead of us and physically blocked out the remaining signs of the struggle that still could be seen. "Let's go around and come up to the street over there," she suggested.

Even as she struggled to keep up with us, Marsha Ellen told us, as she caught her breath, “It’s okay, guys, I need to see this place. All of it. I have to do it for Rune. And for me.” She stopped. “Explain to me what happened. All of what you know so far.” Then she waited, looking sad but determined.

Deputy Dana filled her in on where the wallet was found, where the drag marks had been, and where they led to. It was all approximate now because the signs of the struggle were already fading away under the growth of normal summer vegetation and the recent rain. While they studied the ground, I removed myself to the curved road that led out of the cemetery. I was trying to get my bearings so I could visualize where Buddy G might have been standing when he saw a darkened figure, the one he initially thought was his old frat brother, Rune.

When Deputy Dana noticed I’d strayed away, she called out, “What are you doing?”

“Buddy G told me he came into the cemetery from the Main Street entrance.” I turned to point back in the general direction. “He hadn’t meant to, but he missed the turn onto Cemetery Street. He parked over by the Methodist church and got out to walk. I figure he came out this way.” I motioned to where I thought he would have passed. “Headed that way.” I pointed ahead of me to the grassy extension at the end of Cemetery street. “There’s a nice clump of small trees there that look big enough to hide a good-sized man. If Rune was already on the ground, Buddy wouldn’t have seen him. By the time he thought he saw an old man with a shovel, he was totally spooked, assumed Rune was a no show, and figured he’d get his flash drive back the next day. That’s when Buddy G left by going back to the Main Street entrance.”

"Then what we're looking for is a computer thingy," said Deputy Dana, "that's small enough to fit into a wallet."

"That's about the size of it," I said.

Marsha Ellen chimed in. "And my engagement ring."

"What ring?" Deputy Dana asked.

"Rune had two important items on his person Monday night: Buddy G's USB flash drive and an antique engagement ring," I said. "Marsha Ellen, what do you know about this ring?"

"He was getting it from his grandmother," she said.

"So, it's probably in a nice jewelry box," I mused.

"I imagine so," she said.

"Would the box have been big enough to hold a ring and this computer whatsit?" Deputy Dana asked.

"I think so," I said. I was making a guess based on limited knowledge of these computer storage devices. I had recently seen the ones Alan and James carried around with them. "It would be roughly the size of your thumb. Maybe a little smaller."

"So, okay, we're looking for a jewelry box that a guy who'd been hit on the head, who was suffering from serious brain trauma, with limited time and resources, and who still, somehow, managed to hide it from everyone working this crime scene. Not once, but twice. Is that about it? Or can we move on to his assailant stealing one or both items."

I couldn't blame Deputy Dana for feeling put upon and cranky. I avoided looking at Marsha Ellen altogether.

"It's got to be close by." I insisted. "And I say we start over there at the old travel trailer. He would have seen it or maybe just stumbled across it."

We walked in the general direction of the trailer. Rune would have had to circumvent some bushes and small trees, but it was doable. If Marsha Ellen could walk it, I figured a wounded and disoriented Rune could pull it off, too. Maybe he came here before the attack. I pondered how to figure out that part when we got to the barbed wire barrier of the fence.

"Could he have gotten over this?" Marsha Ellen wondered out loud.

"He could have climbed over or maybe squeezed through somewhere," I said, and began looking for a spot where the strands of wire sagged apart, leaving a gap.

"Over here," Deputy Dana called out. "There's a low spot with a bit of cloth snagged on a barb. Could be from our guy."

I had to agree that it was likely. It was seconded by Marsha Ellen. Deputy Dana pushed the wire down further and we helped Marsha Ellen and her city shoes over before stepping across ourselves. The ground over to the trailer was not as rough as I would have expected. In the dark and after all these days, I could swear I saw the path he must have taken. I led and the others followed.

The trailer looked like an even bigger junk pile up close. It was filled with cast-off items of all kinds: bits of metal, pieces of wood, even plastic odds and ends. The discarded stuff some frugal soul would figure to be important and handy to have some day. The door had an intact padlock. That left the outside. I circled the rusty metal body, gingerly feeling for a cubby hole or slot big enough for a ring box. There were quite a few opportunistic places and I hoped to avoid some serious cuts. Deputy Dana was doing the same by using her flashlight to probe the crevasses. Marsha Ellen hung back with her arms crossed and fist pressed over her mouth.

"Shine your flashlight around this wheel well. I'm not sticking my hand in there," I said.

"Got it," answered Deputy Dana. "I did the one on the other side." She gave it her best shot and straightened up to say, "Nothing."

I had crouched down and when I stood, I found myself looking up at the little wing-like projection on the top edge of the trailer. The designer probably thought it would pass for an indication of aerodynamic speed or sleekness. As I gazed at it, I thought it was off kilter a bit.

"Shine your light up there," I said.

"Where?" asked Deputy Dana

"That wing-like thing. It looks funny, off center maybe. Rune would have been tall enough to reach that."

The combination of our lights revealed a small, dark object wedged into the tight space.

"Oh, my gosh," Marsha Ellen cried out.

"Keep your socks on. We don't have it yet," Deputy Dana said.

None of us were tall enough to reach so Deputy Dana had to boost me up in her cradled hands. It was stuck in there tight and took me a couple of tries to wiggle it loose. When I got back on the ground, I held out a battered jewelry box. One of those old-fashioned kinds flocked with a layer of fuzzy velvety stuff.

"This is it. I know it is." No one could begrudge Marsha Ellen a few tears as she caressed it a bit before opening it. Inside the box was the all-important engagement ring—and nothing else. She lifted the ring out, slid it into place on her left hand, and stared lovingly at it.

"Um, that's evidence. I can't let it go."

"Ms. Deputy," I said softly, "yes, you can. That ring is not the most important thing here. The USB flash drive is, and we don't have it. That flash drive contains the information that might lead us to a motive … and to a possible suspect."

I looked at the joy spreading over Marsha Ellen's face. She no longer seemed quite so tired and beleaguered. I concluded in an even softer voice, "The ring itself is only important to one person here. Let her have this moment. This proof of Rune's true intentions."

Deputy Dana got the message. "Yeah, sure, copy that."

CHAPTER 27

Sunday, June 15, 2008

"Good news, Oliver Carlson is making an excellent recovery," Teeny Mom reported when I came down for a late breakfast. "Kathy called early and asked for you. I told her you were sleeping in, since you had the day off. She told me I could come by. So, I went and saw Oliver for a brief chat. Well, no more than a hello. I had a longer conversation with Kathy."

"So, he's out of danger?"

"Yes. He and Kathy have been interviewed by the sheriff's investigators once already. Doctors have him scheduled to go home on Wednesday."

"That seems awfully fast to me," I said. "He looked so, so terrible last night."

"Well, they think he had a series of small strokes, TIAs, before suffering the larger one you all saw. He was lucky to get the help he needed in time to prevent major damage. They are treating him for dehydration and a high glucose level when he checked in. His doctor has him on a blood thinner while the staff is plying him with fluids and a low-sugar diet. They have a boatload of doctor appointments scheduled in the near future. But for now, he's alert, talking, and trying to piece together what he did since last Monday."

"Wow, that sounds so incredible," I said. "It's so great. For him and his family."

"Strokes are being handled differently these days. Something to do with … Wait a minute, I wrote it down," Teeny Mom stopped to flip open the small notebook she carried with her. “Here it is. They call it neuroplasticity. The brain can reorganize itself and form new connections after an injury. Interesting research going on with strokes and this other thing that’s called,” she checked her notebook again, “aphasia.” She stowed the notebook back in her purse. “Kathy said he specifically asked for you to come by.”

“I can do that?”

“Just stick with regular visiting hours. Either Kathy or Evelyn will be there.”

“Evelyn would be—”

“Evelyn Gunnarson, Albin’s wife, Rune’s aunt. Those Gunnarsons have been family friends for ages. Kathy, Evelyn, and I were friends in school and have managed to stay in touch since then.”

“He did ask to see me, you say. Does this mean he remembers me from Saturday night?”

“That’s just what Kathy told me. He’s working on his memories and his speech. I think your favorite deputy put in a good word for you.”

It was a short climb upstairs to the patient rooms. I entered to find a television providing a low level of noise but no entertainment—Oliver Carlson was sleeping. A gray-haired woman rose from a cushioned chair to greet me and introduce herself as Kathy Carlson. “I’m glad you came. Ollie will be so excited to finally meet you now that he is back in the real world, as he likes to say. Deputy Johnson told us you were instrumental in finding Ollie in time. The doctors tend to be cautious, but I can tell they’re pleased with how fast he’s progressing.”

“That’s what Teeny Mom, excuse me, Christina, told me.”

"No need to fuss about names. I've been calling her Teeny since kindergarten. And that is more years ago than I care to admit. Ollie's speech is still uneven, choppy, but I think you two will be fine. Sit down, will you?" She gave her husband enough of a nudge to get his eyes open. "Honey, you've got a visitor. This is Shelley Anderson. She helped find you last night."

Oliver Carlson struggled to get himself upright. Kathy fluffed up his pillow and used the electric controls to raise him into a position more to his liking. "Will it be okay for me to go find Evelyn in the cafeteria?" she asked.

"I'll be fine," he said, then turned to me, "Yes, you talked a lot." He studied my face and wagged a finger at me. "I wanted to say something. Important." He reached for my hand and held it with a light papery touch that wobbled slightly. "Let's find the memory." He closed his eyes to concentrate. "Yes," he sighed softly as if sifting through layers of fog. "It was … small, I think. Red. Pretty." He opened his eyes and asked hopefully, "Did you find it?"

"Well, sir, you did try to speak to me. I heard you say 'kinda smell horse'."

"I said 'kinda smell horse'?" he said looking mystified.

"No kidding," I said. "That's what it sounded like to me. You had a great deal of difficulty in getting the words out. I figured 'kinda smell horse' was a clue that I took to mean 'find a small house'." I explained the steps I went through trying to decipher his cryptic message and how it led us to the hidden jewelry box at the trailer. I hoped taking him back to that time and place might aid in the recovery of other memories. "Do you remember any of that?"

I could practically feel the effort he made to further probe his mind. “Sorry,” he said, slowly shaking his head. “No. Out of reach.”

“Do you remember talking to anyone else? Maybe earlier in the day?” He shook his head again. “What about Rune Gunnarson?” His face brightened.

“Ah, yes. Monday. Very busy. Albin asked for a favor. His nephew wanted a story. Colony money just the ticket. My favorite topic.” He stopped to chuckle. “Not obsolete when they bought in. Bad timing. 1857 Panic. All that paper made useless.” He splayed his fingers out and uttered a dramatic “Poof” to represent the sudden departure of the Bishop Hill Colony’s investment.

“I did some research into that time period,” I offered. “Teeny has an uncut sheet framed in her bedroom.”

“I helped with that,” he said, as a fond smile spread over his face.

I noted that his smile produced a much more balanced expression than the one I’d witnessed before the ambulance and EMTs arrived. “I was wondering,” I started to say before he preempted my next question.

“Why the shovel?” I was going to say yes, but he’d already launched into his story. “I carried it like I was treasure hunting.” This got a hearty laugh out of him. “Set folks buzzing every time. Trying to guess. Too much fun. Not bad for business. Retired the old shovel. Knees bothered me.”

“You were putting on a prospector act?” I gasped in exaggerated disbelief.

He swatted my feigned indignation away. “Made time for young man. Told him the story. He took photos. Asked for more. Cemetery his idea. Midnight. Did not expect him. Young folks.

You know." I gave him a stern look and he winced ever so slightly before going on. "Why not. One more walk. To the Edwards. Couldn't hurt." He heaved a bitter sigh. "Wrong. So wrong." He sank back into his thoughts.

I allowed him a moment to reflect, then prompted respectfully. "What happened next?"

"Lydia Holder made coffee. Once a week. We talked."

He had been distracted by another topic, and this story stalled, too. I thought I knew why. "She had the best collection of Bishop Hill artifacts outside any museum, didn't she?" I said.

"Fabulous," he recalled fondly. "I buy it all. To save."

"So," I began, hoping he'd reconnect with the story I wanted, "you parked at Lydia Holder's old house."

"Yes." His nod betrayed a slight tremor. "Walked Cemetery Street. Me and shovel. Out for adventure. Like old times," he said, with an increasingly weary look. His energy level was dropping.

"Did you meet up with Rune?"

"Yes, I did. There before me."

"Did he say why he got there early?" I asked.

"Surprise for sweetheart. Treasure hunt for her. He still wanted night pictures. We left for river."

"I guess that explains the hidden engagement ring," I said.

"That was treasure?" Carlson paused. "Thoughtful guy. Strange, but thoughtful."

"He was all that," I replied. It was then I realized there had been more to Rune. I had let my anger overshadow my memory of his better qualities. He could be sweet, kind, and goofy enough to plan a treasure hunt for Marsha Ellen. A valuable antique ring surrounded by junk would appeal to his offbeat sense of humor.

We shared a few moments of silent reflection. I reached out to give his hand a little squeeze. The slight touch got him going again. "I remember the river. He left first," Carlson continued soberly. "Nature called. Used the bushes. Then went back. I heard voices." His distress grew as he relived the last moments of what he remembered of Rune. His wife picked up on it as soon as she cleared the door.

Kathy Carlson held two cups of coffee. She passed one to me as she pulled out packets of cream and sugar from a pocket. "Looks like he's had enough for now. Try to understand. He needs his rest. Please feel free to come back another time."

"Yes, ma'am. I do understand and appreciate your time." I selected a few packets of creamer. After my experience with institutional coffee, I opted for a couple of sugars as well. I shouldered my bag ready to leave but hesitated when I got to the door. "Mr. Carlson, who did you hit with your shovel?"

"Too dark," he said. "Whacked him hard. Made handle loose. Laid that sucker out. Next to Rune." He was stopped by a wheezing fit of coughing.

"Yes," his wife said, massaging her husband's back. "The sheriff's investigators are thinking that whoever Ollie hit must have gotten up and knocked him down—before running away. Oh, honey," she whispered. Oliver Carlson let his wife wrap her arms around him.

"Thank you, sir," I said, and left them to comfort each other.

CHAPTER 28

I left Oliver Carlson's hospital room with a brain packed with so many ideas, so much information. I had to share or write down or do something before I burst. I lifted my gaze from the carpet in time to catch sight of Marsha Ellen coming toward me with a determined look and an armful of flowers.

"Those for Mr. Carlson?" I asked. She nodded. I hooked her elbow and spun her around. She started to sputter something about her mother wanting the flowers delivered. "I got it all." I'd meant to say the whole amazing story but what came out meant the same thing. "Come on," I said, as we quick marched to the elevator. I pressed the button for the lobby. "We gotta talk. Downstairs. Now."

We stepped out of the elevator in time to waylay a surprised Michael J for Just In the Neighborhood Anderson. I hooked his arm, too, and steered them toward some empty upholstered chairs by the fireplace.

"Michael, how did you know I was here?"

"I heard the ambulance call last night and got the rest of the story from Dana a while ago. Your mom told me you'd be here. So, I thought I'd swing by." He yawned as he glanced between his cell phone and his pager. "I can't stay long. Sadie's out in the rig, and I have a date with my bed."

"Seriously," I interrupted, "you've got to start going places without the tow truck. Ladies are going to start to wonder about you." I mugged an appropriately silly face.

"Oh, yuck," Marsha Ellen exclaimed as she sat. "Well, at least I came without a dog. Will she be okay without you?" she asked Michael, as she tried to figure out the best thing to do with her bouquet of colorful flowers.

"She'll be fine. New sights and smells will keep her busy." Michael sat next to Marsha Ellen. "How is Mr. Carlson doing?"

Marsha Ellen pointed a finger at me. "She knows. I didn't make it as far as his room."

"He is doing amazingly well," I said, as I maneuvered a chair within reach of my friends and perched on the edge. "We had a long chat, and I got some great info on Monday night. It really tired him out so let me fill you in." I proceeded to recap everything Oliver Carlson told me about Monday's meetings with Rune: the afternoon interview, the photos, the plan to meet that night in the cemetery for more photos, up to the would-be treasure hunt he had planned. "Marsha Ellen, I have to say I fail to see the romance in that plan of his."

"When he moved in, you know—to our place, he could never find anything. Treasure hunts became a thing for us." She kept herself together.

"In that case," I said, "it was very cool."

I directed myself to Michael. "Okay, Mr. Deputy Wannabe, why did you omit the factoid about the shovel's handle being damaged, loosened up?"

"Come on, you should know by now how Dana is about an ongoing investigation. She only told me now because she knew I'd be talking to you guys anyway." He squirmed in a delightful way.

"Okay, fair point," I relented. "But since Rune's blood was not on Carlson's shovel, it lets him off the hook, in my book."

"And does that place Buddy G for Good Bet on the hook and into your book?" queried Marsha Ellen.

Michael gave us leery looks. "I thought we left those kinds of jokes back in high school?"

"Have you heard any J jokes actually come from my mouth?" I demanded. He shook his head with an air of cautious reserve and remained silent but couldn't stifle his next yawn. "Then fine," I said, trying not to yawn myself. "We're good."

I glanced over to Marsha Ellen. "No J jokes on Michael Anderson ever again. I swear," she pledged with a lifted hand. I also raised my hand and repeated the pledge. Michael remained quiet and appeared unconvinced.

"Now, back to Buddy G," I said. "I think his involvement can be easily verified by reviewing Nikkerbo's security tapes from Friday. Marsha Ellen, remember Lars admitted he was watching us on the monitors? And, well, he was tracking Buddy G, too."

"When you ditched me and ran off to collect our favorite Buddy," she said. "At least Lars was good company."

"Okay, but Lars is always good company," I said. Marsha Ellen grinned at that. Michael glowered. "Oh, come on Michael, don't you have your own crush with a certain deputy?"

He played the indignant card while I gathered my thoughts and returned to the business at hand. "Now, when Buddy came over Thursday night for supper, I don't recall him fussing with his head, like he'd been injured by a shovel. I'll ask Teeny Mom what she remembers but I'm thinking we can rule out both Carlson and Buddy as likely perpetrators."

"Who does that leave?" Marsha Ellen asked.

"Our Mr. MAD Man, aka Bill Smith, probably aka something else, and—"

Michael cut in. "I'm going with a Nikkerbo connection. The timing is right. Stressful corporate meetings. Secret information on a USB drive leads old frat boy Buddy G to recruit Rune." He nestled further into his chair. "And your MAD Man hasn't acted up lately."

"Good points," I admitted. "Said computer device goes missing and Buddy G doesn't go into panic mode about that. In fact, he isn't in any kind of a hurry to leave the cabin and get back to his job."

"He doesn't want to go back to work because he knows he was the real target in the cemetery. It's the only thing that fits." Marsha Ellen broke in with a conclusion I hadn't gotten to yet. "That makes me so angry," she growled. "Rune must have been in the wrong place at the wrong time."

After waiting out a few beats of awkward silence, Michael interjected, "I thought you'd want to know that based on new information, deputies are searching barns in and around the Bishop Hill cemetery."

"Barns?" I said with disbelief. I looked to Marsha Ellen, but she didn't appear to be too interested in barns at the moment. She went back to absently mindedly fussing with the flowers she held. There didn't seem to be any way to put them down without damaging them. "That must have come from Dana. She told me to talk to him, keep him awake, while we waited on the ambulance. When he tried to speak to me, it sounded like 'kinda smell horse'. I told her about it and now they are taking it literally. Poor Dana."

"Horses are generally found in barns." Michael said. "They've started close in and are working their way through everything big enough for a horse. The current theory is that Carlson dropped his shovel but picked up some of Rune's stuff before staggering off. No one knows how far he'd have gotten after suffering some kind of stroke and all."

I settled back into the nicely padded chair. “The pros can handle it. Let them go off and search barns for USB thumb drives. Dumb drives. Whatever.” That sounded more like Dana than me. I’d been hanging out with her too much.

Michael produced another yawn and announced it was time for him to leave. We called out our goodbyes as he hustled for the main doors and his waiting dog. I turned to Marsha Ellen to check if it was okay for me to split as well. I expected a nod. As I watched her pick at the paper wrapping for her flowers, I experienced a sudden jolt of clarity. Marsha Ellen caught the glow in my face and quietly said, “You’re doing that thing again. They’re looking in the wrong places, aren’t they?”

“Could be possible,” I whispered back. “My place is closer.” I could tell she briefly considered mounting a protest, then caved.

“Okay. Fine. But you have more to tell me about this madman business, don’t you?”

She had me there. “Yes, ma’am. Not a problem.” I answered.

CHAPTER 29

Of course, what I meant by my place was the red brick house I shared with Teeny Mom and Uncle Roy. Marsha Ellen wasn't the only one of our old high school group having to move back home. I hadn't meant to stay past summer, but my life was veering off on a significant detour, so I was home for a while. Michael Skip the J Joke Anderson had his own apartment in Galva, but it was only a few blocks away from his folks. He lived at one end of a tree-lined street and his job at Anderson Brothers Garage, run by his uncles, was at the other end, closer to the downtown but still well within radar range of parental types. I considered that a near miss that did not count. He was back at home, too.

When I pulled into the driveway, I made room for Marsha Ellen's car behind me. I couldn't help but notice Dana's cruiser parked where it could be easily seen from the cabins of the Ox-Boy Campground across the road.

Dana waited until we parked, then strode over to join us. "Will someone explain why I should be here now instead of later when I'm driving my route and I've got it scheduled?" She stared at me.

"Let me guess," I said, "Michael suggested you shouldn't wait for your drive-by." She inclined her head enough for me to take it as a yes. "Extra time showing the colors is a bonus, is it not?" Another nod of sorts. "Well then, here we are. Let's adjourn inside," I said.

Teeny Mom watched as we trooped in the back door and requested enough room for all of us to sit together. "That would mean the dining room table," she said. "Give me a few minutes to clear it off. Shelley, check the coffee. You may need to start a new pot."

"That would be so lovely, Shelley," Dana cooed. We exchanged sweetly insincere smiles as I went to see to the coffee. Marsha Ellen wanted to follow but still had a bouquet of flowers to deal with.

"Your table awaits," Teeny Mom announced and motioned to the larger dining room table. "You ladies starting a new club? The Three Musketeers, or is it more of the Pippi Posse?"

Dana pronounced an emphatic, "No to three of anything. And what's with a Hippy Posse?"

"Pippi's Posse," I explained, "as in Pippi Longstocking, was a bunch of us disaffected Knox art students hanging out and complaining about the unfairness of departmental rules, extra hours of work for little or no credit, favoritism for certain male painters over that of talented females. Stuff like that. You wouldn't be interested."

"Unfortunately, you're likely to find those conditions existing anywhere and everywhere," Teeny Mom said. "I'm glad you guys got together for moral support."

"Yes," I said, "we did stir things up a bit. Actually, I think the Three Musketeers might be a better fit for our latest endeavor." I handed Dana a mug of coffee. "You could be our D'Artagnan. A friend and the fourth—"

I was cut off by the deputy's forceful, "No, I can't."

I took a moment to process that claim. I didn't necessarily agree with that and wished she'd give us a chance. "Then why are you here?" I asked.

"Michael suspected you two might be up to something after today's visit with Mr. Carlson, and since he couldn't make it, he hinted, rather strongly, that I might find it enlightening too." The deputy started to pout. Not at all becoming.

"Relax, I get it. But Mr. Carlson said the sheriff's investigators had already been at the hospital. They must have believed his story since I didn't see any guards outside his room. I can't imagine we have information you don't already have," I said. Marsha Ellen chose that moment to ask Teeny Mom for a vase so the deputy couldn't see her struggle to keep a straight face.

"Yeah, well, you just might," Dana said, with a grumble that turned into more of a sigh. I gave her a skeptical look and waited for more. Marsha Ellen and Teeny Mom surreptitiously waited for more. The deputy did an admirable job of calming herself. "Shelley, you were in with Oliver Carlson. I'd really like to know what he told you. There, I said it."

I looked confused. "I'd thought you'd be in on all the interviews."

"I patrol the zone assigned to me. I report anything suspicious on my watch. I direct traffic. I pick up after the crime scene team and such. I'm not an investigator, not yet."

I shifted my gaze between Dana and Teeny Mom and started telling Carlson's story. "First of all, Carlson was having you, and everyone, on with the shovel and pail act. He wanted people to think he was digging for treasure. It was all a sport to him. He wasn't seriously out for anything but playing a prank. And give a little boost to his coin business."

"But what did he see in the cemetery last Monday? Anything important?" the deputy asked.

"Plenty," I said, as I got down to business, "but not enough for a positive ID on who killed Rune." I saw Marsha Ellen stiffen, clench her whole body. She took a breath and loosened up. That urged me on. "At least not directly."

I turned back to the deputy. "You told me the blood on Carlson's shovel wasn't Rune's. You showed me photos that proved he had been struck by something else. What you didn't say was that Oliver Carlson had used his shovel on the bad guy with enough force to mess with the handle. Like, loosen it up."

An "Oh, my gosh" came from Teeny Mom.

"Quite right," I said. "Carlson knocked the guy down, but this guy got up and with enough strength to attack Carlson. Push him down. Did something that might have triggered Carlson's first little stroke, a TIA. Like they told you, Mom, he had a series of them, up until the last bigger one we saw on Saturday. Those TIAs must have left him able enough for searchers to miss him, but not well enough to get back to Galva. That was as far as I got with my visit. His brain is recovering, reorganizing, and he may remember more later. And then maybe we'll find out how and why he moved his car down to the Edwards. I don't know what part his wife, Kathy, has in all this because some of those bags by the back door looked new. What I do know is there's solid DNA evidence on the shovel that can be matched at some point to prove who killed Rune. Carlson shouldn't be considered a suspect.

"Which brings me Buddy G. We had him over for supper on Thursday night. I saw him at Nikkerbo on Friday morning. Dana, you drove him to Cambridge, and he was there for the rest of Friday. I never noticed him acting like he had a head wound. Did either of you?" I made sure to include Teeny Mom in this question.

"Not me," Teeny Mom said. "He was down, depressed maybe, but he had good reason to be, with his friend, Rune, murdered." She reached over to give Marsha Ellen a gesture of support and comfort. "I didn't notice a wound."

"I had him in my cruiser for the ride to Cambridge," Dana said. "Then I turned him over to the investigators and I was out of the picture, so to speak."

"The security tapes at Nikkerbo might be helpful," I said. "I'll look at them the first chance I get. That will probably be sometime Tuesday."

"In the meantime, I'll keep watching the twit's cabin when I'm on my rounds. He's been instructed to stay put here." Dana resumed her official deputy persona. "Same with our Mr. MAD Man."

"Okay," Marsha Ellen said, "how many bad guys are we talking about here? And explain what the deal is with this 'mad man' you keep talking about."

"Sorry," I said. "Our use of Mr. MAD Man is a play on license plate initials that we started doing for the guy in one of our cabins." Marsha Ellen looked confused. "Look, the facts we have on this guy right now say stay away from cabin three and avoid his MAD car. I think Michael was right when he said the important thing to focus on is the connection to Nikkerbo, the meetings that went on earlier this week, and the missing USB flash drive. All those people are either here now or are scheduled to return shortly. One of them considers the information on that computer device to be worth killing for. We have time to gather more information and plan ahead to keep Buddy G from becoming the victim he was meant to be."

"Look guys," Dana said, "I'm okay with Michael and you guys being Musketeers, but I'm not cut out to be a fourth Musketeer."

"You are so," I countered. "You're a fighter. The upholder of the law. You're the one and only Deputy Dana."

"Okay. Enough." Dana said, almost blushing. "Let's just see how things shake out. Now, I've got to get back on duty." Teeny Mom handed her a travel cup of coffee to go. "Thanks, Mrs. …"

"Call me Teeny, everyone else does. And Dana, you're welcome to our coffee any time."

As soon as we heard the crunch of the cruiser's tires ease out of the driveway and fade into the distance, Marsha Ellen said, "I was waiting for her to leave."

"Marsha Ellen," Teeny Mom began, "she's a deputy. She has to be careful with how she interacts with you, us—"

"Civilians?" I offered.

"Precisely," Teeny Mom said.

"What I meant to say," Marsha Ellen continued, "was that it's time for Shelley to tell me, us, about the brainstorm she had at the hospital."

"Ah, you're right. I got so sidetracked that I forgot about the flowers you brought for Mr. Carlson."

"What?" Teeny Mom exclaimed, clutching at her heart in a pantomime of disappointment. "Those weren't for me?"

"Well, they are now," Marsha Ellen consoled. "I'll get Mr. Carlson some fresh ones tomorrow." She pointed at me. "I know that l-thought-of-something aura you get."

"Right," I said, "I'll be right back."

I dashed upstairs to my room to retrieve the paper flower, the so-called rose, that Rune had somehow fashioned and left to be found in his car, discovered later by Michael J for Justly Chivalrous Anderson and given to me because of the accompanying note. I explained it all to Marsha Ellen when I came back down with the frumpy creation.

"I was watching you fiddle with the wrapping paper for your flowers, and it came to me in a flash. I thought it was out of character for Rune. As you said, Rune and I were not getting along and, of course, he planned on proposing to you." This was becoming quite uncomfortable, but I had to forge ahead. "Anyway, I needed a closer look-see at this…." I held up the flower-ish thing and kneaded the lumpy excuse for a stem. "Okay, this definitely has possibilities."

"It's a good thing Dana and Michael aren't here to witness this," Teeny Mom said. "You'd be making their lives miserable."

"Oh," I said. I stopped what I was doing long enough to speculate, "Would that be the whole chain of evidence thing?"

CHAPTER 30

A chill of apprehension gripped me as I realized the paper rose-thing I held in my hand now presented me with a dilemma. "I have to turn it in don't I. But—"

"But if you do, we'll never see it again," Marsha Ellen exclaimed.

"It's not even unwrapped," I said. "We don't know for sure if the USB drive is what's making this so lumpy."

"That's why turning it in now is the right thing to do," Teeny Mom declared. "And the legal thing. Remember you've been told to stay out of trouble."

"Yeah, but," Marsha Ellen and I protested in unison.

"Buddy G gave the computer drive thing to Rune," Teeny Mom said. "He told us that much."

"How do you think he got it in the first place?" Marsha Ellen mused.

"Work, I guess," I said. "I don't know for sure. Chicago or …" I stopped to ponder a different angle, "perhaps somewhere closer. Say, someplace like Nikkerbo."

"Okay," Marsha Ellen said, without going further.

Teeny Mom took the moment of silence to add, "Well, maybe when this young man was filling out his cabin card last Sunday, he sort of asked who I had to help me with my computer when it, um, had issues." She was drawing out her words with hesitant unnatural timing. "I thought of your friends from school, those brothers."

I believed she was admitting to something that left me speechless and thrilled. Marsha Ellen, also momentarily speechless, came around first. “We could just come out and ask, Buddy G. Find out how the computer-memory-thumb-drive thingy came to be.”

“It won’t hurt to feed him again,” Teeny Mom suggested. “He’s been living on bar food for days now.”

“Have any barbecue leftovers?” Marsha Ellen asked eagerly, her eyes wide in anticipation.

“Lots of it since Roy boycotted the new recipe,” Teeny Mom said.

“More for us, then,” I said, rubbing my hands together. “May I be the one to extend the invitation?”

With a sharp nod of approval from Teeny Mom and a softer “yes” from Marsha Ellen, I tucked the paper flower into my pocket and set out on my mission. I resisted the urge to unwrap my prize. They were watching me. Besides, it probably made a better prop as it was.

I walked across the Smoketree road and down the drive between the cabins. The cabins were situated in pairs. Numbers one and two to my right in front of the restroom/shower building were currently unoccupied. Cabins three and four on the left had recently held William Hanson and Walter Kleinmann, respectively. At the far end of the drive were cabins five and six. Charles “Buddy G” Guyer, was ensconced in cabin five. Six was Uncle Roy’s cabin studio and the closest to the Oxpojke Trail.

I gave cabin three a cursory look and noted Mr. MAD Man was still in residence. I headed toward cabins five and six. I knocked on five’s door and waited. Hearing nothing, I stared at Buddy G’s car, parked right where it should be. I tried again and listened intently for footsteps. Nothing.

However, the sound level emanating from of Uncle Roy’s cabin was way out of the ordinary. Puzzled, I went over to knock. The door opened onto Uncle Roy and his guests: Buddy G and a stocky figure wearing a black leather jacket with dark jeans. I hesitated.

"Shelley," Uncle Roy gleefully called out, "Glad you dropped by. Come on in."

I stood still in the doorway. He did not take that as a clue that something was bothering me. "Come on in. We're not going to bite." His jovial manner didn't stop me from considering possible excuses to leave. I came up empty.

"Shelley," Buddy G spoke up, "you are certainly welcome. Our little self-help group needed a snack break anyway." He turned toward the black leather jacket. "Jill's stomach has started complaining."

I recovered enough composure to acknowledge, "Well, food is the reason I'm here." Trying not to stutter or further embarrass myself, I said, "You all are all invited up to the house." I looked to Uncle Roy for some guidance. He beamed a broad smile back at me and waved the others out of their seats. "Come on, guys and gals, let's go."

I wanted them, this trio, to walk in front of me but the guys, Buddy G and Uncle Roy refused. That left me leading the way and walking close to the leather-clad Jill-person.

I felt obligated to start the polite small talk. "Um … Jill," were the only words I could manage. It didn't help that they came out sounding more as a question than anything else.

Sparing me from making a further pathetic attempt to form a coherent thought, she said, "Yeah, look, I'm sorry about misdirecting you guys. But I had to be careful."

Careful! She had to be careful.

Buddy G came up to my other side and asked, "Is Marsha Ellen here?"

"Yes," I said, and saw signs of impending distress cloud his face. "Buddy, she's been out to the cemetery, were they found Rune, and handled it pretty well … considering." I didn't know what to expect out of their first meeting. I offered a tired cliché. "Let's just see how it goes."

Uncle Roy came up from behind and clapped a friendly hand on Buddy's shoulder. "You're doing the right thing, young man. Hiding out doesn't solve any problems." He directed similar encouraging words to Jill. "You'll see. It's going to be all right. They'll understand when you explain."

This new Uncle Roy was amazingly upbeat, positively sparkling. I had no idea where it came from, but it was a welcome change.

We filed into the kitchen where I stood back and left Uncle Roy with the honor of introducing his new-found groupies. "Teeny, Marsha Ellen, this is Jill and I trust you all know Charles here. He wants us to call him Buddy G."

Marsha Ellen stepped forward with a ready smile and an outstretched hand. "Welcome, Jill," she said. She acknowledged Charles with a nod and coolly addressed him by his nickname. "And Buddy G. Rune did speak of you."

I'd hope that Buddy G would be the first to speak, but Jill took the lead. "Thank you for inviting me, us. The food smells delicious. I love barbecue."

She seemed quite personable, and I wanted an explanation for this epic failure. How could we have mistaken the identity of our MAD Man? There must be more to it than a black leather jacket. Jill was tall and sturdy, not gorgeous, but attractive in a practical way. This could be a solid pioneer woman who could deliver her own baby in the morning and cook a big meal for the harvest crew in the afternoon but with a trendier wardrobe and a unisex haircut that had grown out just enough to demand some attention. I had to find the right question to ask. I weighed my options and went with a safe, but trite, inquiry. “Well, I wanted to ask you about your car.”

She turned toward me in a way that subtly separated us from the others and answered with an air of defensiveness that didn’t bode well for a long conversation. “What about my car?”

“I saw it in Galva last week. It’s my current dream car and I wondered … uh, how do you like it?”

“I like it fine,” she said. “Yeah, it’s a good car. A birthday gift.”

I thought about asking what year it was and settled on a question about the mileage. She seemed okay with that and then in return asked, “Do you really like that car?”

“Yes, ma’am,” I replied without lying.

“Okay, I can show it to you.” She made a pretense of fumbling through a rather nice-looking designer bag. She had excellent taste in leather. She sighed, “I don’t have the keys with me. I must have left them in my cabin. I haven’t had it all that long. The night you saw me in Galva I was going in for some gas.”

“You remember seeing me?”

“Sure, I’m good with faces, and cars of course, and I’ve watched you come and go enough times since I’ve been here to know yours.” She must have realized how creepy that sounded and added a defensive explanation. “I’ve been keeping to myself during my stay, but I’ve become attuned to the rhythm of the rural life you’ve got going on out here. I like it. It’s a nice change for me.” She displayed a growing degree of self-consciousness. “I was just glad my dad was able to put me up here for a while. Your mom’s been very patient with me, too.”

"I don't mean to pry but, well, I mean, we kind of thought a guy, a Bill Smith, was registered to that cabin. Ah, your cabin."

She gave me a long sideways look, then sighed again. "Yeah, well, that was me trying to be inconspicuous and apparently failing. Look, you better let me explain."

I was still nervous, but at least she didn't scare me as much.

Turns out that Bill Smith was really Jill Hanson Fischer, whose only crime was marrying into the wrong family. She was in the process of divorcing an abusive husband with unsavory business partners. She'd needed some alone time in the middle of nowhere and I had to admit that we usually had plenty of nowhere most days. Winter was even better. She appreciated that and said she wanted to stay until after Midsummer. She asked for a little patience, some consideration, and lot of discretion on our part. I gave her my word on my silence. But the minute she left I'd have one great story to tell about the mad man who wasn't what we expected.

While Jill and I talked I stole an occasional glance over in Marsha Ellen's direction. It looked like Uncle Roy and Teeny Mom were acting as mediators between her and Buddy G. Hearing no outbursts nor seeing any physical acts of violence meant things were going pretty good considering the circumstances. Jill and I drifted over to the food and began filling our plates. That appeared to be the invitation for the others to join us around the dining room table.

We ate with the usual polite conversation of a shared meal: pass this, hand me that, want any more? Buddy G and Jill were clearly ravenous. Unburdening themselves each in their own way left a void to be filled with barbecue. Teeny Mom basked in the praise of such healthy appetites. Uncle Roy seemed to have developed an intriguing blend of host, mentor, and counselor. He was doing so well. I almost hated having to break the spell by asking Buddy G about the paper flower with the suspiciously lumpy stem. Almost.

CHAPTER 31

We were all still gathered around the table when I drew the paper creation out of my pocket and held it out like an offering. After all this time and handling the paper flower looked less and less like it had ever been anything close to a rose.

"Buddy," I said, "tell me about this."

"Oh, that looks like one of the flowers my niece made for me. She gave me a pocket full before my trip down here, saying they were lucky. Where'd you get…?" He stopped himself. "Is that from…?"

"From Rune's car," I finished for him. "I believe it was meant for me." Marsha Ellen sat stiffly and stared at Buddy.

"Yeah," Buddy said, "I gave Rune one of those flowers. I assumed it would play a part in one of his pranks." He fell silent with his gaze fastened on the object in my hand.

"Okay," I said, "I couldn't help but notice how bulky the stem section is. Like something is wrapped up in there. I haven't opened it—"

"It's just a piece of candy."

"Not a USB memory drive?" I asked.

"Nope, just candy." He studied me and added with all seriousness, "You thought the memory stick I gave Rune to hold for me, the one he was supposed to bring to the cemetery, was in that flower?" I nodded and he went on. "So, it still hasn't been found?"

"No," I said. "As far as that goes, the only clue I've had to work with were the few words Oliver Carlson whispered to me before the ambulance came."

"Oliver Carlson," Buddy repeated. "He had a story Rune wanted to chase down. His reason to be here. Other than mine, that is."

"Other than yours." Marsha Ellen finally spoke up. Her coolness turned icy. "What was so important that…." She stopped when the words froze up in her mouth.

"Please," I jumped in to relieve the strain on Marsha Ellen. "Explain to me what happened. I want to understand. Start from the beginning."

"Beginning? Of course."

Buddy began by going back to his father fixing him up with his first job at a large Chicago bank. He was handling home loans and feeling great about helping people live their dreams of home ownership. He had a free rein. Anybody could get credit for a down payment, and he was making impressive bonuses. The atmosphere was like being back at the frat house on campus where it was "Party hearty" and "What's class attendance done for me lately?"

It took a while for him to realize that something wasn't right. His mortgage clients were struggling. Some were in danger of defaulting on their loans. He started looking within his bank and asking around. Checking out what others in his position were experiencing. Most everyone called him a buzz kill and told him not to worry. The bank's loans were bundled up into huge packages. Everything was backed by a triple-A rating. Mortgages have been solid investments since forever, so no need to worry.

But he found a few people with another story. They had done due diligence on their investments. Researched some of those huge loan packages. Their take was very sobering. The kind of loans Buddy was making in the subprime market were over leveraged and seriously bad.

He began to falter at this point of his story. "All the warning signs were being ignored, or…"

I leaned forward. "Or what?"

"Or I was being lied to and manipulated." Buddy's clenched fist hovered over the table as if he wanted to pound out his frustration. "That's what I meant by saying my job had turned toxic. I had to find out who was right. And yes, I looked. I found the evidence that convinced me that making all those risky loans was really, really awful."

"How did Rune come into the picture?" I asked.

"I had no choice but to leave the bank. I began working for Hemcourt Enterprises, but that toxic environment surfaced again. My new boss, Walter Kleinmann, got interested in mortgage loan deals. I couldn't talk him out of it. He wouldn't listen to reasonable persuasion.

"Rune gifted me with a duct-tape wallet as a young frat brother. He looked up to me back then. I'm sure it meant a great deal to him, the gesture of giving and sharing a moment. I doubt if I felt any warmth at being the recipient of a cruddy homemade thing I didn't want." He winced under Marsha Ellen's stare and looked to me. "I'm sorry. I was like that then: all about image, getting ahead, making easy money. I was so sure the slick and shiny was my future."

I'd been in such a place myself and could feel the heat of his shame. "What?" I prompted.

"What led me back to Rune? Well, I found it again—the wallet. Like it was meant to guide me to him. I'd heard Rune had graduated with a degree in journalism. I knew his family had solid newspaper connections. It would be easy, I thought. I still had the raw data from reports, emails, and such from when I worked at the bank. We'd get together and combine the old data with the newest to hash out the story of corruption and greed. It would get out into the world. We'd be heroes."

"That didn't happen," I said sadly.

"Kleinmann may work for Mr. Hemcourt but he is also a business partner with my former boss at the bank. They are working together on this project, this sales pitch for…."

Buddy looked around the table and realized he was perilously close to losing us. He switched gears and tried painting a different picture. "Think of it this way: there's a tainted package that these guys are hot to sell, to get off their books, and they want Mr. Hemcourt to be the next buyer."

"But judging by what I saw of last week's meetings, that didn't go so well."

"Yeah. Kleinmann started getting suspicious of me and my lack of enthusiasm for his big project, his deal of deals. He told me to stay here until he got back. We had to make the sale or else." A dejected Buddy shrugged. "Turns out I had to stay anyway."

"Buddy," I needed to refocus his attention to the USB drive. "Tomorrow will be one week since Rune walked into the cemetery and failed to walk out. You had the thumb drive ready to go when you met up with Rune." He nodded. "Did you bring it with you from Chicago?"

"No," he said. "I was having problems with my laptop and got hooked up with a tech guy, James something, through your mom."

"Call me Teeny." she said, using her comforting mom voice to inspire the warmth of a caring friend.

"Sure thing, Teeny," he said politely. "I followed through with your recommendation. He got my laptop back up to speed again by running antivirus software. He happened to have a USB drive with him. I got him to download the old bank files I had stored on my computer. Plus, some recent emails between Kleinmann and me. Then I convinced him I needed everything deleted so no snooping boss would find anything incriminating if they did a quick search of my files. I could have done it myself, but he was right there with memory stick and wanted to be helpful. He made sure I understood how he could make the files permanently gone if I wanted. I insisted that he make sure everything was gone for good."

"So, Rune was to be your off-line backup as well as your co-conspirator," I said.

"That was the plan," he said with resignation.

"Does anyone else know you had a local source for the USB drive?" I asked.

"I never mentioned it to anyone. Just you, your mom, and the guys from Galva. I couldn't confide in anybody at Nikkerbo."

"Great, then I think I have another plan," I said impulsively. "If I can get another USB drive, the same kind, I'll have a decoy."

"But I don't have the files to download."

"No problem," I said, making it up as I went. "What I need to know is who has to have that thumb drive so badly they'll steal it from me." Buddy G wore his confused face. "Buddy, whoever that person is will be our prime suspect for—"

"Murdering Rune instead of you." Marsha Ellen voiced the thought I was afraid to acknowledge. It was a plausible theory. Her saying it out loud made it real and intensified the hurt—and the fear. Teeny Mom immediately moved to her side to provide comfort and support.

The color drained out of Buddy G's face. Eyes tightly closed he started to sway a bit. "Buddy," I said, grabbing his shoulder and shaking, "stay with us."

"I was meant to be the target, not Rune." With effort he pulled himself together. "Marsha Ellen, I'm so sorry."

"Look, Buddy, we've got to catch this guy in the act of snatching the decoy. Connect the dots. That's how we can best help Rune." I paused. "And keep you alive, too."

That did not bring the color back to his cheeks.

Before Teeny Mom could voice her objections, Uncle Roy added his opinion. "I think we can do this." He glanced over to Teeny Mom and added a quick, "Safely. We can make sure everyone is safe."

"There are lots of details to work out before Mr. Hemcourt's executive crew shows up for Bishop Hill's Midsommar Festival," I pointed out.

"You only have two days," Teeny Mom informed us with no small amount of apprehension. "They're due to check in on Wednesday."

Jill, who wasn't Bill, took that opportunity to be the first to leave our impromptu dinner party with the excuse of getting back to her job of staying out of sight and out of trouble. Buddy seconded that motion and offered to escort her to her cabin. Uncle Roy loitered in the kitchen long enough to make sure they were out the door and out of hearing range before he remarked, "I don't know who is protecting who with those two." Then he left for his cabin.

Teeny Mom adjourned upstairs, and I finally had a chance to talk to Marsha Ellen.

“Are you settling back into your old room?” I asked.

“It feels weird, but yes, things are going okay. The folks, mom especially, are being very supportive.” She studied the engagement ring on her left hand like she was trying to memorize every detail. “I haven’t talked to Rune’s parents lately,” she said with feigned disinterest. “I suppose they’re making funeral arrangements. If they are, they haven’t included me.”

“Oh my gosh, I forgot all about that. If there’s anything I can do for you be sure to let me know.” I moved forward with a small gesture of helpfulness, but she drew back from me. I was momentarily stunned. “Is it me or Buddy?”

“Oh, Shelley, it isn’t you. I just don’t know what to make of Buddy and everything he told us tonight.” She stared at her ring again. “I need some time.” I agreed to give her whatever she needed, and we walked together out to her car.

When alone in my room I wrote my first email to James Viklund, one of Galva’s tech wizards, and described what I needed. We exchanged a series of messages around midnight and assured me that he’d be able to match the missing USB drive from what he had on hand. I would soon be in the fake USB business. That, at least, left me feeling optimistic. I decided it was best to quit for the night. Since I had the next day off, I’d have the luxury of sleeping in. I was totally ready for that. Before I turned the lights off, I stared at the collage to my birth mother I had hanging on the opposite wall and whispered my wish. “Tell me the right words to say to Marsha Ellen to let her know how deeply sorry I am for how I treated Rune.” I waited … and nothing came. “Right, I must find my own words. Might take a bit longer.”

CHAPTER 32

Monday, June 16, 2008

I arrived at Oliver Carlson's hospital room shortly after noon. The remains of his lunch still littered his tray. He pushed it aside and motioned for me to occupy the bedside chair. I looked around for Kathy, his wife. "Relax, missus went home. Preparing," he said, and gleefully pointed thumbs up to himself. "Getting sprung tomorrow."

"That's just amazing," I said. "You look so much better than the first time I saw you. And yesterday your speech was hesitant. Like you were searching hard for each and every word."

"Yes, quite right. Today is smoother. I feel better, too." He straightened himself more upright in his bed. "Going for a walk soon."

I took that as my signal to ask, "Have you remembered anything new about last Monday?"

"Not much. No picture of man in cemetery." He tapped his forehead. "Lord, I have tried." He reached out to pat my hand. "I wish to help more. That poor young man."

"When we came in the back door, you know, before we found you, there were grocery bags like someone made a delivery. Or was that you?" I asked.

Carlson shook his head, "Not me. Do not remember driving. Doubt if I could. No idea how car moved."

"Then who? Your wife?"

"No. We had a spat. Went in different directions." He watched for my puzzled expression and nodded, "We have 'time out' corners. She goes to Geneseo. Shops with her sister. I camp at Holder place. Work on Lydia's collection."

"By collection you mean the piles of books, newspapers, and such." I paused to recollect the sheer volume of paper the old house contained. "Some things are in better condition than others. Some, I hate to say, might be beyond saving due to water damage." I'd experienced a deep sense of loss on the night of Carlson's rescue. Still did, in fact. "Herb Anderson would have said, 'This too can be saved.' Sadly, not everything can be saved."

"I know. So much there. I do my best." He studied his hands. Opened and closed them a few times to test his grip. "They are working. Getting stronger. I will get back soon."

"If you weren't out shopping for food and Kathy was in Geneseo, then who brought in those shopping bags?"

"Had to be David."

"Do you mean David Ekollon?"

He nodded. I gasped. "Why him?"

He hung his head in disappointment. "Never you called back, did I."

"I chalked it up to you being busy … and all," I said, motioning to the hospital bed.

"I was not busy," he said, as he massaged his knees and stretched out his leg muscles.

I remained quiet, silently urging him to go on.

"Sorry," he said, "Use them or lose them." I nodded agreement and tried to think of a way for him to get to the point of the story he had started. He began again all on his own. "Lydia welcomed all into her home, such as it was. She did little things, acts of kindness, and such. Wanted to lure in visitors. Did not take much for David. Once he had been in, saw Bishop Hill history everywhere, he could not stay away. Lydia became convinced he helped himself. She could not keep him away. Instead, she hid things. I could not talk her into another way. Take a stand with him." He flashed a scornful frown, and stated emphatically, "I owe him no favors—he owes me." He pointed to his chest, then shook his head. "He owes Lydia."

I gave that speech time to soak in before I said, "Thank you for telling me why you never returned my calls and messages. I totally understand your position." I hesitated. "And I'm guessing that this time he used some badly needed groceries to gain access to the Holder collection."

"He used my weakness. My confusion. I was afraid of what he could do. What he did."

"Well, he certainly didn't try to get help for you."

"But you helped me. I will always be grateful." He gave me a heartwarming smile and reached for my hand again. "If I can do anything for you, please, let me know."

"It was my pleasure to be there for you," I said, finally knowing what that platitude meant. I found it difficult to make a case for my own needs, but time was a factor, and I didn't have any to spare. "Sir, there is something you can do for me."

"I'm not sure what my husband can promise you right now." Kathy Carlson had returned. I rose, preparing to vacate the bedside chair, and she waved me back down. "Ollie has rehab scheduled for weeks to come. He must get his muscle tone and balance back. And I'm sure you can tell he's still recovering his speaking abilities."

"Yes, I understand. You see, I first thought something in the house would be the key to your 'kinda smell horse' message, but I went in a different direction. I didn't have any luck finding a computer storage device Rune had with him. What I need most is another visit inside your Bishop Hill house."

Oliver and Kathy Carlson looked at each other in a way that made my heart sink. My getting another chance to search for the missing USB drive didn't look at all promising. I preempted their refusal by making a promise so wild they had no way to say no to me. I left their hospital room with conditional approval that if neither of them was available to supervise a search then an off-duty deputy could stand in for them to protect their property. I had no idea how I could make good on my end of this bargain, but I'd bought myself a little more time to work things out with the only deputy I knew well enough to ask for a favor.

I stewed over my dilemma all the way back to Bishop Hill. How to approach Deputy Dana with this proposal without sustaining serious bodily injury to my person? As I neared the red brick house, I put the situation on hold until I could check my email to see if I had any new messages from James Viklund. Sure enough, he would have something for me tomorrow when I returned to work at Nikkerbo. He could drop it by my office.

I texted back asking if there was any way I could get it before then. Today I had a free afternoon. My day tomorrow would likely be filled with preparations for the Midsommar festival weekend. He promised to do his best. That was progress. Time would tell if our combined "best" efforts would be enough.

The rest of my day involved online computer browsing, re-reading George Swank articles on Bishop Hill's obsolete currency, and checking my email frequently. By late afternoon I finally received a terse message from James. "McKane's. 8 PM. Pizza."

I arrived at McKane's a little before the appointed time. According to the noise level the bar side of the business seemed to be enjoying a nice crowd for a Monday evening. The restaurant side had a few solitary diners staking out their claim to the best tables, preparing to linger over coffee and dessert. One table held Albin Gunnarson, Rune's uncle, and his wife, Evelyn. The instant he saw me, he motioned me over.

"I'm glad you came in," he said. "I'm working on a follow-up story for this week's paper. This saves me a phone call. Please, have a seat if you can spare me a few minutes." I hesitated as I glanced at Evelyn for approval. She returned the patient sigh of the long-suffering spouse and nodded for me to sit down.

"Well, I am here to meet some people," I replied as Albin pulled out a chair. I'd spotted James and his brother, Alan, in a back booth. "They are here already." I waved at them, held up five fingers, and hoped they got the message that I'd be there in five minutes.

Mr. Gunnarson saw everything and reassured me with, "I'll make it quick. It's about Oliver Carlson and how he was found last Saturday night. I got most of the story from Deputy Johnson. I just need something from you that would make a good quote. You remember how we used to do it."

"I sure do," I said as I took the offered seat. Working with Mr. Gunnarson for the local paper had been one of my best writing opportunities from high school. He was my first editor and made it a great learning experience.

By the time I left Mr. Gunnarson and made my way to the back to join Alan and James, Michael J for Just Had to Come By Anderson and one pizza had arrived. The brothers sat together on one side of the booth, which left me no option but to slide in next to Michael. I gauged the size of the pizza and the number of hungry guys and declared, "There isn't enough food here."

"Relax," James said, "another pie is coming."

I placed an order for decaf coffee when the waitress swung by to check the table.

Alan snickered, "Wimp."

"Dude, I have to show up for work tomorrow morning." James slid a new USB drive in front of me.

"Oh, thank you. It looks … so small." I held it up to get a better look.

Michael placed his hand over mine to swiftly push it down, then withdrew it just as quickly. "You might not want to flash that around."

"Oh, look out, a computer joke!" Alan dissolved into snorting giggles.

A somewhat more serious James said, "You might want to scuff that up a bit. Rub some dirt on it. But not too much." He leveled on my blank stare. "Duh, it's been to the cemetery. Am I right?"

"And who knows where else," a smirking Alan chimed in.

"Okay, yes, you figured that out," I said. "So, it looks realistic. What happens if I plug it into my computer?"

"Well, first off, *don't*," James said with emphasis. "Let our would-be thief have the honor. I embedded a Call Home feature with all the emails and such.

"I assume those would be fake emails?"

James and Alan exchanged strained glances and appeared rather guilty about something. "This has the real stuff on it." I surmised. "How? Buddy thinks all his sensitive information was erased. Gone."

"Sure," James said, "I made his USB drive and erased the data from his laptop. And yes, it is permanently gone from his computer. But what he doesn't know is that I distracted him a bit and made an extra copy. It's good to have insurance in case he ever came back and desperately needed that info again. I've seen it happen."

"Yeah, it happened to me," Alan said, without the snarky attitude this time.

"Okay, I get it," I said. "But what's this 'Call Home' thing? What does it do?"

"Let's me know when someone downloads the data and, you know, tries to access it," James said, as he waited for the spark of recognition that didn't come. "Shelley, you want enough juicy stuff in there to keep a thief busy for our purposes."

"Which is?" I asked, wondering if we had conflicting goals.

"For finding a location, the computer IP address," James said. "We wait for your thief to log onto a network, then we can monitor everything from a safe distance. Which is better for you, right?"

"It's going to work," Michael said with confidence. "You just have to wave it under enough noses for someone to take the bait, literally."

About that time the second pizza showed up and we all dove in for a hot slice. Michael paused long enough between bites to say, "Shelley, remember how you talked me into going back into Herb's workshop because, how did you phrase it exactly? Oh, yeah, it felt important to see it again."

"Yes, I remember," I said. "I also remember how reluctant you were about helping me."

"At first," he said, passing up his next mouthful of pizza. "I really didn't spend that much time inside Carlson's trash castle, you know, and I'm sort of having that same feeling. I need to see it again. Having a decoy doesn't eliminate the need for the original evidence. Might yield useful fingerprints. DNA even. If you find any way to go back inside to look for the original USB drive, would you mind if I came along? We could get lucky. No searching through any barns."

I asked, "Now, who exactly do you mean by 'we'?"

"You, me, and Dana," he answered.

That I understood to be a golden opportunity.

"I'll work on it," I said. "What day would be good for you guys?"

"Dana usually has Wednesdays and Thursdays off. What with Midsommar coming up I'd better check with her. I can get back to you."

"That'll be great," I replied, with a surge of optimism. Things just might work out.

CHAPTER 33

Tuesday, June 17, 2008

Tuesday morning had everyone at Nikkerbo preparing for a two-pronged attack plan for the rest of the week leading up to the village-wide festival day on Saturday. First, the public events for Nikkerbo's participation in Midsommar focused on workshops and entertainment that included a heavy emphasis on family-friendly programming and music. The planning had taken place over the past few months and everything should go smoothly. Most of the staff might have been new to Nikkerbo, but, like me, not strangers to Bishop Hill-style celebrations.

Second, the non-public business meetings that were scheduled for Mr. Hemcourt's top executives, most of whom would be staying at my family's Ox-Boy campground or within reach of Nikkerbo, were now a part of my new responsibilities as assistant to Mr. Hemcourt. I typed up meeting minutes, organized information for reports, and made copies so each person had their own folder.

I found Mr. Hemcourt strangely annoyed at the last-minute addition of a new associate who, in an unguarded moment, he called an odd choice for Walter Kleinmann's financial consultant. Director Ekollon was nervous about all that and more. He knew his performance would be graded. On the other hand, all I had to do with my higher level of responsibility was to ensure that all parties involved had what they needed to succeed. I envisioned my work to entail a lot of running errands and maybe a few cases of innovative problem solving. I felt up to the challenge.

Lars was Lars. He went about his duties with an air of confidence that I truly admired. To be that self-assured was amazing to watch. Every now and then he'd emerge from Mr. Hemcourt's office like they'd had a private meeting for two. Or perhaps it was for three, since Lars had stopped hiding the fact he was there in the most part to represent his uncle's Stockholm-based business interests in connection to the Chicago-based Hemcourt Enterprises.

Mr. Hemcourt's people had meetings planned for Thursday and Friday leaving Saturday available for touristy fun at the various Midsommar Music Festival events held throughout the village. They were due to begin appearing the next day. Teeny Mom had everything ready for them.

I also was prepared for their return. Michael J for Just Be Prepared Anderson had me convinced that one of those executives would be very keen to lay his or her hands on the USB flash drive that Charles "Buddy G" Guyer had created and that Rune Gunnarson had briefly held in his possession during his ill-fated visit to the Bishop Hill cemetery. We still didn't know where the original USB drive was, but Alan and James, Galva's techie brothers, had created a reasonable facsimile. It was the perfect bait. They'd been in and out of Nikkerbo making sure our computer systems were in good order, so they never had time to say more than a few words to me. I left them to do their thing and I did mine.

I sat at my desk scrolling through my emails, sorting them by importance and deleting the useless time-wasting spam, when I came across an interesting one from Rune's uncle, Albin Gunnarson. He wanted me to confirm a couple of facts about my participation in finding Oliver Carlson. I replied promptly since I knew he was facing his deadline.

I heard a series of quick taps before Lars entered. "Pardon my barging in on you," he said politely. "That is how you would say it? I wonder where that comes from?" He settled himself into my one extra chair. I nudged a small bit of black plastic within sight.

"'Barging' sounds like it might be related to a river boat term. Other than that, I have no clue." I tried to gauge his interest in the item in front of me. A complete lack of awareness seemed to be the case here, so I asked, "Do you know what this is?"

"*Ja*, a computer memory device. From one of those brothers, perhaps? I can't tell one from the other," he said.

"No worries," I said, "the results are usually the same." I weighed my history with Lars over the past summer and decided to trust him with the real nature of the USB drive and how it could be used it to set a trap. "There's data on here ready to engage someone long enough for a Call Home feature to work," I said.

"Call Home?" he repeated, and thinking it over said, "That makes it traceable. *Ja*?"

"*Ja*, I would say so." He gave my attempt at Swedish a sympathetic nod of approval. "Now," I said, picking it up, "I could use some help on how to give this little beauty the best chance to work its magic?"

Lars and I thought through some scenarios without deciding on which might be the best. It all depended on what opportunities opened up. I received an incoming text message from Teeny Mom. One of the executive types had checked in early—one Walter Kleinmann with a new helper who wasn't nearly as fresh-faced and likable as Buddy G. Teeny Mom had expressed her opinion with a frowning emoticon. Her computer skills were growing by leaps and bounds. I found it totally awesome.

A single firm knock on my office door gave us scant warning. Ekollon chose that moment to enter. Lars excused himself but made no haste in leaving. David "The Dragon" Ekollon could do nothing. Or chose to do nothing. I wondered which was the case.

He closed the door after Lars left. In the past I'd have started going through scenarios trying to figure out if I'd made a mistake or done something wrong, even if it were only in his mind. Not today. Not after speaking with Oliver Carlson yesterday and hearing about his and Lydia Holder's suspicions about Ekollon's actions. This could be the perfect time to have a cozy chat about our feelings pertaining to Bishop Hill artifacts. I believed we shared a common interest and level of commitment to preservation, but the line had to be drawn at theft.

"I just had the strangest conversation with Oliver," he began. "He actually didn't seem to want to talk to me. He directed me to speak to you. Now, why would that be?"

I motioned to the seat that Lars had vacated. "Why don't you have a seat."

"No, thank you." He stood calm and composed in his usual khaki pants and dark tweedy jacket.

"Have it your way," I said smoothly. "What did Mr. Carlson have to say exactly?"

"Just that I should discuss certain issues with you. He hung up without any further explanation. I thought our friendship deserved more consideration on his part."

"How far back does this friendship go?" I inquired in a pleasant voice.

Ekollon drew a sharp intake of breath as he assumed the guise of the put-upon innocent. It was so not going to work on me. I waited for an answer as he fussed at a speck of lint on his sleeve.

"Well, if you must know, we met while taking the same American history lecture in college. I was majoring in American studies and he was fulfilling a core requirement. We discovered shared interests during long car rides back home: Bishop Hill for me and a farm outside of Kewanee for him." He smoothed his mustache as his patience began to wane. "How does this matter?"

"I just wondered how you could take your day off and help him out by delivering groceries but not get him medical help?" I watched him shift from one awkward position to another. He finally sat down.

"I only knew about the spat with his wife. He seemed fine otherwise," Ekollon said.

"He was having small strokes, TIAs. You didn't notice?"

"No. He was his usual self. Very private. Very circumspect. I followed his instructions. Left some basic provisions inside the back door and offered to return as often as I could."

"Did he instruct you to hide his car?"

"Yes," he said bluntly.

"You didn't think that was a little odd?"

"Of course, but I've known him to do the outlandish stunt every now and again."

"Look, he didn't say anything about not trusting you around Lydia Holder's stuff?"

"Oh, that," he said. "Sadly, Lydia became convinced I had taken things, artifacts. It was a shame that our relationship had to end on that note. I enjoyed her company."

"Why would she believe that of you?"

"Because her memory was failing," he said with conviction. "She couldn't remember our transactions. I purchased some documents when she needed the money. I gave her receipts on those occasions. Other times we traded for the things we each needed."

"You never took anything without her permission?"

He grew quiet. His indignation and nervous movements stilled.

"You did. You took things."

"You saw that house. What it had become. The haphazard storage. Irreplaceable documents ruined by a leaking roof. Colony clothing disintegrating to the touch. I could not stand by and do nothing. It was an intolerable situation. She simply lacked the ability to protect the bulk of her collection and refused to accept assistance from anyone."

"So, you stepped in to save history," I said curtly. "Much like you stepped in to protect Mr. Hemcourt's painting?"

"That was different," he exclaimed. "It wasn't a genuine Krans. It was a cheap knock off."

"Oh, I don't think it was that cheap."

"Well, you wouldn't since your uncle painted it. Still, I had to remove it."

"To protect what exactly? Nikkerbo's honor? Or that of the Hemcourt family? Or was it for the honor of the Prophet Karl Hemson?"

When his sudden and complete silence failed to move me, he uttered a cold, "You'll never understand." With that he strode to the door and left.

"I wouldn't say that." I whispered at his retreat. I knew what the painting meant to him. How much Hemson meant to him. And how he believed in the connection between the two. He would have been fine with me taking the blame for the disappearance of the painting and letting all the disturbing questions die away. His job security would always come first. I was an annoying inconvenience.

The USB drive had been on my desk in plain sight for the entire duration of our little discussion of professional ethics. No temptation there.

My day was winding down when Mr. Hemcourt called me into his office. I entered carrying a yellow legal pad filled with scheduling notes, printouts I thought would be useful, my cell phone, and a handy USB drive. I seated myself and for a moment entertained the thought of how much I looked like an old-fashioned secretary sitting at the ready for dictation or whatnot. I made sure that the thumb drive was clearly visible.

"Ms. Anderson," he said as he turned to me, "I wanted to ask you for a little extra help in preparing for my upcoming meetings with Walter Kleinmann and William Hanson." He paused to check for my agreement. I nodded and uttered the required yes sir. "Good." He continued, "What I need most is to gain a sense of where these guys are coming from. Their moods. Confidence levels. I'm afraid that's a rather vague request, but I need all the input I can get in order to make my best choice. As you know all too well, I have to choose a new chief financial officer to succeed Thomas Gubben. It's between those two and I have to admit that I'm having difficulty."

"How can I help?" I asked, not totally sure how I could make my input valuable.

"I need you to get a feel for them. Any impressions they leave with you. I value your opinions. Talk to the people they've interacted with so far. Like Christina, for instance. She'll be checking them into their cabins. Her instinct about people has always seemed right on the money."

"That is a fact, sir." And I did have some recent experience with her accuracy.

"The more information the better." He started rearranging small items on his desk. "More than what I'm getting from them. Sure, Walter and Bill say all the right things, but I'm fielding conflicting advice from my usual sources. I've got a bank breathing down my neck about loan security on one hand and these guys talking up investment opportunities that don't appear to involve anything of real tangible value on the other."

That rang an alarm bell with me. "Anyone mention mortgage-backed bonds or such?"

"Yes, I think so. It gets confusing when they start in with the initials and what sounds like made-up words."

"Sir, you should talk to Charles Guyer. He seems very knowledgeable about these things. He tried to explain it to me and had to resort to a really simple explanation. I bet he can give you a detailed briefing on investments and what kind of pitfalls to avoid that you would find valuable."

"Charles Guyer, I know him, don't I?" Mr. Hemcourt asked.

"He was the young man here for last week's meetings."

"Ah, yes. I recall him now. I made some inquiries about him. Not a team player it seems. Is he still here?" He tilted his head to better study me. "Why would he still be here?"

"It's a long story, but rest assured, he is your man."

"Okay. Can you connect the two of us?"

"I most certainly will do my best." I answered. "In fact, how about tomorrow morning? What's a good time for you?"

Mr. Hemcourt agreed and set a time for an early meeting. That was all he needed from me. He and Ekollon had already gone over the scheduled events. I left wondering if I might have saved Nikkerbo from an odd partnership with corporate types who would seek to profit by other people's losses. I also left with the USB drive that had failed to arouse any interest with its presence.

CHAPTER 34

Wednesday, June 18th, 2008

My day at Nikkerbo began with getting Mr. Hemcourt and Buddy G formally reintroduced and supplied with coffee and homemade pastries. After the morning staff meeting, I spent the greater part of the day outside marking out the boundaries for the placement of vendor booths, game and activity locations, and a first-aid station complete with ambulance parking. Plus, I now knew more about portable toilets and the associated humor than would ever show up on my resume. I couldn't wait to get back to the red brick house for a shower, a change of clothes, and some sunburn cream.

I found Teeny Mom eager to tell me everything about her day. Walter Kleinmann had checked into his Ox-Boy cabin a full 24 hours before his first meeting with Mr. Hemcourt and the other expected businessmen. According to Teeny Mom he made a disdainful show of spurning Charles "Buddy G" Guyer's cabin five. I guessed he wanted Buddy G to feel slighted at being replaced. However, without the occupant's car in sight it was obvious that he had wasted his efforts.

Unlike Kleinmann, his new tag-a-long underling took no special interest with the occupant of cabin five. After settling into his own cabin, he strolled the length of the drive seemingly to familiarize himself with the layout of the campground. Teeny Mom insisted his cursory perusal of the automobile parked outside of cabin three interested him far more than the location of the restroom/shower building. She said he spent way too much time eyeing Jill's car, the one with the MAD license plate that had had me stewing over phantom mobster connections for the better part of the past week. In Teeny Mom's opinion, he was more of a menacing presence than Jill had ever been in her tough-guy disguise.

Teeny Mom had a grand old time filling me in on all these juicy little details. I waited for the new arrivals to drive off on the likely quest for fast food before walking over to Jill's cabin to check out if she had noticed the car inspection. She met me in the doorway and quickly pulled me inside. So yes, she'd noticed.

"Did you see those guys?" Jill's otherwise healthy complexion had turned into an anemic shade of panic.

"Teeny Mom told me about them."

"That bald dude in the shiny business suit. What do you know about him?"

"All I know for sure is that they're together for upcoming business meetings. He's the new Buddy G," I said as calmly as I could. "Teeny Mom said he seemed interested in your car."

She wrapped her arms around herself, paced over to her bed, sat down with a heavy plop, and tried rocking herself to calmness. I gave her time to find some peace before I asked, "What's with this guy?"

She stilled herself and said cautiously, "Nothing. It's probably nothing." That last statement brought on a fresh wave of anxiety and the last bit of color drained from her cheeks.

"Okay," I said. "If you won't talk to me, fine, talk to Buddy G or Uncle Roy. Maybe they can help."

"I texted Buddy and your uncle. Told them to stay away for the time being."

"Oh, I doubt that will work with Uncle Roy," I said with a pessimism well founded in experience. "Do you want to come up to the house?"

"No. But thanks for the offer. I'm sure I'll be okay," she said, and seemed genuinely grateful.

By the time I left Jill was looking better and getting some color back into her cheeks. I made sure she programed my number into her cell phone.

I intended to check on Buddy G for my next stop but halted when I spotted his car pulling into the driveway of the red brick house. Buddy G had come to me.

I entered the kitchen door to the sounds of happy chatter and followed the voices to the front parlor where I found Buddy G holding court with Teeny Mom and Uncle Roy. With a buoyant change in mood, he was reporting on an amazing meeting with Mr. Hemcourt. It seems that Buddy G's detailed accounting of the travails of investing had an attentive audience who wasn't intimidated by a barrage of initials and neologisms. He took the time to explain them to us as simply as he did for Mr. Hemcourt: MBS, for mortgage-backed security; CDS, for credit default swaps; CDO, for collateralized debt obligation; and FICO scores, the system for credit ratings used by lenders. I wasn't interested in that much information, but Buddy G was having a great time recounting what had to have been the interview of a lifetime.

I let it all flow over my head until I had a chance to ask a question. "You really spent the whole day with Mr. Hemcourt?"

"Yes. He wanted to know everything about me. Especially everything involving Mr. Kleinmann and Mr. Hanson. I've never talked that much. I lost track of time. Didn't realize it until I obviously got hungry." He patted his stomach. "It was his suggestion that we break for lunch at the local café." He turned somber at this point, and I knew he referred to The Lutfisk Café. "We talked about how Rune and I had met up there … that last day." Buddy G fell into a silence that showed signs of stretching on too long.

"That must have been uncomfortable and awkward," I suggested.

"It was, at first. But he was so patient, so understanding, and curious. I just kept talking."

"What happened next?" I prompted, hoping to avoid another stretch of silence.

"Mr. Hemcourt invited me to sit in on the upcoming meetings. I explained how I didn't want a confrontation with Kleinmann. Not after spending most of the day shooting holes in any investment scheme he might have to offer for Mr. Hemcourt. Then I thought of your decoy plan and how important it was to be on hand to show I wasn't in possession of any USB drives."

"I'm glad you're going to be there tomorrow, because your original still hasn't turned up." I noticed another shift in his mood. He was suddenly smiling way too much. "You've got something else to tell, don't you?"

"Mr. Hemcourt offered me a new position within the company. I'm more than ready for a change of scenery."

"That is wonderful news," I said, and Teeny Mom and Uncle Roy joined in with their own congratulations. Buddy G soaked it up before returning to the issue of USB drives.

"I assumed the one I created was still missing," he said. "What's new about the fake USB drive that is the center of your scheme to trap Rune's killer?"

I produced the item in question and told him about today's results, or rather the lack of any interest so far, and passed it over for his inspection.

"Yes, that certainly looks like what I had last week," He said, before turning melancholy and handing it back to me.

I knew he had started thinking about Rune and the cemetery again but before I could say something consoling, Teeny Mom interrupted. "Shelley, come and help me in the kitchen. Buddy G, you are staying for supper."

Her tone conveyed the message that neither of us had any real choice in the matter. I followed her into the kitchen where I discovered the night's star ingredient. "Sweet corn!"

"First of the season. Roy brought it in saying it was picked fresh this morning," she said. "He wants to grill some burgers and Buddy G is going to help him."

"Does Buddy G know he's about to have a cooking lesson?" I asked.

Teeny Mom cocked her head toward the sound of male voices and smiled. "I think he's finding out right about now," she said. "We'll let them work out the details. In the meantime, you can get started on shucking the ears. I'll get the water heating on the stove."

We worked side by side at the sink. Teeny Mom peeled the overlapping leaves of the corn husks down toward the bottom of the ear, revealing the yellow-and-cream-colored kernels of our preferred hybrid variety. With one swift and sure move she neatly snapped the leaves and stalk away from the edible core of goodness and handed the ear to me so I could strip away the layers of silk left over from the corn's fertilization process. One delicate and somewhat sticky strand of silk for each kernel meant a lot of work and a lot of mess. We were soon up to our elbows in green leafy shards and diaphanous threads, but the finished pile of clean ears grew at a steady pace.

"So, Buddy G had a good day today," she began. "I haven't seen anything of Jill. How are you doing?"

"Okay, I guess. Better than Jill. That new guy with Kleinmann has her badly spooked. I have the feeling she's holding something back." I shouldn't have said that last bit out loud and flinched. I hoped it wasn't enough for Teeny Mom to notice.

She stopped handling the corn for a moment and tried to make eye contact. I made the mistake of shying away. "Okay, Jill isn't ready to talk," she said. "So, what's bothering you?"

I hesitated, searching for a way to express my disappointment. "All I got today was a lot of nothing. No reactions to the USB drive. I don't think I really expected something to happen right away, but it's made me wonder if I'm making another mistake."

"What do you mean, 'another mistake?' Since when are you making mistakes?"

"Since the trap in the archive room. That was my idea and it almost got me … shot."

"Okay, that was not so great, but Dana came through and that frumpy little man got caught embezzling funds."

"And he went to the hospital."

"Yes, he got shot. Thankfully, it wasn't you," she emphasized. "What else?"

"I was wrong about Mr. Carlson and the buried treasure bit."

"He had everyone fooled," she said firmly. "What else?"

"I was wrong about who was the intended victim in the cemetery."

"Again, everyone went with the seemingly obvious." She mulled over what she said for a beat then added, "If Sheriff Henry thought otherwise, he hasn't let on." She ripped the leaves off another ear of corn. "And it's good to be reminded that things are not always what they appear to be. For instance, Bill Smith was really Jill Fischer. One more example of why we should keep ourselves open to possibilities that we consider outside the normal or the expected."

I nodded in half-hearted agreement.

Teeny Mom accepted it at face value. "Good. Now, what else?"

"What else?" It hurt to know the answer to that one. "How about the way I treated Rune so badly on his last day. How snotty I was to Marsha Ellen—at first. She is talking to me. She seems okay. But deep down I'm afraid there won't be any way to come back from this. I may have lost my best friend. Forever."

Right there at the sink amid corn husks and wispy strands of corn silk Teeny Mom put her arm around my shoulders and bent her head in toward mine. We stood like that until we heard Uncle Roy call out, "Charcoal's getting hot. We need some meat."

We separated. Teeny Mom went to the refrigerator to fulfill the protein order, while I added another clean ear to the ready-to-cook pile.

"You know," she said before backing her way out the screen door with the tray of raw patties in front of her, "there's a way fix it. Say you're sorry. And really mean it."

"But—"

"Better late than never." The back door banged closed on her final word.

She left me to figure out how and when to make amends with Marsha Ellen.

CHAPTER 35

Thursday, June 19th, 2008

Last week's headline for the *Galva Prairie Pioneer* announced the finding of a body in the Bishop Hill cemetery. That ensured the local newspaper had a ready-made audience eagerly awaiting this week's edition of updates and follow-up stories. I joined the ranks of the curious at The Lutfisk. I had met up with Albin Gunnarson, Rune's uncle, at McKane's the other night. He had wanted a usable quotable for his story and I needed to see how he handled it. I told myself it was now part of my job to stay up to date on how the sheriff's investigation was playing out to the public. With the big festival weekend coming up, Bishop Hill's image was important, but I worried about how Marsha Ellen would cope with another round of publicity. That was more important than tourism.

I awaited in front of The Lutfisk's counter to pay for my paper and place an order for toast and the all-important mug of coffee when I noticed heads turning my way. It made me nervous enough that I changed my mind when it was my turn to order. I quickly tucked the folded newspaper under my arm, secured my caffeine, and left. There would be time to investigate the meaning of those looks later.

Today's agenda for Nikkerbo would entail the final preparations for the influx of visitors for the big festival day on Saturday. At this point it meant staging and stocking all the supplies needed for the children's make and take crafts, checking out the movie venues for accessibility and seating, suppling the refreshment stations with water, and my personal favorite: making sure employees and volunteers were dressed in colony-era costumes.

Over the years our family had built up a reliable supply of hand-me-down blue chambray shirts, denim skirts, and straw hats. I had splurged once on a custom-made item, a brightly colored colony-style shirt made from the boldest tomato fabric I'd ever seen. I'd worn it for Teeny Mom's *OK Art Fest in the Meadow* last summer and for Nikkerbo's gala opening, at least until I saw Lars with his posse of adoring admirers; then I covered it up with a jacket. Anyway, what I brought in for the coming weekend would be safely in line with the usual docent attire seen throughout the village. I helped some of the others with their ensembles, making repairs and adjustments as needed. We had pretty much commandeered the break room for the afternoon.

Lars came by to show off his Swedish folk costume. The handwork was expertly done and impressive. It used silver jacket clasps of a style I hadn't seen before. All of us fussed over it until Ekollon came in seemingly to look for something in the condiment cabinet. His somber presence smothered the festive atmosphere and everyone but me scattered for the cover of other pressing work.

"How are things going so far with the business meetings?" I asked. "I've been needed here, as you can see."

"Apparently, a bit better in the discipline department than this little hen party," he allowed.

"Then no weapons of mass destruction detonating in the board room," I said to his glowering disapproval. "Just pins and needles in here," I added brightly. "Nothing larger than these scissors." I showed them off with a practice snip. "Oh yes, we did luck out when a portable sewing machine showed up. That'll have to be added to next year's list of necessities."

"If you must know," he located and claimed a new container of flavored creamer, "there was a bit of tension early on when that young fellow, Guyer I believe, insinuated himself and his opinions into the agenda."

"I heard he and Mr. Hemcourt were getting along well." I picked up the apron I'd been working on before Lars had shown up and finished turning under the lower edge, securing it with several straight pins.

"Yes, the young man seems to have found favored status … for the moment. A source of irritation with some of the others. The meetings are proceeding smoothly enough as far as I can tell. Now, I must get back." He paused at the doorway long enough to say, "Do try to keep the merriment under control and the volume level down a notch."

"Yes, sir," I replied, amazed at what was subdued behavior for him. I wished I could have been there for Buddy G's entrance. I would've bet money that part of his reception had more to do with what he didn't have, as in a certain USB drive, than what he was contributing to Mr. Hemcourt's business plan. How, I wondered, could I work in a sneek peek of my version of the missing computer memory device? I held up the apron for inspection. "Does this need a pocket?" I quietly asked myself. I considered the all-around usefulness and answered, "Yes, most definitely."

I set the apron aside so I could take advantage of having the room all to myself for a few minutes. I retrieved my copy of the Galva newspaper and read what Albin Gunnarson had to say about recent events. I'd gotten most of the way down the first column before my jaw dropped open. As I read on, I swung from disbelief to anger.

Gunnarson had used my comments for more than a couple of incidental quotes. I wasn't just a sideline. He'd used my words to make it sound like I was the only one in Oliver Carlson's house until the ambulance arrived. That was bad enough. Then he turned his attention to the house, using Mr. Carlson's own words to describe the conditions in which he had been found. My anger morphed into panic when I realized what had happened; Mr. Carlson had recovered more of his memories from the night Rune was murdered. My chance for an orderly search of Mr. Carlson's Bishop Hill house—the trash castle, as Michael called it—had evaporated.

I debated who to call first. The obvious choice was Dana. Did I dare call her on her day off? She might not want to talk on the phone. We needed to meet face to face. Should I try Michael first? No, I thought to myself, I must trust Dana. I tapped in her number.

I approached the delicate topic of Oliver Carlson's Bishop Hill house with trepidation. It was a barely habitable structure, but I talked about how it was still packed with Lydia Holder's belongings and her impressively large collection of early Bishop Hill memorabilia. I stressed that there had to be some really important artifacts in there. Things that belonged in an archive or a museum. Places where they could be kept under protective temperature-controlled conditions. What worried me was I might have crossed over into babbling, but I wanted her warmed up to my real reason for calling, to ensure she was on board for another search for the missing USB drive.

Dana's deputy senses must have tuned in on my dilemma. She told me frankly, "It's okay to talk about revisiting Carlson's

Bishop Hill house. It's not a crime scene. Oliver Carlson was a person of interest in the death of Rune Gunnarson, but that has been cleared up. Today's newspaper made it clear you've been in contact with him, so is there something you need from me?"

"Yes," I answered, relieved that Dana's forthrightness freed me to also be direct. "I asked if I could return to the Bishop Hill house. Carlson and his wife agreed to let me in for another search as long as there'd be someone there to supervise me. They are really sensitive about, shall we say, inventory loss. So, with you on board we're good to go, and hopefully find the USB drive Rune was holding for Buddy G." Michael had certainly been correct about her readiness for another search. She agreed to meet up at McKane's later to discuss the details.

I got off work on time, stowed my colony clothes in the back seat, and only intended to stop by the red brick house long enough to change into something more casual, then drive on to Galva and my meeting with Dana. So, seeing her waiting with Michael in our driveway was a total surprise. Same with Marsha Ellen leaning against her car.

Dana was dressed in a nice T-shirt and stylish jeans, definitely off duty. Same with Michael and Marsha Ellen. I parked in my usual spot and greeted everyone. "Hi guys. What's up?"

"Well," Dana started, "Michael and I are here to talk about how to do an effective search. And strangely enough—"

Marsha Ellen cut in with her reason for showing up. "I stopped by to tell you that I'm officially out of the apartment and our deposit refund is in the works. When I saw the meeting, I decided to stay. Whatever is going on here, if it involves Rune, I'm in." She glowered at Dana daring her to try any form of dissuasion.

"Right," I said. "I don't have a key yet, and this arrangement is only good if Mr. Carlson doesn't feel up to being there himself."

"Okay, that sounds fair enough," Dana said. "In any case I think Saturday's music festival provides us with the best opportunity to go in for another look-see for the computer whatsit," she said. "Besides, I had other plans for tonight anyway."

Michael added, "Me, too."

Marsha Ellen chose to look enigmatic.

"Okay," I said, choosing to ignore all the implications. "Today's newspaper article by Rune's uncle gave out way too much information, on one hand, and added some misinformation with the other."

"That last hand would be the one where you pretty much did everything by your lonesome self." Dana sounded rightfully miffed.

"I had no control of how Rune's uncle was going to write that piece." I huffed an exasperated sigh of my own. "He went for maximum drama."

"He made it sound like Carlson had picked up something. If it's from Rune, well, it's in there now," Marsha Ellen said with some urgency.

"Right," I said. "We must get in soon, because Kleinmann came back early and he's not alone."

"That would be your current main suspect?" Dana asked, and I nodded. "Not the MAD license plate guy anymore? The one staying at your campground. That I've been surveilling." Her agitation level grew with every point she made.

"The MAD license plate thing didn't pan out," I said. Dana stared daggers at me. "She didn't do anything."

"She?" Dana answered and flashed a devilish grin as possibilities grew in her mind. "Oh, this has got to be good."

A confused Michael asked, "What am I missing here?"

I gave a shortened explanation of the role reversal that went with the suspicious Bill Smith becoming the more likable Jill Hanson Fischer all over again, which Michael J for Jovial Anderson thoroughly enjoyed even though he pretended to be aggrieved that it hadn't been part of the conversation at Monday night's meetup with Alan and James.

When all the joking about my cluelessness died down, Dana took us through the basic steps of searching a structure and securing evidence in a way that would preserve fingerprints. Afterwards, we all agreed that, like it or not, we had to make our plans for meeting up late Saturday afternoon when most villagers and visitors would likely be out of the way. The concerts in the park would be over at 4 p.m. Followed by a procession from the park to the Colony School for the decoration of the Maypole. The barn dance was scheduled to start at the school at 6 p.m. By then I'd be done at Nikkerbo, Marsha Ellen would be finished with waitressing, Michael promised to be awake, and Dana would use her break time. It was up to me to obtain a key.

CHAPTER 36

Saturday afternoon, June 21st, 2008

Lars had the day off, so it was up to me to close and lock Nikkerbo's doors at 5 p.m. after making sure the building was clear of stragglers. We'd had a respectable day for visitation, and I had begun composing a list of the suggestions offered. The idea of extending the horse-drawn wagon rides up to Nikkerbo's parking lots seemed fine until one thought about the slow-moving horses on the main two-lane road leading into town. We'd have to work out another way to shuttle people out to Nikkerbo's corner. Tractors seemed like a better bet than large animals prone to bolt and run if startled. I added that last thought to my list before closing down my computer. Eager to get on my way I checked the time and hoped finding a parking spot on a festival day wouldn't be too difficult. Having some kind of shuttle service between Nikkerbo and Bishop Hill sounded better and better.

I waited for Marsha Ellen outside the restaurant where she worked. She still wore her waitressing attire, a ruffled bib front pinafore. I wore my Colony outfit of chambray shirtwaist, denim skirt, and an apron made of red-striped ticking. We formed a quaint tableau of old-fashion charm if you didn't count Marsha Ellen's modern handbag. I left my shoulder bag in the car but carried my cell phone and keys in my skirt pocket. The USB drive was in my apron pocket. Michael caught up with us in the parking lot of the Methodist church. Dana, in her uniform, would meet up with us at the rear of Carlson's Bishop Hill house.

Our route was basically what Buddy G had described. He had started from the Methodist church, went under the large trees that lined the entrance lane, passed the headstones and monuments, and followed along as it turned toward the west and became Bergland Street. Rune would have walked up Bergland Street from the west to meet up with Mr. Carlson for the continuation of their interview.

We exited the cemetery near where the struggle had occurred all those nights ago and came upon the scene that once had been taped off. Nature had been busy reclaiming the spot. Hardly any physical trace was left, but it was planted well enough in my memory. I pointed out to Michael the abandoned trailer further down the northern grassy extension of Cemetery Street where we had found the engagement ring.

We continued walking east down the grassy section of Bergland Street and approached the back door of the old Holder house. Oliver and Kathy Carlson had wanted to participate in the Midsommar activities in the park and supplied me with a key to get inside. They would join us later.

We had plenty of daylight to work with. Midsummer being the longest day of the year meant that the sun would set around 8:30 p.m. Dana, in full deputy mode, met us and passed out disposable gloves and refreshed her instructions on how to conduct our search: draw the window shades down, keep any flashlight beams pointed low and off the windows, search methodically so as to keep the backtracking to a minimum, and look for the odd thing out of place. The something that does not fit in. Handle all evidence with care. We needed fingerprints.

After unlocking the back door, I entered and was again awestruck with the sight of massive amounts of clutter everywhere. It grew outward from the battered plaster walls. In the makeshift bedroom only the immediate space around the bed was clear. However, this time I noticed subtle differences: a new layer of chaos had been added to the disorder.

"Guys, this doesn't look right."

"How can you tell?" Marsha Ellen asked.

"It just looks … worse," I said.

"Worse than the disaster it was," Dana said. "Remember, the ambulance crew worked in here. And our forensics team went through."

"But look at this stuff." I pointed to the various bits of torn wrappers that had once held sterile gauze pads, tubes, and needles—all that the EMTs needed to stabilize Mr. Carlson before taking him to the hospital. "There is another layer of debris on top of it. We didn't do that. I don't think trained investigators would do that either. I think the place has been searched recently." Dana gave a thoughtful nod.

We divided up the rooms: Marsha Ellen and I stayed with the bed, Dana went to the front room, while Michael said he'd look outside for a basement or root cellar and check the outbuildings.

I stared at the bed which still had the impression of a body pressed into it. I picked up the book that was nearest to me and started flipping pages. It was the ledger book that recorded the early history of the town of Bishop Hill. Marsha Ellen had found it last Saturday and left it as it was. I, too, recognized the names of Colonists. I became so absorbed I momentarily forgot our propose for being here—to search out the items mentioned in the newspaper. I also thought back to the clue Mr. Carlson whispered to me before they took him away, "Kinda smell horse." It hadn't meant small house, but what else could it be?

For privacy, we made sure the paper pull-down window shades were drawn as low as we dared move them. They were so dry and brittle they looked like they might crumble and turn to powder if handled too roughly. Fortunately, someone had sewn some muslin curtains that were in much better shape and could be tugged close. Marsha Ellen and I used our cell phones as flashlights as the ambient light began to fade.

I knelt to swing the light of my phone under the bed. "There's some shoes under here. Maybe men's shoes."

I turned off the light and pocketed my phone before retrieving the shoes. I gingerly felt inside them and came up empty. Then I stopped to consider what was within reach of the bed: a nightstand with a drawer, a shelf above the headboard, some books on the floor. I'd made a quick scan through the books and was disappointed to find nothing stashed inside the covers or within the pages. Certainly not a thumb-shaped flash drive. I pulled out the drawer preparing to give it a good search inside and out. Nothing. I needed to ponder the next move and sat down on the mattress only to spring right back up with a yelp. It seemed to come alive beneath me.

Marsha Ellen used her phone light as we lifted together and uncovered the plastic grocery bag that had supplied the crinkling noise that so startled me. We inspected the contents closely and found Rune's cell phone and keys, but no small flash drive.

"Why can't it be just a little bit easier?" Marsha Ellen moaned.

I was busy with my own questions. "Why would Mr. Carlson pick up Rune's things and hide them here? Was I wrong about him?"

"Do you think so?" Marsha Ellen said. "That he—"

I threw out a sharp, "It can't be Mr. Carlson."

I listed the main arguments. "There's no motive. The weapons were different. The timing is off, according to Buddy

G's statement." I tried to put myself in Mr. Carlson's place. "So, if I were him and I'm wounded. I'd look for help. There's nobody. I feel threatened, afraid. I become desperate. I'm in Lydia Holder's house and I use her example. I hide the things I most want to protect. Rune's things. The evidence. Then I hide myself."

"Well, whoever was searching here before us never got this far or they would have found this sack."

"Okay. They were interrupted. Good thing we have a deputy with us."

"Look, if Rune's stuff is here," Marsha Ellen pointed out, "the computer gizmo he was holding for Buddy G can't be far away." She placed the shopping bag into a commandeered pillowcase and carefully laid it nearby.

"Famous last words." I groaned and slumped against the headboard. I found myself staring at a potted plant on the nightstand. It had been on the windowsill. I'd moved it when I closed the curtains. I pulled out my improvised flashlight and aimed it at the painted flowerpot. It shone brightly against the wilted foliage and faded blossoms. Its vibrant red color could almost make it pass for a living thing. It was totally out of place among all the dust and debris.

"You remember what Dana said?" I asked slowly.

"She said quite a lot. One thing alone does not stand out to me," Marsha Ellen said.

"She said to look for what doesn't fit in," I said. "Or words to that effect." I switched off my light and repocketed it as I pointed to the flowerpot decorated with a Swedish Dala horse. "That. Maybe…?"

Marsha Ellen laid her phone aside so she could poke around the pot's surface a bit. Then she grasped the dead plant and lifted the dried clump of dirt out and set it aside. She tilted the pot so I could see into it. There, tucked away in the bottom, was a flash drive protectively wrapped in plastic. She dumped it out onto the bed and shone her light on it. The flash drive looked just like the decoy Alan and James produced for us. We gave each other the fist-bump of success.

Marsha Ellen pointed to Buddy G's USB drive like she was afraid to touch it. "You should take it."

"No," I said. "You keep it till we get back together with Dana and Michael." I patted my apron pocket. "I've got the other one in here. Let's not get them confused.

"Good deal," she said, and carefully placed the plastic wrapped flash drive into the pillowcase. "Dana is in the front room. I'll go find her."

When I noticed Marsha Ellen hadn't come back into the bedroom in a timely fashion. I went to look for her. I found her standing still and looking scared. A serious looking Dana stood next to her with a hand resting on the handle of her gun. I held back the question I wanted to ask. Instead, I gave her the equivalent look for "What's going on?"

Dana made a two-fingered walking motion and pointed outside. Straining, I heard the footsteps of someone disturbing the brushy growth that edged the old house as they crept along. Michael making his way around the house, I wanted to say. Or not. I strained to listen for more and was aghast to hear the splash of liquid hitting the wooden siding. Followed in short order by a click and a whoosh.

The odor of burning fuel wafted in. I also detected the smell of burning wood. Nice wood. Wood that had been aged by over a hundred years of post-colony use.

Marsha Ellen screamed, and we ran for the back door. Smoke was beginning to seep through the cracks even before we got there. Dana held us back.

"We can't open it. Too dangerous. There's no getting out this way."

We ran for the front door. I turned the glass doorknob and nothing. I pulled. It didn't budge. I pulled harder and the doorknob came off in my hand. With no way to open the door, running out of time, we looked at each other and screamed, "Windows!"

But which one? They all had mounds of stuff, newspapers and magazines and unmarked boxes, barring access. I choose one with the most useful height and grabbed a sturdy looking book to break the glass if need be. I toppled over a stack of magazines which created a ramp that was too slippery to get traction.

Marsha Ellen got to another window and unlatched the lower half of the six-over-six window. She pushed up in the center and cracked it open. Dana joined her, and they got the crack widened far enough for us to slide through one at a time. But first, the screen had to be pushed out. I picked up another old village ledger much like the one I'd seen before. I had no time to be sentimental; I used it to jab out the screen.

Dana yelled, "Go, go." I tossed the improvised tool outside and wiggled headfirst after it, wishing I didn't have to contend with my long denim skirt and apron. Strong hands grabbed me under the shoulders and roughly pulled me through.

Before I could stand up those same strong hands proceeded to grab at my pockets. I heard fabric tearing. I swatted at the hands and was shocked when they slapped me back. I thought about yelling at Michael J for Jerk Anderson to stop messing around, but I was too busy trying to protect myself. The struggle ended with me curled into the fetal position.

I heard Marsha Ellen yelling for help. Running footsteps fading away. More running. Then the real Michael helped me up and away from the window before asking if I was hurt. I mumbled no without really checking; I just knew my main body parts were intact. I stared down at the remains of my apron pocket. My cell phone was on the ground, but the flash drive was gone. I'd wanted to find a way for the bad guy to get his hands on the USB copy with its Call Home feature, but I never dreamt of this scenario.

Dana yelled "Clear!" I got out of the way as she came through the window in a dive with a tuck and roll landing. She rose into a crouching position and drew her weapon.

Michael pointed and called out: "Bald guy. Dark cloths. Headed for the road. Turned left."

"Got it," Dana replied, and gave chase up Berglund toward Bishop Hill road. Michael helped Marsha Ellen get through the window with the pillowcase filled with Rune's possessions. While Marsha Ellen and I made tracks away from the burning house, Michael took off after Dana. I feared they were headed for the park and into the mass of people returning from the Colony School after the celebration of the Maypole.

I made the emergency call and prayed the firefighters would come quickly, but quick could be a relative term since Bishop Hill had a volunteer fire department. The closest guy, the fire chief, lived six blocks away. Some of the others had to come in from their farms. It all took time. The Carlson's Bishop Hill house might not have much time.

I felt the increasing heat and mourned the imminent loss of so much irreplaceable history. We moved further away from the burning house to a spot where we could sit down to wait for help to arrive. I didn't shed any tears until the first wave of volunteer firemen pulled up in full turnout gear and sprang into action. The chief directed us to move further away, so we crossed the street to watch from a neighbor's yard. People gathered around us. I was relieved to see Oliver and Kathy Carlson among the curious sightseers drawn by the commotion, smoke, and flames. Kathy stayed with us while Oliver struck out to find the fire chief to make sure he knew the homeowner had arrived.

There are many times when a volunteer fire department, no matter how well trained and prepared, cannot respond soon enough and they are left with hosing down a basement or a chimney or whatever was left of a structure. Not the case today. Oliver Carlson's Bishop Hill house was in luck.

CHAPTER 37

The firefighters worked hard to knock the flames down. With the drama diminished and the sun setting, the crowd of curious onlookers dispersed. The locals returned to their homes. The out-of-towners retreated to their vehicles for the journey back to wherever they came from. Kathy Carlson began insisting her bone-weary husband leave for his own good. He refused to budge until the fire chief promised to call him later.

I lost track of Michael and assumed he, like Dana, had to get back to work. I watched as Lars escorted Marsha Ellen to her car. However, the dramatic relief did not last long—I reached for my car keys and only found a torn pocket. They had to be back by the house, near our escape window. When Michael had pulled me off the ground, I had reached for my cell phone first but hadn't thought about the keys until now. I made one attempt to retrieve them and was sternly rebuffed by the firemen assigned to keep people away from the still smoking crime scene.

I ran to catch up with Marsha Ellen and Lars so I could get a lift from them. As I got near enough to hear their voices, I heard him tell her, "There I was on my way through the park when this man ran past me. Your friend, Michael, yelled for me to 'get the bald guy.' I chased him through the park, all the way back to the schoolhouse. I could not catch that skunk before he drove away in a dark car. I feel terrible. I was the only one close enough. Something about the license plate stays with me. The letters spelled out MAD. Is that not an odd thing to put on one's car?"

Marsha Ellen emitted a strangled yes about the time I caught up, gasping for air. We stared at each other for a heartbeat before she ordered me to get into her car.

So much time had been wasted at the fire scene that there seemed to be little point in rushing back to the Ox-Boy cabins across from the red brick house. Still, Marsha Ellen made good time getting past the knot of cars by the Colony School. From the back seat I heard a brief blast of a western tune and the caller's instructions to do-si-do. Hard to believe that the square dance was going on as scheduled. I wanted time to stand still and let me catch up.

Marsha Ellen turned onto Smoketree road and sped up. I cautioned her to take it easy on the hills or we would go airborne. I left it to Lars to talk her down to a safer speed while I used my cell phone.

I tried Dana's number first and got nothing. I got Michael to answer. Well, sort of. I told him I was on my way home and he gave me a gruff "Be there soon" and disconnected.

Marsha Ellen called over her shoulder, "Is everything okay back there?"

"I don't know."

Our speed ticked up a notch. I fought the sinking feeling in the pit of my stomach.

The roof of the red brick house emerged from the darkness as strobing flashes of the red and blue from a Henry County sheriff's cruiser reflected off it. The surreal scene gripped me so hard I failed to note the ambulance coming up from behind. Marsha Ellen slowed down and pulled over to let it go by. It roared past with so much disorienting noise I covered my ears, trying to block some of it out. Marsha Ellen took up the chase and called out, "Almost there."

Dana emerged from nowhere to wave us into the driveway in front of the red brick house. The ambulance swung into the driveway for the Ox-Boy cabins. It stopped close to number three, Jill's cabin. Mercifully, it cut off the siren. I was out the door and around the back of the car before Dana stopped me.

"Shelley, no. Stay back. Give them room to work. I'll tell Teeny you're here." With that she quick walked across the road.

Marsha Ellen and Lars joined me. "Thank you," I told them, while inside I was crooning to myself, *Please. Please.*

"Look at that," Marsha Ellen said, as she pointed, "The Smoketree has claimed another victim."

"No more MAD car," said Lars.

I stared at the wreckage. There was enough damage to put it permanently out of commission. I got a strange, disembodied sense of drifting out of my body for a moment. I wondered how far the driver could have gotten. With a startled jolt I knew he made it to cabin three. And then Teeny Mom was by my side. She grabbed me, turned me away from the smashed car, and shielded the sight of the ambulance from me as best she could. "Honey," she whispered, "I'm so glad you're here."

"What happened?" I answered. "Who's hurt?"

She choked back the catch in her throat. "It's Roy. He's alert. Trying to talk some. He's going to be okay," she said, as much to reassure herself as well as me. "He's strong. He's going to be fine."

"Was it that car?" I pointed to the wreckage at the base of the Smoketree. "How?"

"No. Not the car."

I didn't give her time to say more. I broke free and started for the road. I encountered a sheriff's deputy that looked a lot like Dana. Tears blurred my vision. "Let me go," I cried.

Dana shook me and shouted, "No, Shelley. You have to help *me*. I need you here."

She stared into my eyes until I responded with a barely coherent, "What for?"

"You know more about this Jill Hanson Fischer than anyone else," she said. "Like, how well does she know her way around here? Where she might be headed to?"

"Chicago, I guess. They all came from Chicago. The southwestern suburbs mostly. Why?"

"Because Jill is driving. Her car was stolen and crashed into that tree. Our perpetrator was wounded. We've got a hostage situation and I need some insight into how she's going to act. Sheriff Henry has roadblocks set up at several points on Interstate 74. Would she go that way or another?"

I gathered my thoughts as best I could. "She'd get on 34 and follow it to Galva. She drove there before. She can stay on 34 until Princeton and Interstate 80." I paused. "I don't see her, them, going west. East makes more sense. That's how I'd go."

"My thoughts exactly," she said, and stared into my eyes again. "Shelley, I need to go now. Michael is coming soon, and I need you to ride with him. Help him with the radio. Watch for traffic. Whatever he needs. You got that?"

I started to protest. She gave me enough of a shake for me to respond with, "Okay, I've got it. Michael. Yes. I'll help."

"Shelley, it's Musketeer time. I'm counting on you."

With that she took off in her cruiser with lights flashing but no siren. She meant it when she said Michael would be here soon. He pulled up in the Anderson Brothers' biggest tow truck and waited for me to climb in. I looked back to Teeny Mom and saw her nod and shoo me away. I squeezed in next to Sadie who immediately began licking my face hard enough to make me sputter and beg her to stop. Michael pushed her away, handed me his cell phone, and gunned the engine as he followed Dana's cruiser north. When we reached the Page Street extension, Dana went right, and Michael turned left. The cell phone came alive with text messages containing ten codes and cryptic directions totally foreign to me. I repeated all of them to the best of my ability.

"Michael, you can't possibly expect to catch up to anyone, driving this monster," I said.

"Right," he said, "not catching up. More like getting in front of them."

I recognized a name from one of the phone messages. "Michael, are you planning on taking the Ulah road?"

"Yes," he hissed, clearly not wanting any discussion. I had to persist.

"Ah, Michael, the Ulah road is one lane. How—"

"Look, I'm going and everyone else has to get out of my way."

Sadie and I sat still as we closed in on the turnoff for the narrow road and its equally narrow bridge. The dog had to have felt my nervous tension level soar. She whimpered just enough to get Michael's attention.

"The general plan is to force them to turn off 34 in Galva and go north, then west on 81, and finally through Ulah back to the Page Street Extension. Makes a big circle. Right. Buys us some time. All I have to do is get into position on 81 north of Ulah. Odds are they won't want to hit me. So, yeah, we'll be okay."

"Who's this 'we'?" I asked. "Your plan is going to take more than two vehicles. There are too many backroads around here."

"First, they don't call the business Anderson Brothers for nothing." Michael flashed the devilish grin I remembered from high school. The one he used just before he got into real trouble. "Plus, I've tapped into the world's best pool of reserve talent."

"And you've been working on this plan for how long?" I asked.

"Oh, I don't know, a few minutes or so. Don't look so worried. We've been in training for action just like this."

"And the sheriff is okay with this?"

"Well, quite a few of us are in the sheriff's auxiliary. Now hush, my turn is coming up."

On a good day, a nice sunny day, the Ulah road can be fun for a couple of young kids. If given the choice of roads to take back to Bishop Hill after shopping in Cambridge, my brother and I always clamored for the "lumpy bumpy" as we called it way back then. Right now, it was a single paved lane, in looming darkness, at higher speeds, in an unwieldy service vehicle. I was ready to freak out. Sadie, however, was steady. Her example helped me immensely. Until we got close to the bridge … the one-lane bridge … with headlights coming at us. Michael tensed his grip around the steering wheel, and he set his jaw in determination. He was not going to stop.

"Michael!" I yelled, "Honk the horn. Do something. Get *them* to stop!"

He lifted his left hand and had it ready when the approaching lights disappeared.

"What happened?" I called out in a voice weakened by terror.

"They could've turned into that hog farm up by the corner—or they dipped below a hill." He did not slow down. "We'll know soon enough."

One minute. Two minutes. We were over the bridge and in sight of the intersection with Highway 81. Left was Cambridge. Right was Kewanee. I wanted to ask which way. He turned left and then a fast right turn into a short lane, someone's field access road. All he said was, "Where's my phone?"

I handed it to him and he quickly scanned his messages. "We made it in time. The show will start any second now."

I rolled the window down and craned my head outside to look for a car. I was instantly hit with the rank odor of a nearby hog farm. Headlights were definitely coming at us and this time they were followed by the now-familiar red and blue pulses from a deputy's cruiser. Michael turned his yellow warning lights on, checked the road behind him, and backed onto 81 to form the blockade. He leaned on the horn for extra measure. I don't think I was breathing at this point. The light show kept bearing down on us and I kept thinking: *Turn! Turn! Now!*

And they turned.

The lead vehicle went by so fast I couldn't register anything about it other than dark and sleek. It made the turn and started fishtailing on the loose gravel of the shoulder. The deputy took the corner more slowly and in better control. They zipped out of sight.

Michael straightened the big truck out and turned back the way we came.

"Are you sure you want to do this, uh, follow them back to Ulah?" I asked tentatively.

"Yup," he said in reply.

We didn't have to go far before we ran up behind the deputy's cruiser stopped on the narrow shoulder of the road, its lights flashing streams of red and blue. They illuminated a farmyard with the front end of that fast, sleek car rammed against the side of a large containment tank. Liquid oozed out from riveted seams popped open by the impact. The once-fancy muscle car had found the source of the pungent odor I'd experienced before.

Perhaps just moments before … it was hard to tell with my sense of time becoming distorted and unreal.

The car had clipped the fence of a hog pen on its way to the tank, and the animals were discovering their newfound freedom with enthusiasm. There was the irate farmer, armed and yelling at the driver, who was struggling to get out of the car and away from the reeking mess. Deputy Dana advanced on the scene with her pistol drawn, calling for the farmer to back away to safety. The farmer replied with some coarse words about just who needed to back safely away while swinging his weapon in wild menacing arcs. When the passenger side door opened and a bald man dressed in dark clothing emerged with a gun in his one good hand, the farmer naturally took aim. Deputy, farmer, and Michael were shouting for the bald man to stop and drop his weapon. Of course, nothing stopped him until the bullet from the farmer's rifle narrowly missed his head, struck the containment tank, and released even more of the foul-smelling liquid. The bald man dropped his gun, sank to his knees, and raised his hands in submission.

CHAPTER 38

Deputy Dana handcuffed her prisoner and called in to report her status. The farmer surveyed the damage to his property, the loss of his livestock, and demanded to know who was going to pay for it all, and if he could press charges. Michael and I approached the driver, who was on hands and knees retching between gulps of contaminated air. We each grabbed an arm and hustled back toward the road. Dana called out for no one to leave the scene. I gave her a thumbs up response. No talking required therefore minimal breathing.

We escorted our willing captive to where the lights of both tow truck and county cruiser pooled to confirm who we were holding onto. "Jill!" I exclaimed.

A surprised Michael asked, "This is the one you thought was a guy and is really a—"

"A woman," I interjected, then tried to form a coherent question. "Jill, are you okay?"

Jill wasn't able to choke out any words that I could understand. Michael went to his truck for water. He came back with enough bottled water for each of us humans and one to fill a dish for his dog. Sadie lapped up her fill, relieved herself nearby, and then pricked up her ears. The loose hogs made her herding instincts kick into gear.

"Sadie, no. Stay," Michael ordered. He turned to Jill with an equally commanding voice, "You've got to tell us how you got … here." He opened his arms in a gesture meant to encompass the whole chaotic scene.

Jill swallowed enough water to sputter out, “He had a gun. Made me drive. So many turns.” Her eyes were streaming tears, I couldn’t tell if she’d started crying or if it was the cumulative result of the fumes coming from the ruptured containment tank. “My car. He stole my car. Did you see it?”

“Yes, I saw it smashed into the Smoketree,” I pointed to the bald man being held by Deputy Dana. “I remember when he showed up at the campground. You were so scared. You were an instant basket case.” Then it dawned on me. “That jerk over there is your husband, isn’t he?”

“Soon to be ex-husband. We’re getting a divorce. At war over….” Her voice failed her. After another swallow of water she added, “Everything. That car came from my parents. The MAD on the license plate was for ‘Mom And Dad.’ George, the sleaze bag, cheated me out of it. I took it back. Tried to hide it here.” I could tell she had real tears flowing. “Now, now it’s gone again.” After drinking more water, she gave me a sorrowful appraisal and asked, “You know what happened at the campground, don’t you?”

“Not really,” I said. “I got there just after the ambulance. Got a quick glance at your MAD car. Teeny Mom was okay. Uncle Roy was hurt. Then Dana told me to help Michael in the tow truck. I had to leave.” I bit back my growing sense of dread.

“Your uncle Roy was very brave. He saved us,” Jill stammered.

“What do you mean—was?” I felt pressure building up in my chest. There was only a split second before I launched myself at her. Michael caught me and held on while I angrily demanded “Tell me what happened!”

Jill recoiled. "Look, George was ranting about a huge mess he had to clean up. I thought he'd start shooting people if I didn't cooperate." She started some fresh sobs.

Michael only loosened his grip when I promised him I was good. I regained control and calmed myself by trying to place the pieces into some kind of order. "So, he, that moron over there, shows up. Steals your MAD car to drive over to burn down that old house. The one that my friends and I just happened to be in."

"I swear I know nothing about a fire. I heard a crash and ran out of my cabin. I saw him stagger out of what was left of my car. I couldn't believe what he'd done to it. I screamed at him. He was having trouble with his arm; it must have been broken. He yelled back, ordering me to drive his car. I refused. That's when I saw the gun." She paused for a ragged breath. "So did Roy."

She stopped again. "Roy and Buddy had come up behind us. Teeny was crossing the road coming toward us. Roy dove for the gun." Tears welled up again. "The gun exploded so close to my ear I couldn't hear anything but the ringing. But I do know Roy didn't fall. Not until George used the gun to hit him on the head. I was dragged over to that car." She pointed to the manure-soaked muscle car. "He made me drive. Told me to go north to Interstate 80. I started out by going to Galva on 34 because I knew that way. I don't know how it happened, but, somehow, I kept running into detours and construction and stalled trucks. When I took that last turn … well, I just knew I couldn't go on any further. I had to make it all stop." She motioned to the farmyard. "I didn't know such things existed."

She brushed her tears aside. "I'm so sorry. For everything." She hesitated for a moment then asked, "What is making that awful smell?"

Michael and I locked knowing eyes. We'd both grown up with the answer to her question, but I left it for Michael to repeat his favorite version.

"My Uncle Bill always said, 'That's the smell of money.'"

I nodded in agreement.

CHAPTER 39

Sunday, June 22, 2008

I returned on foot to Oliver Carlson's Bishop Hill house early Sunday morning. I felt weighed down with a combination of fatigue and grief as I waited for a chance to get closer and search under our escape window for my lost car keys.

Thankfully, most of the fire damage had been confined to the rear of the house where a lean-to structure had been added to serve as a covered porch and provide more storage space. But there still could be a lot of smoke and water damage to the contents of the tired old house. No telling how much of Lydia Holder's legacy would be lost forever. I sincerely wished Mr. Carlson good luck in his efforts to save what was left of all this history.

It looked to me like two fire fighters had been stationed there all night. I greeted them by asking politely how things were going. Not bad, they said. No flare ups or extreme hot spots to worry about. They had shed the cumbersome coats that were the main part of their turnout gear. They still had to tromp around in the thick pants and heavy boots carrying shovels. I imagined fire duty turned their gear into walking saunas.

"Are you the one who made the fire call?" one of them asked.

"Well, yes," I said.

"You did good," the first one replied. No judgment on his part on whether or not I should have been in someone else's house.

"Yeah," the second one chipped in. "This place was prime tinder. Old house, dried up wood, stuffed with fuel like this. It would have gone up fast. Whoosh!" He demonstrated with an explosive hand gesture.

"Come on, man," said the first one. "Don't scare her. You and I know how a fire moves in this type of construction," he chastised.

"So glad it didn't go whoosh," I said, unsure if I wanted to know more.

"You got that right," said the second guy.

"What about the arson?" I asked, wondering how much they'd be willing to tell me.

"Chief said he saw signs of tampering from the outside. Residue from an accelerant," the first fireman said. "Rags stuffed under some siding." He scratched his head. "Like someone tried to set a slow fire, failed, and came back with some gas."

"Wait, what did you mean by 'this type of construction'? This isn't timber framed?" I asked.

"No," he said, motioning to the house. "This is balloon construction. There's an air space in the walls that runs from the bottom sill to the top. Fire has to breathe. If it gets started at the bottom it follows the air currents up to the attic. Once it's there we're cutting holes in the roof. And praying for a miracle."

"Usually it's the wiring," said the second fireman. "An old house like this sits empty for years, well, of people anyway, then someone comes along and starts the electric up again. All those unused circuits." He grimaced at the thought.

"Sure, unused and substandard, nowhere near up to modern codes. It's usually a sad story," the first fireman said and shook his head. "I don't care what you were doing in there, miss, but you all saved that house as much as us."

"Thanks, guys," I said. "By the way, did anyone find some keys? Maybe over there?" I pointed to the open window. "I couldn't get the front door open. That's where I had to push the screen out." I felt my face flush a bit as I pointed to the ruined ledger. "Then some guy grabbed me. Uh, helped me out. I don't know where they landed. Any sign of them?"

The firemen looked at each other and exchanged shrugs. The second fireman offered, "Nah, go have yourself a look. Be careful, though. Don't go messing around too much or the deputies will have our—"

"Save it man!" the first fireman interjected. He turned to me and said, "Look, we have to watch for any signs of the fire starting up again. Keep people away, you know, mainly for safety reasons." He shouldered his shovel and nodded to his partner. "We've got to check things out over there." The two of them walked toward the back of the house and out of sight.

I took that as my cue to get busy and then get lost. I walked over to the window, ignoring the dented and battered ledger lying in plain sight, and examined the churned-up grass, weeds, and the bushy remains of old flower plantings that still crowded in on the foundation of the house. Finally, I was rewarded and bent down to retrieve my prize. For an agonizing moment I wanted to pick up the ledger, too. I could save it from further exposure to harsh sunlight. Carefully dry it out. The contents might still be readable.

"This too can be saved," had been Herb Anderson's trusty motto. But in this reality, I had no control. I couldn't take liberties like Ekollon might have done. I made myself leave the ledger on the ground. I hated to give it up but looting, for whatever sentimental rationale, was still a crime. I had to trust that Oliver Carlson, or someone, would take care of it. I turned my back to walk away but stopped after a couple of steps. The dilemma had me frozen. I couldn't take it with me. I couldn't abandon it. I resolved the issue by handing it back through the window. A personal compromise I could live with, but one that won't stay private for long.

A casually dressed and tired looking Dana had pulled up in her own vehicle. "I saw what you did there."

"Did what?" I asked, with all the innocence my embarrassment could muster as she parked her car and got out.

"Tampered with evidence."

"That wasn't evidence. Not really." I went on to make my case. "It's old water-soaked paper that's going to curl up when the sun hits it. It'll become so brittle when its dry it'll crumble as soon as someone touches it. That's not much in the way of evidence. Besides, my fingerprints were already on it."

"What are you doing here so early?" she asked, stifling a yawn.

"I had to rescue my car keys." I displayed that evidence.

"That's why your car was up on the road parked all by itself."

"I wasn't able to get any closer yesterday. And Michael dropped me off at the house last night. Or this morning. My sense of time has let me down. And speaking of drama. Chases, crashes, and such. What happened with Jill and her almost ex-husband?"

"Well, we weren't talking about them," she said. "But I can say that someone is waiting for her father to pick her up. And a person in custody is waiting in a cell for his lawyer to show up. However much good that will do."

"Why say that?"

"Both of them required a good deal of clean-up before they could be interviewed. Not unlike me and my car." She frowned. "The male in question was informed he would to be charged with first-degree murder and aggravated arson. He had enough time to think about his options and became quite cooperative."

"How could he have murdered Rune? He only showed up at the cabins on Wednesday."

"Well, Wednesday wasn't his first time here. After I'd gotten myself cleaned up, I ran a check on him and found a credit card receipt for gas that makes a strong case for him being in the area before Wednesday. If he followed Jill, I'm thinking we'll confirm more sightings of him and his car before long."

"So, Jill's attempt at a disguise never had a chance."

"Nope. Certainly not with Kleinmann in the picture."

"Kleinmann?"

"There just might be an arrest warrant in the works with that name on it."

I gasped and began forming a question before I was cut off.

"No more," she said, with a dismissive wave. "You need to get your car and go home. I need to find those fire spotters. And remember," she sternly cautioned, "no talking about this to anyone. And that means Teeny. Musketeer honor." She made me repeat that last part before cracking a smile as she left.

I pulled into the driveway of the red brick house and parked on the far side between the barn and the back door. I was surprised to see Teeny Mom framed in the kitchen doorway. She waited for me to gather my things from the car before descending the steps.

"Nice to see that you had success," she said. The worried expression never left her face as I got near enough for her to take a closer look at me. She failed to relax.

I jangled my keys and said, “This much is okay.”

I squeezed by her and entered the house. She followed. When I’d unburdened myself of bag and yesterday’s work material, I sat down at the kitchen table. Teeny Mom joined me but only for a moment before immediately standing up again. I gave her my usual prompt. “Well, what have you heard?”

“Dana was here, and we talked a bit about last night. I can’t believe someone would intentionally do such a thing.” She shook her head, sighed, and remained standing. “But after what happened in the cemetery, I guess anything is possible. At least the skunk who set the fire is in jail.” She wrapped her arms around herself in a consoling hug.

“That’s a good choice of words,” I said, with a passable smile. Hoping to relieve some to the tension I felt. “Why was Dana really here? Other than talking to you, I mean.”

“She came by to check out the cabins. Who was here? Who was gone? Nose counting, I guess.”

“Buddy G must still be here. I saw his car. Jill’s, too. Has she or anyone made arrangements for getting her MAD car towed away?”

“Later today. It goes up to Cambridge. Evidence. Her father stayed on and she’ll ride back with him.”

“And Uncle Roy?”

She took a sharp intake of air, held it for a moment too long, then revealed the reason for her anxiety. “The hospital called. Roy has had a setback of sorts. I have to go in and find out what it involves.”

“Do you want me to drive?”

“Please,” she said.

I rose from the chair. It was her turn to receive a soothing embrace.

CHAPTER 40

Saturday, August 9, 2008

Bishop Hill had perfect August weather for Summer Market, or Sommarmarknad in Swedish. The morning clouds dissipated by noon and the humidity fell into the bearable range. The corn was tall, green, and not quite to the tasseling stage, so the pollen count was also manageable. With David Ekollen off pursuing his new career as a consultant, Nikkerbo's part in the village-wide celebration was my responsibility, and I genuinely appreciated nature's cooperation.

Mr. Hemcourt had wanted to stage a significant craft event at Nikkerbo for this year. He considered our Midsommar activities merely practice. Sommarmarknad needed to make a bigger splash. His words, not mine. I'd been shocked when David Ekollon accepted the challenge back in June. I'd thought it a doomed endeavor without having a proper amount of lead time for planning and contacting possible vendors and artisans, most of whom had their show schedules set at least a year in advance. It had all the makings of a disaster waiting to happen, and it would have been if not for one significant happenstance—Oliver Carlson.

Mr. Carlson, as my new-found friend and benefactor, provided a first-class exhibit of his collection of obsolete currency. Bishop Hill's 1857 Western Exchange notes took the center spotlight. He used his connections to supply fellow coin collectors, personal friends, who each had their own interesting displays and merchandise to contribute.

Marsha Ellen and I hit up our Knox art school contacts for creating booths, at discount prices of course, and the results ranged from austere to flamboyant. By early this morning Nikkerbo teemed with art and artifacts, trinkets and treasures, the campy and the crafty.

My busiest day yet with Nikkerbo was winding down. I'd been moving constantly between the inside coin dealers and the outside artisans making sure minor snags wouldn't grow into major problems. It was late afternoon and with all the visitors gone it was time for the exhibitors to gather, eat lasagna, and relax. I had one last job set for myself: to thank everyone personally.

I thought I'd start with the Oliver and Kathy Carlson first and figured they'd be inside Nikkerbo, close to the food and enjoying the air conditioning. I headed in that direction but was waylaid by the outstretched hand of Michael Just a Minute Anderson. He shared a picnic table with a uniformed Deputy Dana Johnson.

"I'm surprised to see you guys," I said. What really surprised me was how easily I'd slid back into my habit of making up cheesy nicknames. After last June's wild ride that ended at the hog farm, I simply couldn't disrespect him like that anymore. I painted on a smile and hoped neither of them noticed any awkward hesitation on my part.

"Shelley," he said, "thanks for letting my guys go through the chow line first."

I looked around for Illinois Army National Guard uniforms and seeing none I asked, "Where'd they go?"

"Teeny and the other ladies helped us dish up carry out containers. They wanted to get over to the meadow, so those folks felt safe to come here and eat knowing their booths were being protected. I'm headed that way directly."

"That's so thoughtful of you guys," I said. "You all work so well together. Everything went so smoothly the night of the great car chase. Midsummer will never be the same for me." I paused for thought. "But it really wasn't a chase, though. More like a bunch of decoy diversions forming a giant backroad circle. I'm still impressed with how you got everything so coordinated and so fast."

"Well, those guys have trained together for a long time," Michael said, then added with a sly smile, "and they were more than willing to help out with, shall we say, a little tactical exercise." Michael pulled out his cell phone to waggle in front of me. "Surely you remember, you gave us some technical assistance."

I nodded and turned my attention to Dana. "I'm glad you're here. Is there any news about the decoy USB drive? I know it probably got lost at the hog farm and I'm sorry to keep asking you. I just need to keep my hope alive."

"Actually, that's the reason I'm here. Finally, some activity was traced to a person you might know." She used her cell phone to confirm the name, "Yup, one William Hanson."

"No, I don't believe it," I said. "How could that be?"

"Best narrative we have is that after the car crashed into the holding tank at the hog operation, Jill Hanson Fischer's soon-to-be-ex hubby passed the decoy memory drive to her. Or he wanted to ditch it fast and planted it on her. Either way, it ended up in her father's possession."

"And he used it? Why now, after all this time?" I found it confusing. "He seemed so nice. So together. So…."

"So up to here," Michael waved a hand to indicate the eye-level depth of his disdain, "in the stock market scheme Buddy G was talking about."

"I remember him making arrangements. I wonder if he was ensuring he'd be on hand for whatever was going on. I was surprised when he wasn't made CFO, Chief financial Officer. Buddy G edged him out. So, will Hanson be arrested?"

"That's the sad part," Dana sighed. "Hanson might not be guilty of any crime related to the stock market schemes. No grounds or some such. Now, George Fischer and Walter Kleinmann are still in big trouble for arson and murder. Both are looking for ways to work out better plea deals by dishing dirt on each other. The lawyers are quite busy."

"But isn't Hanson guilty of fraud, or conspiracy, or some serious crime like that?"

"Not necessarily, but you'll have to talk to someone else besides me. Someone who knows more about legal loopholes and such. It might come down to what he knew and when he knew it."

"Well, if tricking people out of their money isn't a crime, then it should be." I huffed. "Maybe Marsha Ellen will know more."

"Marsha Ellen," Michael scoffed. "Are you kidding me?"

"I heard that!" Marsha Ellen announced as she walked up to us. She thumped her food tray down next to me and demanded "What's going on here?"

"The decoy USB thingy woke up and fingered William Hanson's computer," Dana said. "We were speculating about the implications."

"Charles and I are working on an exposé. Rune's uncle Albin is helping us." Marsha Ellen slid into her seat. "Good thing we found the original USB drive with all the emails. It's all admissible, if it ever becomes a court case, like the one coming up for those hedge fund guys." She paused to reflect. "You know, those two were arrested in mid-June. Right around the time of our fire." She shuddered. "I hate thinking about how close we came to dying for digital data."

"Yeah, that was a close one," Michael muttered before changing the subject. "How's Lars taking that?" he asked. Then clarified. "Your spending time with Buddy G and all."

Marsha Ellen flashed him a coy smile. "Our working together might be why Lars is serious about his invitation for Shelley and me to visit Sweden. Oh, and Charles doesn't want to go by that nickname anymore. Not with his promotion."

That silenced Michael. "I need to get going. My food is getting cold. You guys have a good one." Michael couldn't depart without giving some advice with an added wink. "Be sure to do Sweden before winter. It gets dark and cold."

"Thank you for that sage advice. And thank you for everything else," I called out before turning my attention back to Marsha Ellen. "I have to thank you, too. You made so much of this day possible."

"I was glad to help out. But seriously, you're the one with the organizational talent."

I noticed Dana eyeing Marsha Ellen's plate of lasagna. "Dana, have you eaten? I've heard there's a ton of food in there."

"There sure is," Marsha Ellen seconded.

"Okay, save me a seat," she said to Marsha Ellen. Then imitated an ominous movie quote with "I'll be back."

Dana and I went inside Nikkerbo. The smell from the kitchen made my mouth water and stomach growl, reminding me that I hadn't eaten much during the day. It would be so unladylike to present myself to others in this condition. I followed Dana to the end of the line.

I began chatting with the lady behind me by asking, "How did you like the speech Mr. Hemcourt gave?"

"Oh, I'm so glad he thanked Oliver and Kathy. They are longtime friends. We do a lot of the same shows. When Oliver asked us to come here, why, we dropped everything and … well, here we are," she said, fluttering brightly. "And I've heard such good things about the lasagna," she added with a conspiratorial smile.

"Thank you so much for coming." I decided to take a chance with a personal question, "If I may inquire, how has the show been for you so far?" I was fully prepared for an evasive answer. Some folks prefer to be vague about their financial affairs.

"Oh, my dear, it's been grand. Mr. Hemcourt certainly has taken up his late father's passion for coin collecting. He purchased some of our finest specimens. If y'all do this again next year, be sure to let us know. My husband and I will be back in a heartbeat." She lowered her voice to confide, "Mr. Hemcourt's purchases from the other vendors will probably bring the same response."

"Mr. Hemcourt will be pleased to know that," I said. "Circumstances didn't allow much time to prepare for this show. I certainly think next year will be even better."

"Well, he has just been a dear. Showed us, everyone really, that old Liberty Head nickel of his father's. Told us all about the tragic loss of the original family portrait. I can't remember the name of the painter."

"Olof Krans," I answered. "He painted Mr. Hemcourt's great-grandfather's portrait in 1897."

"Oh, yes," she said. "That was the first portrait. Such a shame about the fire. Now the second one…?"

"Krans often revisited favorite images and themes. Thanks to an eye witness we know for certain that the second portrait was created in the summer of 1915. In fact, our witness was the centenarian honored at the opening ceremony with pulling the cord to unveil the first ever public viewing."

"She is an impressive lady," she said. "But I don't understand why it looks the way it does."

"That painting was hidden soon after it was finished. Krans died the following winter. It was lost to all of us until recently. It was decided to display it as is for the time being," I said.

"Well," she said, "I enjoyed the exhibit. Such interesting stories about those three paintings, the two by Krans, and that other one—"

"The modern reproduction created by a local artist." I filled in the blank hoping that would be enough information for her. The artist was Uncle Roy and the talks about provenance were on hold for the time being.

"I see," she said. "Y'all do good work here, dear."

Our conversation was cut off because it was our turn to begin filling plates. A new pan of fresh lasagna was waiting. Amy Anderson, Michael's mother, was handling two plates at once. "I hope that isn't for Michael. I saw him leave."

"No," Amy said. "He's with his guard buddies. Great Auntie Pearl wanted seconds."

I scanned the room for the familiar white top-knot bun. "But I don't see her."

"She's holding court over in there." Amy pointed to a group of people clustered together, obscuring my line of sight.

"I can't believe she's still hungry after eating up all the attention," I said with a grin.

"Well, between the opening ceremony at the Krans exhibit and visiting with former students tonight, she'll need these extra calories to keep going. Do drop by when you can. She keeps track of your, um, exploits, if you will. Please excuse me," Amy said, and headed toward Pearl's crowded table.

After I piled my plate up with every bit of food I could safely carry, I looked around trying to locate Oliver and Kathy Carlson as well as Teeny Mom and Uncle Roy. I spotted them sharing a large table with an empty seat hopefully saved for me. I angled myself around all obstacles and headed in that direction.

I wondered how the conversation between Uncle Roy and Oliver Carlson was working out. Last June's run-ins with trouble left both of them with head injuries, but with strikingly different degrees of impairments. Mr. Carlson was able to talk to me. Okay, with some hesitation and shortened sentences, but we understood each other. He seemed to get progressively better every time I visited him while I was trying to figure out what to call this first-of-its-kind Nikkerbo Summer Market event.

I'd been dealing with the dilemma of names since early June. I couldn't come up with anything better than colony this, festival that, and other unsatisfying results involving Olof Krans. There seemed to be nothing new to tap into. No image that hadn't already been used countless times. Oliver Carlson may have been the behind-the-scenes force of nature making it all possible, but he refused to have his name used in advertising.

At one point I felt that it should have been called the Lydia Holder Memorial Art Festival, since her house with its over-stuffed rooms remained so near the heart of what had brought Rune Gunnarson, Charles "Buddy G" Guyer, and Oliver Carlson together on that fateful night in the cemetery. I felt she was owed some recognition.

The same with all the stories I'd been privy to over those early weeks of June. So many centered-on the topic of money: in its old and new forms, both real and imagined, the quest to possess more of it by any means, and the length an outlaw would go to repay a chivalrous gesture. These themes began to resonate and merge with the shadowy image of Oliver Carlson, shovel at the ready, always on the prowl. I couldn't use his name, but the next best thing was an amalgam of everything else. We agreed to christen Nikkerbo's premier Sommarmarknad event The First Annual Bishop Hill Treasure Hunter's Invitational.

Uncle Roy's recovery of his lost language skills was making slower progress. Teeny Mom bore the brunt of his frustration at understanding speech, whether it was his own or someone else's. A downturn in his general mood was the most alarming result. I hoped coming out for this event would go well for him. He needed an ego boost.

Teeny Mom saw me approaching and waved me in for a landing. I successfully set down my drink and used the free hand to gingerly lower the plate of food into position. Two cherry tomatoes rolled over the edge and into my hand. I stared at how neatly they fit together in my palm. If I rolled them around a bit, they nestled back together.

"Like Fischer and Kleinmann trying to escape justice," I said. Teeny Mom looked puzzled. "Dana told me that George Fischer is busy ratting out Walter Kleinmann, his boss. Kleinmann brought Fischer in to destroy incriminating emails that Buddy G, sorry, Charles Guyer had saved on his computer. That started the whole business with the memory drives." I dropped the tomatoes onto my plate. "Between the newspaper article and me flashing the decoy USB around Nikkerbo Kleinmann must have thought a house fire would solve all his problems. It just didn't work on the first try."

Uncle Roy uttered a contemptuous, "Baboon bottom."

I looked toward Teeny Mom, "What do you think he meant to say?"

After a moment's reflection she answered, "I think it's pretty clear—Walter Kleinmann is a baboon bottom."

The tension around the table dissolved into laughter. Neighboring tables cast sympathetic smiles our way. Uncle Roy relaxed and appeared totally pleased with himself. It was great.

Later, the room cleared leaving Talli and me with the last of the cleanup work. She gathered up the table linens into great piles to be laundered. I boxed up the table decorations.

"I saw you talking to Pearl Anderson," she said. "She's a good one for wisdom and advice."

"Not unlike you," I said.

"Oh, sure, give me, what, another fifty years or so and I'll be right up there with her."

"She said to make my own story true. I've been thinking about that. What is my story?" I looked around the now deserted room. "This place was full of the people who gathered around food and lingered in conversation. All part of a community. I like this," I said. "I know I didn't do it all by myself. I was handed all the parts and pieced together this gathering of treasure hunters. It makes me feel good. I can see why Ekollon liked this job so much. So much so that he never wanted to share any of it. But I won't use his methods."

"You'll have your own way of doing things," Talli said. "That can be your story."

"But I want more than that. I am confident that Lydia Holder's collection will end up here and it will have our best efforts at conservation and preservation. I want that to be a part of my story."

Talli approved with a subtle nod. "And are there more parts?"

"I want Krans's last portrait restored properly and displayed with the true accounting of its provenance. So many stories intersect here: Krans's; Hemcourt's; Carlson's; Buddy G's, excuse me, Charles. And Rune's—" I stopped short. "Is it wrong of me to want so much, while Rune is … still gone?"

"He isn't gone as long as we remember," Talli said. "And I'm sure there will be justice for him."

"Yes," I said. "And there will be a Treasure Hunter's Invitational here as long as I am able."

"That's the spirit." Talli said. "Pearl was always the best teacher. Now, did she tell you anything else?"

"She said to 'take it to the Swedes'. I think she meant the 1915 Krans. My Krans. My treasure. I know it is in rough shape after being hidden all those years, first by Krans himself and then by my family. Someday I'd like to get it restored to how she first saw it as a young girl in Altona.

"That's what preservation is all about isn't it? Saving all the artifacts we can. Keeping the past intact," I said. I looked down at the Colony outfit I had on. "This is exactly what I was wearing when I crawled out of that window. I patched it up." I tried to straighten my skirt and press out some creases. "So, am I pretending things are the same and nothing has ever changed?"

"Things have changed, haven't they?"

"Yes. We can keep our connections to the past, but we have to live our own lives, now. I guess that is what I really want. To be free to choose a path that is my own but not be so far away from home, this home, to feel lost. All the stories, the real connections to the past are safe within me, aren't they?"

"Definitely. And that is a good place to start a new story," Talli said. "Now, let's close this place up.

AUTHOR'S NOTE

Bishop Hill is a state historic site and a national historic landmark with innumerable stories to tell about the life and times of a Swedish utopian society founded on the Illinois prairie in the 1800s. I chose the avenue of fiction to tell my tale of mystery. I used my imagination to create names, characters, businesses, organizations, and institutions wherever I could, or otherwise used them fictitiously. Historical figures, events past and present, and geography were likewise subjected to my imagination and altered for this work of fiction. Any resemblance to real life is wholly coincidental.

A young Olof Krans did join the Bishop Hill Colony and later used his self-taught painting skills to document the colony's early years. Those who want to learn more are encouraged to continue their journey by reading further or visiting the real Bishop Hill in Henry County, Illinois. There are many knowledgeable people to help you on your way.

ACKNOWLEDGEMENTS

From the beginning, I wanted my second Bishop Hill mystery to have money, specifically the obsolete colony currency, and preservation as major themes. *Shadows Over Bishop Hill* is not just any second book. Its timeline begins immediately after the first book, *Clouds Over Bishop Hill*, ends. I needed the June Midsommar festival as a plot point along with the unfolding financial scandal with subprime mortgages coming to light in the summer of 2008. Incorporating all that information was a difficult task for me as a writer and I passed the challenge along to my editor, Misty Urban. Through helpful comments and astute suggestions, she helped me clarify my intentions and create a better book. Thank you, Misty.

Henry County Sheriff Kerry Loncka provided expert input that helped shape my narrative. Sometimes it is more import to know what won't work than what will.

Ron Loetz, a retired Davenport Deputy Fire Chief, helped me with detailed information about fighting fires. Jack Hawkins, retired Bishop Hill Fire Chief, presented the experience of the volunteer firefighter in a small town.

Special thanks for computer advice and logo design go to Michael Davidsaver. He saved me time and anxiety.

A big thank you to Kaitlea Toohey for a cover design that captured the essence of my novel with efficiency and skill.

I wish to thank my early reviewers Xixuan Collins and Dan Moore who were very generous with their time and talent.

I still consider myself a product of the Midwest Writing Center. I always had access to workshops, information, and support to help me whenever I needed it.

Thanks to the patient members of Writer's Studio who listened and gave thoughtful, constructive feedback whenever I read excerpts from my manuscript. Phil Turner, Mike Bayles, and Steve Lackey always gave me their expert input. Special thanks to Dan Moore for sharing his astute editing skills.

Thanks to all my Beta readers: Ann Pieper, Susan Strodtbeck, Judy Benson, Jodonna Loetz, Cynthia Irwin, Eloise Graham, Janet Latchaw, and Larry d'Autremont for constructive comments, finding embarrassing typos, and offering kind words of praise. They all gave me something.

I reserve my most special thanks for my husband, Mark. He has always been the reader I relied upon the most for advice and editing skill. He's been a loyal fan and morale booster whenever I needed it. This book wouldn't exist without him and his confidence in me.

ABOUT THE AUTHOR

Mary Davidsaver is a graduate of the University of Iowa who lived in Bishop Hill, an Illinois state historic site and a national historic landmark for twenty-four years. She wrote for local newspapers and won an Illinois Press Association first place feature photo award. Since returning to Iowa, she has won two Iron Pen first place awards, was the first local writer to win the Great River Writer's Retreat contest and was honored as an Outstanding Literary Artist by the Midwest Writing Center.